STERLING CLAY

L.B. DUNBAR

WWW.LBDUNBAR.COM

Sterling Clay
Copyright © 2024 Laura Dunbar
L.B. Dunbar Writes, Ltd.
https://www.lbdunbar.com/

Cover Design: Lori Jackson Designs

Cover Model: Chris David

Photographer: J. Ashley Converse

Mountain Cover Design: Jillian Liota/Blue Moon Creative Studio

Couple Cover Design: Megan Dunbar

Character Images: Erika Plum

Editor: Nicole McCurdy/Emerald Edits

Editor: Gemma Brocato

✽ Created with Vellum

OTHER BOOKS BY L.B. DUNBAR

<u>Sterling Falls</u>

Sterling Heat

Sterling Brick

Sterling Streak

Sterling Clay

Sterling Fight

Sterling Touch

Sterling Stone

<u>Chicago Anchors</u>

Elevator Pitch

Catch the Kiss

Parentmoon

<u>Holiday Hotties (Christmas novellas)</u>

Scrooge-ish

Naughty-ish

Grouch-ish

<u>Road Trips & Romance</u>

Hauling Ashe

Merging Wright

Rhode Trip

<u>Lakeside Cottage</u>

Living at 40

BOOKS IN OTHER AUTHOR WORLDS

Smartypants Romance (an imprint of Penny Reid)

Love in Due Time

Love in Deed

Love in a Pickle

The World of True North (an imprint of Sarina Bowen)

Cowboy

Studfinder

THE EARLY YEARS

Legendary Rock Stars Series

Paradise Stories

The Island Duet

Modern Descendants – writing as elda lore

May you be a butterfly (or a phoenix) and rise from the ashes, transformed.

1

———

[Mavis]

"What the hell are you doing?"

The gruffness in his tone was the last thing I expected, although I'm familiar enough with his voice which currently sounds like he smoked a pack of cigarettes when I know he doesn't smoke.

"I—" I blink, stunned as the heavy downpour hammers at my skin.

For late September, the weather has been unpredictable, and this sudden deluge came out of nowhere. I hadn't been to Sterling Falls since summer a year ago—nearly thirteen months—but I needed to be here. While I no longer had a home, I wanted to be somewhere more welcoming than where I'd been.

This was no pleasant greeting, however.

I'd debated even stopping. The mountain was dark, the hour late, and the trees around us drenched in rain which created an ominous atmosphere. Witnessing a pickup truck pulled off to the side of the road should have meant nothing to me. Stopping on the dark highway would be dangerous and foolish as I was a single mother with my six-year-old child in the backseat of my car. But I recognized the logo branded on the side of the truck, and noticed the hood propped up and a man bowed underneath it. I pulled over because it wasn't just any man beneath that hood. He was someone I knew, sort of.

With my hazard lights on and a quick check of Dutton sleeping in the backseat of the VW Jetta, I set the parking brake and exited my warm, safe, *dry* vehicle to see if the man needed assistance.

Now, piercing blue eyes narrow at me. Eyes like ice when they'd been nothing but kind over the last five years. His silver hair is plastered to his face, charcoal-colored from the wetness of the rain. His leather jacket reflects how soaked the material is, suggesting he'd been out in the storm for a while. Standing here only seconds, the rain has seeped through my own layers of a heavy sweater and long-sleeved tee, plus my jeans. My entire body shivers from the unrelenting rain, making my sodden, cold clothes cling to me, chilling me to the bone. If Clay has been out here longer than I've stood here, he must be miserable.

"I thought you might need help," I call out over the thundering downpour, my voice sheepish as I stand a few feet away from him. I hate this about myself. Hate how I cower. How anxious he makes me.

I wasn't afraid of him. No, Clayton Sylver—Clay—would never harm me physically.

What frightened me was how attracted I'd been to him from the moment I first met him. A kind smile once upon a time. A friendly greeting whenever I entered his local business. The teasing banter he shared with his employees, reminding me his jovial behavior was nothing special toward me. His behavior was simply who he is—a good man.

So, his narrow-eyed glare and sharp words throw me off like the onset of this September storm.

Clay glances over my shoulder, the light from my hazards blinking red behind me. "You're getting drenched. You shouldn't be out here."

Does he mean in the rain? Or simply out in the openness of the late-night road? Or maybe he even means I shouldn't be returning to Sterling Falls after all that happened. However, that might be my own fear talking. Fear that as much as I loved this town, I might not be welcomed back here.

And I'm doubtful I've ever made an impression on Clay Sylver. I've simply been a customer over the years. A woman who thought she was decorating a house to make it a home. A woman designing a backyard for a child to play. A woman duped by the wrong man when the right one didn't know I existed.

I've been crushing on Clay Sylver for a while now.

"I thought you might need help," I repeat, a little stronger, forcing myself to hold my head a little higher as I take one giant step closer to him. My cold fingers are clasped together, tightening until they feel like they might crack. The rain is painful, like a harsh baptism, pelting my face and continuing to make me blink. My own hair is plastered to my cheeks like Medusa's snakes, but I don't reach for the strands. Instead, I remain stone still staring back at Clay.

I only want to help.

Holding my breath, I wait for him to tell me he doesn't need me. Whatever caused his vehicle to be pulled to the side of the road, hood up, isn't my concern. Considering a flashlight is propped up near the engine, though, the situation doesn't look good for him.

Clay slowly turns his head, glancing back at his truck.

Swiping a hand over his hair, which does nothing to remove the water in the continued downpour, his shoulders fall, and he gazes back at me.

"I guess I could use a ride to town."

I nod once. "Need help with anything in your—"

A sudden hand, held upright, palm outward cuts me off. "Just get back in your car. I'll be right there." Frustration fills his voice. Maybe even defeat. He sharply turns back for his truck, and I watch as his broad back hunches. He hitches up the collar of his leather jacket as if that could prevent any further rain from hitting his body.

I spin away from him as well and briskly walk back to the Jetta. Once inside, I shudder and glance in the rearview mirror to check on Dutton again. Still peacefully asleep when he typically hates storms. Lucky little kid.

Reaching for the thermostat, I crank the heat and gaze into the side mirror to check on Clay's progress. The hood of his truck is closed. The brightness of my hazards flash in measured time, flicking across the slick, dark road, and colliding with the front of his vehicle.

While looking to my left, the passenger door to my right opens, and I let out a squeak, shifting in the driver's seat. Clay's eyes crash with mine. Bent forward, he has a hand on the top of the passenger door. His other arm rests on the roof of my car.

"Are you sure about this?" he asks, eyeing me, noting my surprise. As if I hadn't asked him if he needed the ride.

"Get in," I state quietly, quickly darting a glance to Dutton once again.

Clay tilts his head, door still open, rain hitting his back, and catches sight of Dutton in the backseat. My son's head is tipped to the side, leaning awkwardly on a bed pillow pressed against the window. His mouth hangs open, and he's gently snoring.

Clay's eyes drift back to mine. He pauses another second as if contemplating something but when a clap of thunder rustles through the trees and a sudden bolt of lightning cracks upward from the street before us, Clay settles into my car. He slams the door then shifts once more to check on Dutton.

"Sorry about that," he mutters, side-eyeing me. He shudders once while facing forward then sets his fist to his mouth and coughs. A sharp, barking kind of cough that wracks his entire body. He bends forward as if curling into himself as the hacking continues harsh and deep. Once the spell passes, he sits upright, swipes at his mouth, and tips his head back. He closes his eyes.

"Are you sick?" I question. A fever would be difficult to detect without taking the liberty to touch his forehead. Something tells me Clay would not appreciate my hand on his face.

"Just a cough," he mumbles, his voice still ragged and rough. He swallows hard, and I watch his Adam's apple roll along his throat.

There is nothing *just* about his cough. He could have bronchitis or pneumonia or the flu.

"I work at the Sylver Seed & Soil," he states, like I didn't know, muttering the address just outside of Sterling Falls. "You can drop me there."

I silently nod, turning off the hazards, and releasing the parking brake. Giving another quick glance at Clay, his tense body remains rigid in the passenger seat.

"I'm making a mess of your car." His voice scratches but his eyes remain closed. He smooths his large hands down his thighs, covered in soaked denim. His body shudders once more.

"No worries," I whisper, not half as concerned for my front seat as I am for the man sitting beside me. In the darkness around us, the glow of dashboard lights offers the only illumination, making it difficult to determine if Clay is sicker than a simple cold. The roughness of the barking cough suggests he is.

I glance over my shoulder once more to check on Dutton.

He'd recently gotten over the flu, and I don't want him to be ill again.

"I can call one of my brothers." Clay's voice has me turning my head, meeting those icy blue eyes once more. His pinched expression suggests he'd rather not call one of them, though.

I don't know a lot about Clay, but I know his older brother Stone is the local sheriff. One of his younger brothers, Knox, is a firefighter. Unfortunately for me, I've been acquainted with each of them through their professions, not as a neighborly citizen of Sterling Falls. Clay also has a brother who owns the local bakery, and a sister named Vale.

"No. I'll drive you wherever you need to go." Placing the car in Drive, I cautiously roll onto the mountain highway, curious what Clay was doing out here near midnight. Glancing through the windshield at the slick pavement, I wonder if I should be worried about black ice as the temperature outside has dropped considerably. Or maybe concerned another strike of lightning will burst before us.

"I'm Mavis, by the way." I clear my throat, noting it isn't half as strong as the woman making a rash decision to pull over to the side of the road and help a stranded male driver. "Mavis Grant."

The use of my maiden name with him feels foreign on my tongue when it shouldn't. I hadn't been married. Not like everyone thought.

"I know who you are." His voice is quiet but no less rugged. The tone implies more than recognition of a repeat customer to Sylver Seed & Soil. He knows about my past, or at least the local lore of thirteen months ago.

With Clay's head tipped back while he spoke and his eyes closed, I want to shut my own as if they can hide me. As if it will make the past disappear and protect me from the blaze of history I'm rushing toward.

I shouldn't be returning to Sterling Falls, but this was my

home despite all that happened. Deep down, I once believed I belonged here. Not on the run. Not hiding. Dutton and I have been hidden for long enough.

My parents encouraged me to move on. Start somewhere new, somewhere fresh. That newness meant remaining in Florida with them. But amid the told-you-so speeches, and the pitying looks, I couldn't continue living there any longer. We'd overstayed our welcome. It was time to return to the only other place I'd known.

I can only hope Sterling Falls is forgiving and forgetful, unlike the man seated beside me.

I DON'T TAKE Clay to the Seed & Soil. With him practically passed out in my front seat, mumbling on occasion, and coughing sporadically in a way that wracked his entire body, I drove him to his house. I shouldn't know where he lives. It made me appear like a stalker that I did, but in a small town, it isn't unlikely to know where people reside in and around the town limits. Clay owns a rather modern-looking, sprawling ranch-style house. Taking the winding gravel drive, now pocked with puddles, my Jetta jostles cautiously toward the single-story home.

Stopping at the end of the drive, marked by a line of railroad ties, I turn my head to notice a singular light illuminating the front door and a wall of windows facing us. Somewhere within the house another light glows and a thought hits me.

Does Clay have someone in his life?

He didn't have a wife or steady girlfriend as far as I knew, but a lot can change in a year. I'm hopeful many things are different about me. Still, the soft light offering a welcoming beam from behind the windows has me second guessing my decision to bring Clay here.

Glancing at his slumped body, head resting against the cool glass in a similar fashion to Dutton in the backseat, I argue that I've made the right choice.

Clay Sylver is sick.

Unbuckling my seatbelt, I hesitantly reach for Clay, gently placing a hand on his shoulder and jiggling him.

"Clay." My voice is too quiet, not loud enough to rouse a sleeping man. "Clay, hon—" I quickly cut myself off from continuing the gentle endearment, as if we are more familiar with one another.

Giving Dutton another glance in the backseat, I shake Clay more firmly and strengthen my tone. "Clay."

A smug smile quirks one corner of his mouth higher than the other. A damn dimple pops out, nearly blinding me. "In a minute, baby." His muttering suggests he's dreaming of someone. Someone clearly not me.

The sobering thought has me pushing harder at his shoulder. "Clay," I snap sharply, sparing Dutton another glance, torn between waking my son and needing to wake the sick man happily fantasizing beside me.

Clay's eyes ping open, staring straight ahead a second. His gaze appears unfocused. Those icy blue eyes are distant. Then his forehead furrows, deep creases forming as recognition slowly dawns. His rugged voice harshly whispers, "I'm home."

"No place like it," I softly tease.

His head shoots toward me, those piercing eyes locking on me. His expression suggests he isn't certain who I am despite claiming he knew me earlier, or how he got here. In my Jetta. At his house.

His hand slides to the door handle, and he pops open the passenger door, awkwardly tumbling out of it before catching himself with one foot. Twisting his body without a second glance at me, he slips from my car and blindly presses on the door to close it behind him.

The way Clay sways as he moves forward, staggering side-to-side before reaching his front door, I'd think he was drunk if I didn't know better. He still doesn't look back and I watch with bated breath as he types in a code on a keypad to open his front door. As the door swings open, I tell myself I'm only waiting for him to enter the house. Making certain he is safely inside. Then I'm leaving his apparently ungrateful ass behind.

Through the floor to ceiling glass panels, I watch the outline of Clay moving inside the immediate entryway and further into what I assume is a living space.

Then I watch him stumble, pitch forward, and land face down on the floor.

2

———————

[Clay]

Someone rustles beside me in bed before a voice softly speaking, as if to a child, awakens me.

My head is pounding like someone is jackhammering my skull. My throat is as thick as a forest, yet just as dry and brittle as one in the heat of August. My eyelids are heavy, refusing to open. I'm so tired, and I'm shivering.

Whoever moves away from the bed has taken all the heat and I tug at the blankets finding them already tucked up over my shoulders and beneath my chin. I'm reminded of being a kid, my mother pressing in the bedding around me.

"Gotta warm up my ball of clay, so he can get back outside and play." The memory rushes in, almost as if I can feel her cool hand on my fevered forehead.

I haven't thought of my mother as often at forty-three years old as I did when I was younger. When my ten-year-old self found her slumped over beside my parents' bed, body curled inward, as if protecting our only sister who hadn't been born yet. That was the day my world tipped on its axis.

And right now, I feel upside down as well. The sickening spin of the room has me fighting harder to open my eyes. Someone groaned. *Was that me?* I shiver beneath the layers of blankets.

"Clay?" A quiet feminine voice has me slowly lifting my lids, assuming my sister will be standing by my bed, telling me to get my ass up and get to work.

Instantly, my lids shut again. *What time is it?*

The brightness behind my lids tells me it must be daytime, somewhere past noon. Panic strikes. I have too much to do today, but with my head pounding, I'm slow to recall things on the list. Something about a shipment of animal feed arriving, and the part Perry ordered for his tractor which is in the back of my truck. A warehouse inventory and a check on our Christmas supply for the home merchandise section, and—

"Clay? Honey? Can you try to take these?" A cool hand brushes back my hair before resting briefly on my forehead. Then it sweeps down my cheeks and along my jaw before settling beneath my chin. I burrow into the soothing touch, calming strokes, and tenderness of delicate fingers.

Wait. *Honey?* My sister wouldn't ever be calling me such a sweet thing in such a pretty voice. My eyelids fly open, and I freeze on the face of a woman that takes a second to come into focus.

Long, midnight colored hair hangs over her shoulders. Her face lightly tan, suggesting the coloring might be permanent. Her eyes wide and dark. Her smile weak, sympathetic, hopeful.

Mavis? *Mavis Holland?*

I blink once but can't seem to find my tongue, the muscle dry as dust and swollen inside my mouth.

Mavis Holland is in my house. Squatting beside my bed. What the hell is she doing here? And how did I get here?

The night comes back to me like a trickle of rain. I'd driven a Sylver Seed & Soil truck to pick up a part for Perry. Deciding I was close enough to Glady, I called her. We were a situationship that cannot be defined other than scratching an occasional itch.

We didn't have a schedule. We didn't make plans. If one or the other of us wasn't available or didn't answer our phones, there were no hurt feelings. I hadn't seen Glady in months, and not feeling so great, I should have stayed away. However, I figured getting laid out of convenience would hold me off for another few months. The decision was reckless. Glady turned me out the second she saw me, suggesting I might have a fever and should see a doctor.

Fuck that. I didn't trust doctors. They'd been wrong in the past.

Then . . . the truck broke down on the way back to Sterling Falls. One of my assistant managers warned me the other day something was off with it. One more thing to add to the long list of what needed to be completed. As the CEO, a title still strange to me, and head manager of Sylver Seed & Soil, a family-owned business in which I was one of three family members actively working there, my to-do list didn't stop at the bottom of a sheet of paper but was pages of stuff to be done.

In reminiscing about the stormy night, I realize how I got home is a bit fuzzy.

The thought makes my already thumping head pulse harder, and I continue to stare into the charcoal eyes of Mavis.

She's a strikingly beautiful woman. The kind of beauty that ties your tongue, even if it isn't as dry as the desert like mine is. My heart is racing, and I'm not sure I can blame my fever or illness entirely for that fact. Because there is no doubt that I'm ill, I just can't remember ever being this sick before.

My limbs ache. My eyes wish to close again. All I want to do is sleep and bring back the warmth of whoever was lying next to me.

My forehead crinkles, an action that makes me want to wince from the pain radiating inside my brain.

"Mavis?" Her name is a croak, as if I'm a toad attempting to speak my first word. Had she been the one beside me? How did I get in my bed?

Slipping a hand from the blankets, I attempt to swipe at my face in hopes to clear my head and recall what happened. As I brush my palm over days' worth of growth on my jaw, I wince for real. My cheek feels tender, possibly bruised. *What the hell happened to me?*

"You have a fever," Mavis says, her voice trembly but calming like the patter of water tumbling gently down a stream. "I need you to take these." Two white pills rest on her extended palm.

Struggling to sit upright, my body feels weighed down as if a ton of landscaping stone holds me in a horizontal position. Making it only to my elbow, tipped on my side, I take the pills from her hand, noticing the tremor in mine. Mavis holds out a small glass of water and I sip, the cool liquid not enough to quell the thickness in my throat or quench a sudden thirst.

"Mama?" The quiet voice of a small child has me turning my head too suddenly, causing another sharp pain to flash across my temple. The room sways.

"Just a minute, little bear." Mavis aims her gaze toward the door of my bedroom. When she glances back at me, panicked eyes meet mine.

"What's going on here?" I flinch at the roughness in my own voice. My tone is normally raspy, or so I'm told, but this sound is sandpaper going against the grain.

"You're sick," Mavis reminds me.

"How did I get home? In bed?" My brows cinch again. "And what are you doing here?" I attempt to infuse the question with more inquiry than accusation, but the sound is raw, even to my own ears.

"We can talk about that later. You need more sleep. And maybe something to eat soon."

My stomach loudly rumbles on cue, reminding me I haven't eaten since sometime yesterday.

"What time is it?" I shift for my nightstand, where I typically leave my phone. The device isn't there, but a bottle of acetaminophen is, along with the short glass of water, a washcloth folded over the edge of a mixing bowl, and a package of cough medication.

"It's a little after one."

"In the afternoon?" I bark, as if the brightness in the room doesn't give away that it's daylight outside. Shoving the covers off me in a rush, I say, "I need to meet—"

The room tilts around me as I attempt to sit upright. Mavis abruptly stands and places her hands on my biceps, pressing against me. My eyes are level with her chest which I have no energy to check out. Still, those perky tits are front and center, wearing a Sylver Seed & Soil tee I recognize as one of mine. Her legs are clad in jeans. Her feet bare as if she has made herself right at home. In my house.

"What the fuck is going on?" I bark, sounding like a baby seal.

"You aren't going anywhere, Clayton."

The use of my legal name has me stilling, hoping the room will stop moving as well. With her delicate fingers against my bare skin, I slowly drop back down to the pillow, suddenly aware that I'm naked except for my boxer briefs which feel itchy, as if the material was once damp and dried against me.

Embarrassment hits hard. *Did I fucking wet myself?* Panicked, I glance at Mavis towering over me. Her long hair falls forward like a curtain. Those large dark eyes mirror the anxiety within me.

"Did you undress me?" More barking noises which sound overly harsh occur. I can't control my tone. My throat is on fire.

Mavis glances quickly over her shoulder toward the bedroom door before meeting my gaze again while taking a small step away from me.

For a second, I worry she's planning an escape. She'll run before I get details about how I'm in bed, and I don't want her rushing off. I didn't miss her flinch when I snapped at her, and I don't want her afraid of me. I can't help my tone because of my throat. Still, I take a measured inhale to calm my racing heart.

She wrings her hands. "It's kind of a funny story." However, there isn't a drop of humor in her voice as those nervous eyes scan my face.

"Humor me," I groan.

To my surprise, Mavis rushes forward again and places her hand on my forehead, the coolness reminding me of my thoughts only moments ago of my mother. Mavis's touch is comforting, and instantly I melt back into the pillow beneath my head. *She's* the one who touched me earlier.

Her soothing fingers smooth down my forehead to brush over my cheek, and I wince at the tenderness beneath my eye.

"You fell," she states, as if reminding me when I have no recall of that happening.

"When? How?" Although, with Mavis gently stroking over my face, my body relaxes more. I fall under the spell of whatever she's doing to me.

That feels nice.

A soft chuckle follows my thought, suggesting I might have said it aloud.

"Sleep, Clay," she whispers. The ghost of her breath brushes my cheek, and my eyes want to open in surprise.

Did Mavis Holland just kiss me? Impossible.

She's a married woman. With a child no less. And my thoughts should not be traveling down the path they sometimes lead. Where the crush I have on an unobtainable woman haunts my dreams and brought me to my knees a time or two, when the fantasy became too much, and I had to take matters into my own hand.

Imagining this woman who can never be mine.

A woman who entered my store with a forced smile and a bruise covered only by the edge of a short-sleeved tee.

A woman who stared at me, as if pleading for someone to protect her when it wasn't my place to be near her.

She belonged to another man, and he didn't deserve her.

Not one inch of that midnight hair I want to slip my fingers through.

Not a glance from those dark, hollow eyes which made me weak for her.

Not a kiss from those lips that look soft and thirst-quenching and make my own mouth water for a sip.

No, he didn't deserve her after what he did.

I don't either, especially as I drift back to sleep with images in my head of her curled up beside me, warming my skin, and matching my heartbeat.

The one hammering with desire to keep her safe.

3

[Mavis]

I shouldn't have stayed but I didn't have the heart to leave. Clay Sylver was so sick. I was certain he had the flu, and as much as I didn't want to expose myself to him for fear Dutton would have a relapse, I couldn't leave him.

After watching him fall on his face the other night, I scrambled from the Jetta, grateful to find Clay had not locked his front door when he entered his home. Thankfully, he hadn't broken his nose when he landed on the floor. By the grace of all things holy, I was able to rouse him enough to help him sit upright and then lead him to his bedroom, although he leaned heavily on me. His clothing was soaked. His skin was a cloying mixture of chilly and clammy. Unceremoniously, I dropped him on his bed and stared down at him, a war raging within me.

Stay or go.

I selected option one but first I had to get Dutton from the car. Rushing back to the vehicle, I picked up my six-year-old, struggling with the new weight he'd gained and the deadweight of a lanky sleeping child. I brought him into Clay's house, tucking him in on the couch with a decorative pillow and a throw blanket. Returning to my car I retrieved our suitcases. The two large bags contained most of our belongings. The few other things we owned remain in Florida for now.

Then I settled in to take care of Clay.

As an out-of-work nurse, I told myself to treat him like any patient. Rolling him over was another struggle as a sleeping, grown man is five times the deadweight of a child. I peeled his wet leather jacket from him and wrestled with the Henley beneath it that was sticky and tricky to remove. Clay was hardly disturbed while I held my breath and occasionally let out a laugh at my awkward attempts. His boots came next, easy enough to tug off him, and then removal of his socks that were disgustingly saturated. His jeans, however, were my real dilemma.

I didn't want to feel like I was taking advantage of Clay in any manner, but extreme times call for extreme measures, and Clay could not sleep in wet denim that was suckered to him like a second skin. Gingerly, I popped the button at his waist before realizing they were button fly as well and I couldn't do a simple unzip to relieve him of his pants. No, I had to cautiously pop open each button, working deliberately while quickly, so I didn't disturb a particular body part I had no business thinking about.

Certain the sudden movement of tugging at his waistband near his hips would wake him, I pulled hard and fast.

Clay didn't rouse and, thankfully, neither did any other part of him.

Once his jeans were removed, he rolled over without a glance at me. His entire body shivered while I willed myself not to give him an appraising glance. However, the struggle was real. Clay might be over forty, but his body was tight. His muscles honed from manual labor. His back had divots I didn't think could exist. His legs had definition. His forearms were covered in tattoos.

I tried not to objectify him, but my imagination took flight, wondering how it would feel to have those arms wrapped around me in comfort. How a body that tight pressed against mine might feel like safety. Would his skin be warm like a blanket of security?

When he trembled again, a slight moan added to the quiver. I pulled the blankets up and over him knowing he could really use a shower to warm up and maybe some fever medication. He was burning up.

I should have walked away then. He was safely in his home. He was removed from the rain-soaked clothes. He was tucked into his bed. But I didn't go. I didn't have anywhere pressing to be.

Only a cheap motel some forty minutes away awaited us.

And while I should have laid on the couch next to Dutton, cuddling my little man, then left as soon as the sun rose, I didn't.

Instead, I snuck in a quick warmup shower for myself, helped myself to a T-shirt on the back of his bathroom door, and laid down beside Clay, keeping the blankets around him as a barrier between us. I figured if he woke with me beside him, I could explain myself without a scene in front of Dutton.

Dutton had already had enough scenes in his young life.

However, Clay slept into the late afternoon, and I busied Dutton with our normal routine. I'd been homeschooling him since August which wasn't ideal, and another reason I'd decided to leave Florida. I wanted him to be in a school setting where he could interact with children his age. Plus, I needed a job. I'd lost my nursing position in Florida, which had been another sign to exit the southern-most state. I couldn't continue to rely on the shaky hospitality my parents had given us.

When a heavy knock rattles the front door, I freeze from picking up Dutton's afternoon snack. He'd worked hard in the morning, following the homeschooling curriculum resources I'd found online, and had earned free time to play safe video games on my tablet. He didn't even look up at the interruption, but my breath caught. My hands trembled.

Breathe, Mavis. Breathe.

Setting Dutton's plate by the sink, I head toward the front door where I hear the distinct whirl of the keypad lock unlatching. As the door swings open, I pause beside Clay's couch, wringing my hands together and waiting on whomever might be entering.

With a stunned expression that mirrors mine, I face Stone Sylver, the local sheriff and Clay's eldest brother.

"Mavis Holland?"

"Hi." I weakly wave. "It's Mavis Grant, actually. Nice to see you again, Sheriff Sylver."

Stone is a large man with hair as silver as his brother's. His eyes are a softer blue, though. His presence intimidating while strangely reassuring. He's the law around here, and the impressive uniform he's wearing reinforces that position. Plus, I respect him.

His thick brows crease, the question between them the same one I've been asking myself for the last twelve plus hours.

What are you doing here?

Stone keeps those Sylver-clan blue eyes on me a second before looking around the room. "Is Clay around?"

"He's in his room. He's very sick." My answers sound stilted like I've been caught shoplifting, which I'd never do, and haven't done here. While I am invading Clay's privacy, I wouldn't say I'm breaking and entering. A quick glance at my open suitcase in the corner suggests I might be a squatter in a non-vacant home.

With a heavy exhale, I release my wringing fingers and

smooth my hands down my upper thighs. "He was stranded on the side of the road two nights ago."

Stone's brows rise.

"And there was a storm."

He nods to agree, as if remembering.

"So, I pulled over when I recognized him."

Stone's facial expression goes blank. Not a hint of surprise or suggestion of concern.

"He must have been out there for a while because he was soaked to the bone, and he had a horrible cough."

Stone lowers his head, shaking it side to side while the corner of his mouth crooks in a manner similar to his closest-in-age brother.

"He made it inside the house, and I was set to leave but through the windows, I saw him fall." I point at the floor to ceiling windows behind Stone. The glass panels are like sheets of clear drywall and provide a spectacular view to the immediate outdoors. A large field stone fireplace is the focal point of this room, though. A soft, caramel-colored leather couch faces the hearth while an oversized chair and matching ottoman sit in the corner closest to the fireplace. I'd previously admired the natural color scheme in the slightly masculine room, but now, I explain myself.

"I helped him up and took him to bed."

Stone's head lifts at those words, eyes expressive and wide.

I clear my throat as my face heats. "I mean, I helped him into his bed, tucked him, and then—" And then what? Helped myself to stay here overnight? Made meals with food that wasn't mine with the intention I'd pay him back?

Stone watches me a long, awkward moment before stating, "Clay's lucky you are here."

I want to take that praise and roll in the genuine warmth of Stone's words, but I know better. Luck and I are not friends. We aren't even neighbors.

"I was hoping to get him to eat something and then we'll be on our way."

"We?" Stone arches a brow, glancing around me.

"Do you remember my son, Dutton?" My voice lowers, embarrassed and ashamed of how I first encountered Stone Sylver. A cold sweat breaks out on my neck. I don't know if the sheriff remembers all his cases or if situations eventually blur together. We hadn't lived in Sterling Falls for long before everything fell apart.

How had my life become such a mess?

Oh wait, I know the answer to this one. Because I had a proclivity for alpha-holes instead of cinnamon rolls in my life, and my ex had been the biggest jackass.

"How is he?" Stone asks, his voice firm, but comforting. His question is as genuine as his smile.

I remember when he told me how proud he was of me, for finding the courage and the opportunity to admit to him what had been happening in my life. Like I had done something truly amazing and brave. I didn't think I had, but Stone made me feel like I had.

If only I had gone to Stone sooner. Would it have made my life easier, or more difficult? Leaving came down to timing, and I'd almost been too late to freely make the decision on my own. There are statistics and reports on the number of women who stay in abusive relationships, and volumes written about the psychology of such decisions, but no one understands the toxic position like the woman who lives it.

The hope that he doesn't mean his ugly words.

The desire to believe he loves us.

The way he made me feel during the good times.

The absolute lie in every touch and word and promise.

I focus on those lies to remind myself of what happened to me and Dutton.

My sister would have been so ashamed of me and the mess *I* made.

"He's doing well. Better." I slip my hands into the back pockets of my jeans. "We've been in Florida for a while. But I wanted to come home."

Again, we hadn't lived in Sterling Falls for long, but I'd liked it here. A sense of community existed. People were friendly. Business owners polite. We'd found a routine I appreciated. I'd had a good job. We had a beautiful home.

The thought of that house makes my skin crawl. I won't ever go back there, which was another reason to return. I had insurance claims to collect and the shell of a residence to sell, and I'd made the assumption that being present would speed up the already painfully long, drawn out process.

Stone continues to watch me before glancing around his brother's living room. "If you need anything, don't be afraid to ask."

"Thank you." We remain pinned in place. Him eyeing me; me trying to hold my ground. I should be restating how I'll leave after Clay takes some dinner. I should tell the local sheriff that I'll be staying in a motel some forty minutes from here because it was the cheapest place I could afford on my unemployed budget. I should ask if he's seen or heard anything about Wesley Holland.

But I don't.

Stone nods, then tips his head toward the long hallway that runs the length of the house, the outer wall all glass panels until the end where Clay's bedroom begins. "I'm gonna go check on the invalid." His smile softens again.

I smile in return and relax for the first time in a long time.

4

[Clay]

"You called in sick." Stone enters my room without a knock or additional warning.

The murmuring of voices had carried to my bedroom, and I'd intently listened to decipher all that was said between Mavis and Stone. I'd caught the gist of things, as their lowered voices drifted along the window-lined hallway to the slightly ajar door of my bedroom. What a wimp, tripping over my own feet, and knowing Mavis rescued me from laying on the floor of my living room. God knows how long I could have laid there before I might have gotten up.

"You never call in sick," Stone adds, bringing my full attention to him.

Staring up at the ceiling as I lie on my back, I blink. "Because someone has to run the Seed & Soil."

For as long as I can remember, I've worked at our family-owned business. The farmer's fleet and animal feed store had been our mother's vision combining her two great loves: nature and animals. Upon her death, our father cracked and took the Seed & Soil with him in the downfall. I hadn't gone to college like my most immediate brothers older and younger than me—Stone and Judd—opting out of more years in school and sticking close to what I saw as our family legacy.

While our father shattered the company, like a piece of pottery tossed to the ground, I was there when he died to pick up the shards and reassemble the precious business bit by bit. We still supply farm seed, but we've shifted more to landscaping and garden services. While continuing our animal feed selection, we've included more house-pet food and supplies. A few years ago, we added a general merchandise store with a collection of all things decorative related to home and garden, emphasis on the garden theme. I was proud of what I'd rebuilt. The family was equally thrilled as dividends from the business were split between all six of my siblings each quarter. I had the additional income of being the chief executive officer of the company and head manager, which basically meant I was married to my job.

I loved it but I didn't have a life outside it. And like Stone said, I never called in sick. I couldn't remember the last true vacation I'd taken other than weekends away that revolved around trade shows.

"I'm sick," I snap at Stone, as if I've committed a crime when deep down this is my body telling me I pushed too hard. I'd ignored the tickle in my throat, which turned into a chest-clenching cough accompanied by a lingering headache. Then I stood in the rain for who knows how long trying to work on that damn truck, which reminds me I need to have Perry tow it when it had been his fault I'd been out on a run for a part in the first place.

Actually, the decision had been mine. I should have told Perry I'd send someone the next day, but Perry Foster was one of my best friends, beside my brother, Stone. We did favors for each other all the time without question, and I hadn't been considering my health when I decided I'd be the one to handle his need.

I'd been thinking of Glady then.

With Mavis in my home, in my space, there was no room for thoughts of anyone else, least of all Glady.

"And Mavis *Grant* is here," Stone states as if reading my thoughts.

"Mavis Holland," I correct, reminding us both that she's a married woman.

Stone is a man of observation and, one night, he'd caught my gaze tracking Mavis as she moved about Milton's Roadhouse, the local bar and grill in town. He'd warned me she was a married woman, as if I needed the reminder, but there was something about Mavis that drew my attention.

Damsel in distress syndrome, my brother Knox once told me.

I was a rescuer. My siblings lost count of the number of stray animals I'd brought home until my dad said he'd break the neck of a lone cat one night. The gleam in his cold, vacant eyes since my mother's death told me his drunken ass might do it even if I didn't want to believe he meant it. The man had many faults, but animal cruelty wasn't one of them. He saved his dark, dangerous side for his kids.

"Don't think she's married anymore," Stone states, arching one thick brow. His expression suggests he knows something.

"Don't think I'm interested." The words were harsh, roughened by the scratch in my throat, and in total contrast to the way my pulse kicks up at this news, making me a liar. Just as quick as my blood flow surges upward, I crash, reminding myself I don't have *time* to be interested in Mavis even if I have admired her from afar for years.

Not to mention, Stone was only making an assumption about Mavis's marital status, not stating a fact.

"Sounds like she's been taking care of you."

I scoff. "I don't need taking care of." Smirking, I give him my best fake, gleaming smile to reinforce my comment. I've been a one-man show for forty-three years because I take care of others. The family business. My employees. The women who pass through my life. Stray animals. Plants.

"You're extra ornery today." Stone's broad shoulders lower, questioning my condition.

"I'm sick," I remind him when that shouldn't irritate me. I'm not the one to be easily irritated in our family—I leave that honor to my younger brothers Sebastian or Ford—but lately there's something I can't quite define, a restlessness inside, an unease that feels out of reach to settle. Maybe it's all just another symptom of my illness.

Or maybe I just need to get laid.

Stone meets my eyes a second before looking away, focus aimed toward the window. The same glass panels lining the length of my hallway encompass one wall of my bedroom. I crave natural sunlight and not feeling caged in. The floor to ceiling windows were expensive and a pain to install but worth every penny and profanity cursed once the renovation on this old house was completed nearly a decade ago.

I scrub a hand down my face and roll to my side. I'm only wearing a pair of boxer briefs beneath the duvet, and I stare at my brother, knowing whatever is going on with me isn't his fault. *We* worked hard to keep our family together. Stone had been away at college for four years and had not been a witness to how bad things were getting. How much of a dick our dad had turned into. Not able to find the solution to his heartache in the bottom of a bottle, and yet unable to give up what only contributed to his demise. But Stone never failed to check in daily on the family.

"Is she staying?" Stone asks, turning his head back toward me. His expression is one of concern. My family jokes I have a pattern. That damsel in distress thing. However, once the calamity is rectified, I'm free, whether by her choice or mine is never certain.

"I don't even know what she's doing here," I say quieter.

"Sounds like she rescued you from the side of the road. Why didn't you call me?"

"My phone died." I thought I had it plugged into the charger in the truck, but apparently, I didn't have the plug fully in the outlet. When I realized the damn thing hadn't charged, it was too late. The truck stalled. The storm happened. And I tried to rescue myself.

Like I always do.

AFTER A FEW MORE MINUTES OF interrogation about flu symptoms and a suggestion to rest, Stone leaves. A light, fitful sleep allows me to sense movement within my normally empty home. Hearing the murmur of voices and the lilting laughter of a woman and a child when my place is typically silent.

Ceramic bowls clatter. Water runs. The hum of the television trickles to my room.

Then Mavis appears at my bedroom door, my body sensing her presence before I open my eyes. She comes closer, a strong floral scent giving her away but not overpowering me. Through my congested nose, it's a wonder I can smell her at all.

"Clay? Honey?" Her voice is quiet, as if she doesn't wish to disturb me even though her intention is to wake me.

My eyes shoot open at hearing the endearment and the tenderness in her voice. She offers me a strained smile. One that doesn't light up those dark eyes but keeps them shuttered. *Did Stone say something to her?*

She sets a dinner plate with a bowl on it on the nightstand. "I was hoping you could maybe eat something. I made some chicken soup and brought some crackers. You're taking a lot of medications and need something in your stomach to soak it up."

What I really want is a shower and to change my underwear, but I don't mention it.

She swallows and drops her gaze. "Once you eat, I'll feel better leaving."

Leaving? Where is she going?

My gaze drops to her left hand, the one once graced by a giant diamond. Is she really divorced? Or is she simply not wearing her ring?

She isn't wearing my T-shirt anymore either but her own clothes. Dark jeans. A flannel shirt, open in the front and exposing a fitted tee underneath. A pair of cabin socks cover her feet. She looks comfortable, casual, and *right*, standing in my room beside my bed.

"Where are you going?" My voice is still crackling, and scratchy like sandpaper. My chest constricts at the thought of her leaving my house.

She shrugs, stepping back and wringing her hands together. "I have a motel room rented outside of town. We were headed there when I found you."

"At midnight?" My brows lift. I recall the time being late, the mountain highway dark as black silk, and recklessly dangerous in the storm.

"We got a late start from Florida."

"Is that where you've been?"

She nods, then points at the soup. "You should eat."

Avoidance, I recognize thee.

Slowly, I shift, lifting myself to sit. Mavis rushes forward, tugging my pillows to an upright position behind me and gently pressing at my shoulder so I lean into them. She pulls the covers up to my lap, folding them over and smoothing them over my thighs before she stalls, realizing what she's doing. She stands tall again and takes a giant step away from the bed but her gaze lands on my bare chest. Her eyes widening, the dark color of her cheeks deepening. She likes what she sees, and damn, it feels good to be looked at like that, even if I am sick. I rub a hand down my sternum and over my exposed belly. Mavis follows the trail before pulling up her eyes.

She points toward the bowl. "Do you need any help?"

"I got it." Only, as I reach for the plate, my arm feels limp, and I can hardly lift the stoneware without the bowl on it rattling. The spoon falls off the edge. "Dammit."

Mavis quickly bends to pick it up. "I'll get you another one." Her voice squeaks. Her movements are rigid. Heck, her back is ramrod straight and the desire in her eyes moments ago is wiped clean. Something else replaces that pleasant appraisal. Fear.

"Mavis," I whisper, as if speaking to a cornered cat. "It's okay."

She nods, like she hears me. She knows what I'm saying. But she can't apply what I've said.

She's okay. It's only a fallen spoon.

"I'll be right back." Spinning on her sock-clad feet, she rushes out the door while I hold the plate awkwardly on my lap and eye the soup.

The liquid meal looks homemade with carrots and celery, large egg noodles and chunks of chicken, and I'm certain I didn't have any of these ingredients in my cabinets or fridge. Did she leave while I was sleeping? I hadn't heard her exit.

A coughing attack hits me, and suddenly, the plate on my lap is jostling. The soup sloshes over the edge of the bowl when I lean forward, hacking into my fist.

Mavis rushes back into the room, spoon in hand, raised like a treasured utensil, until she sees my position.

"Shit," she whispers, taking the plate off my lap and running her hand over my bare back. Her warm palm feels amazing on my clammy skin. She doesn't speak while my lungs constrict and my throat barks until the spasm passes and I lean into the pillows behind me, tipping my head backward.

"Did you burn yourself?" Her concern has us both looking at my lap where I've spilled soup all over the sheet.

I groan, suddenly desperate to curl into the mattress and disappear beneath the blankets again. Instead, I shake my head in answer.

"Do you think you could take a shower? Or a bath?" Her nose wrinkles, implying I stink. "The warm water might feel good, and while you shower, I can change the sheets."

"You don't need to do that. You don't need to make me soup. You don't even need to be here."

Taken aback by my tone, Mavis steps away from the bed again. Her hands which were once fussing over my lap are clasped together again in a way I've already learned tells that she's on edge.

I've made her anxious when she's been nothing but kind to me.

"I'm sorry," I mutter, the apology weak and unworthy of what I've said, how I've said it. Without a care to her presence, I fling back the covers and toss my unsteady legs over the side of the bed. "I'll shower."

With my hands clutching the edge of the mattress, I place my feet on the floor and take a deep breath. Mavis steps forward like she'll help me, stops as if reconsidering, and then retreats.

I can't look at her. I'm ashamed of my behavior, of my sick position, and my lack of clothing. She shouldn't see me like this, and she doesn't deserve my irritation. She has done nothing wrong.

Without a glance back at her, though, I stand on shaky legs, and stumble toward the bathroom.

I'D LOVE to stand in the shower for the rest of my life as the steam clears my nasal passages, and the hot water flows over me like heaven. But I don't have the strength, and within seconds, the warmth drains any energy I could muster. I quickly dry off, feeling only minutely better, then tug on a pair of black sweatpants that were hanging on the back of my bathroom door and return to my bedroom.

Where I find my bed freshly made, the plate on the nightstand is swiped clean, and the soup still steaming. All minus Mavis.

"Fuck." I hiss, and scramble on shaky legs down the hallway.

In my living room, Mavis is zipping up a suitcase and telling her son to put a tablet in his backpack.

"I don't want to leave," the child sulks, seated on my couch beside his sack, holding said tablet.

"Time to go, little bear," she says before glancing up at me from her kneeling position. She finishes zipping the case, and stands, settling the luggage on its wheels.

Meeting my eyes, she coolly says, "I replaced the food we ate with new groceries. More soup is in a container cooling on the kitchen counter. You'll need to put it in the refrigerator in a little while. Your sheets are in the washing machine. They'll need to be moved to the dryer in an hour."

She lowers her head. "And I borrowed a T-shirt which was freshly washed and returned to your drawer." As she ticks off the list of things she's done for me, I'm ticked off with myself.

Stepping forward, which takes my remaining energy, I reach for her hand.

Mavis steps back. Her son jumps off the couch, placing himself between her and me. A pair of eyes matching his mother's glare at me.

I hold up both my hands, palms outward, knowing exactly what I've done wrong. "I'm sorry." I swallow hard, tampering down the ache in my chest that she might be afraid of me. "I'm being an a—" My gaze shifts to the kid. "A jerk. I didn't mean to touch you without your permission. I only wanted your attention."

Mavis eyes me warily while placing a protective hand on each of her son's shoulders.

With a deep exhale, I add. "I want you to stay." I could argue that I don't know where the request came from but there's a feeling deep down in the pit of my belly. An ache where I don't feel quite right about her leaving.

"Don't go." The roughness of the words doesn't match the tenderness I intended, the genuine desire I wish to express. I don't want her to leave.

"I haven't been a gracious host, but I have a guest room." I glance down at her son. His hair is the same midnight color as hers and a bit shaggy and long. His eyes are wide and round, matching his mother's set. He's lanky and lean, and small. *Is he wearing a shirt with a princess on it?* My forehead furrows, the question is one I don't have the energy to ask.

"You two can take that room if you don't mind sharing the space." I glance at my couch, willing to sleep there and give Mavis my bed, but my room would be better for my condition. I'm isolated in there.

"That's very kind of you, but we don't want to be in your way. I'm sure you'll feel better in a few more days."

"Days?" I scoff but soften the sound with what I hope is a reassuring smile.

Mavis doesn't smile back. Her hands cover her son's shoulders, pulling him against her. "You've already suffered through two days. I predict you have three more to go, with rest, before you're on the mend."

"Two?" I question, sounding like an owl. Did I miss a day? Mavis brought me home. I slept until late this morning. "It's Tuesday."

She clears her throat. "It's Wednesday, actually."

How did I miss an entire day? Fever fog, I guess.

Without thinking, I step toward her again. She shoves her son behind her and steps back.

I raise my hands once more and add more space between us. Pain strikes my chest like a lightning bolt. *Who hurt her? Hurt them?* While I have a strong inkling of who it was, I don't want Mavis to ever think I'd act in a similar manner toward her or her son. Her suspicion, caution, reminds me of the behavior of my siblings and I around our father, and I will never emulate that behavior and hope to never give off a vibe that I might.

"Please. Don't go." Another bolt of anxiety strikes. If she leaves, I might lose her. The thought is rash, and I dismiss it as addled flu-brain, which coincides with the fact I'm suddenly sweating. I swipe at my brow and take a seat on the couch.

"You should really be in bed. And eat your soup."

"Come tuck me in," I tease, sensing she's the one who wrapped me up when I'd dreamed my mother had. Her touch on my forehead reminded me of my mom. She's been taking care of me, like Stone said, and I shouldn't take advantage of her. I shouldn't request she do more, but something unfamiliar yet soothing warms my insides and has nothing to do with my fever.

Holding my smile in place, Mavis finally interprets my jest, and chuckles. Strained, the sound is still a hint of laughter and breaks the tension between us.

"Take the guest room."

Her eyes narrow. "But you don't even know me." She peeks back at her son. "Us."

"I know you, Mavis."

She's a woman I've secretly coveted when I had no right to want her, and she's been missing for over a year. Now, she's back, standing in my living room, fiercely protecting her son, and I want wherever that strength comes from aimed at me.

5

———————

[Mavis]

Something deep inside me tells me I'm safe here. Clay seems genuine enough in his offer for us to remain a few days, and I really don't want to take Dutton to a musty, old motel. Plus, Clay needs more rest and recovery time, and I want to help him in return for his generosity.

He didn't immediately kick us out.

After helping Clay back to his bedroom and setting him up with a bed tray I'd found tucked in his kitchen, I leave him to his soup. I move Dutton and my things into the guest room we will share, and feed Dutton, then set him up in front of the television, as a means of distraction.

Returning to Clay's bedroom, I find the meal tray on the floor beside the bed and Clay resting on his side, phone in his hand.

"You should sleep," I remind him, handing him another dose of fever-reducing pills. Men are babies when it comes to illness, and I've found doling out their medication when they're sick is best.

Plus, I'm a mom and a nurse. Funny how I hadn't planned on being the first one when it happened.

Clay takes the pills, downs an entire glass of water, and settles back on his pillows. "Thank you."

I nod, bending to retrieve the food tray, but when I stand upright, Clay is watching me.

"I mean it, Mavis. Thank you for being here." He holds out his hand and I want to take it. I want to believe in the sincerity on his face. The warmth in those occasionally icy eyes. The softening around his mouth, flashing me with more dimples. But I don't trust myself.

Kindness could be my undoing, and I don't need to be undone now that I've finally pulled the tatters of myself back together.

Still, I offer him a timid smile and nod. "You're welcome." Holding his gaze, our eyes locked together, a thin bead of sweat trickles down my neck. His large palm remains extended but I'm holding the tray like a shield when I want to drop it and take his offering. I want to know how his rough-looking hand might feel in mine. Would he be gentle? Would his kindness seep through his touch? Or would those large hands turn into fists?

Instantly, I shake the thought. This is Clay Sylver. He'd never act in such a manner.

"Get some rest," I whisper, forcing more of a smile before turning away from him and exiting his bedroom.

Hours later, Dutton has taken his nightly bath and settles into the queen-sized bed in Clay's guest room. We read a chapter from the book we've been sharing nightly together. He loves to read, which I'm thankful for. He loves to draw and dance. Play outdoors and take adventures. And he loves anything princess related.

My ex hated that about my son. *He* swore I was babying Dutton, catering to a whim, making the boy soft. With old-fashioned ideals and machismo off the charts, my ex didn't understand that Dutton was constantly evolving. He needed to discover who he is, and indulging in a phase of princess worship or finding a preference for typically female-defined activities did not make him a girl or gay or any other construct my ex wanted to place on a child.

Because Dutton *was* a child, full of imagination and exploration, and I didn't want to squander, squash, or dissuade him. If he wanted to be a fucking princess, he could be whoever the hell he wanted to be.

And if he did want to be a girl or was gay or wanted to be any newly defined term, I would love him unconditionally. *Un.Con.Ditionally.*

My ex disagreed and that was the final straw.

To my surprise, Dutton never asks about Wesley. A quiet relief fills the empty well once within my son. Although spending time with my parents hadn't done Dutton many favors, being around my father restored his faith in men a teeny bit. My father hadn't been physically cruel or outwardly aggressive. He wasn't verbally abusive or demeaning. Any chastising digs he made were aimed at me.

Cecilia wouldn't want this. The reminder of my sister's perfection was constant. She would have made better decisions. She would have done a better job than me.

"Okay, baby. Time for bed."

Dutton groans. I kiss his head and roll off the side of the bed, taking the chapter book with me. After setting it on the nightstand, I turn toward Dutton, watching him slip deeper beneath the blankets and then I pull the covers to his shoulders.

"Sleep well, my love." I swipe a hand over his dark, shaggy bangs.

He smiles before his expression turns pensive. "Are we going to live here now?"

I kneel beside the bed, leaning on the edge to be at his level. "No, honey. But Mr. Sylver is letting us stay a while."

"Until he's not sick."

I'm not certain how long we'll be here, but I don't want to overstay my welcome and I don't want to take advantage of Clay. Still, canceling the motel reservation for a few nights will make me rest easier knowing the extra money will remain in my pocket for now.

"I don't know, baby. But we're safe here." That's the question he's really asking.

"I don't want to go home," he whispers, recalling our house in town. The beautiful historic place on a gorgeous boulevard off the business district of Sterling Falls. The one bought under false pretense and with money we didn't have. The one purchased with a promise of forever when eternity wasn't a possibility.

"We aren't ever going back." I run my hand through his thick hair and cup it on the top of his head, lowering my forehead to his. We didn't have a place to call home now, but we'd find one. We'd make something great out of the grains of sand we had. The thought reminds me of the princess chapter book we are reading where the heroine has a jar of loose sand she's convinced is magical.

I'll make it happen for him. For us.

First, I need to reclaim what I can of the property loss here. Then, we'll make a plan.

Running the tip of my nose over his, I say, "I love you, little bear."

"I love you, too, mama bear."

That's all that matters in this world.

Hours later, I check on Clay, certain he's sleeping like he had been the last time I checked, right after putting Dutton to bed.

Instead, Clay is awake, staring at his phone again. I remember a man like that, constantly looking at the device like an extension of his hand. He'd been checking on deals he'd dickered and checking in on the other people in his life.

"Mavis?" Clay softly calls my name in the darkness of his room. The only light is naturally floating in from the outside and the illumination of his phone.

"Just wanted to check on you one more time before I go to bed."

Clay has rolled to his back, and he slowly sits upright. He wears a T-shirt when he wasn't earlier. He's kicked off the blankets once covering his legs and his black sweatpants are tugged up to below his kneecaps. The fever medication must be kicking in if he's warm.

"Is Dutton all settled in? Everything good for him?"

I smile at his concerned questions. "He'll sleep like a hibernating bear cub in that bed. Thank you."

Clay slowly lowers his head but looks at me with a playful gaze. "Will you sleep well in there?"

"I'll be just fine." I feel exceptionally comfortable here. Too safe. "Thank you."

Silence passes between us before he asks, "Were you wearing one of my shirts earlier?"

I chew my lower lip, warmth creeping across my cheeks. The other night, I'd taken advantage of a clean, warm shirt because I hadn't thought to bring my own nightwear into the bathroom with me when the desire to shower occurred.

"Did you shower in here?" His gaze wanders to the open door of his bathroom as if reading my thoughts.

I chew my lip harder, uncertain how to explain that I'd taken liberties when I should have asked permission.

A wide, bright smile curls amid the heavier-than-normal scruff around his mouth. "Damn," he whispers. "I missed it."

Uncertain for a second if he's toying with me, or teasing, my lower belly flutters at the thought he might be *flirting* with me.

Don't be foolish, Mavis.

"And you in my tee." Clay hums. "Can I tell you how much I liked seeing you in it?"

The T-shirt was nothing special, and for a moment, I simply stare at him, wondering what he's doing. Men like Clay Sylver don't flirt with women like me. Broken ones. One trying to pick up her own pieces.

Still, relief washes over me. He isn't angry that I used his shirt. He is not upset that I helped myself to a shower.

I chuckle as the truth hits me. He's definitely teasing me like he'd joke and wink at the elderly ladies in town, making them feel a little desirable with his innocent banter.

"Clayton Sylver, I think that fever is muddling your brain."

He laughs before a coughing fit chokes off the happy sound. Rushing to his side, I'm hesitant to help him, uncertain if he'd want my hands on him as a form of comfort. Unable to relieve his cough, I hate feeling so helpless.

When the chest-clenching subsides, Clay takes the glass of water I offer him and drinks. Setting it back on the stand himself, he glances up at me towering over him like a mother hen.

He lifts his hand as if he wants to take mine again. I glance down at how he reaches forward and then retreats. Earlier, I'd overreacted. He wasn't going to hurt me. He simply wanted my attention. Still, I'd gone into fight mode. Dutton's attempt to come between us brought out my mama bear claws. Dutton was the only thing that mattered. His safety. His protection.

"Did you sleep in my bed the other night, mama bear?" The term stiffens my shoulders. Had he heard Dutton and I exchange such a thing? Or can he simply read me?

"I—" Helping myself to his bed was more . . . intimate . . . than borrowing a shirt and sneaking in a shower. Before I can try to explain my reasoning, which was shaky at best, Clay speaks.

"I might have liked that, too." He winks and my face flames.

He *is* flirting with me. Or maybe this is just carefree banter. It's been so long I don't know how to tell the difference.

"I'll be staying with Dutton tonight."

Clay digs his teeth into his lower lip while his eyes focus on mine, like he's fighting the pull to let his gaze roam down my body. An appraising scan meant to scorch my skin. He's drinking me in with only a stare, and I want to be swallowed whole. I want to be touched in a way I don't feel threatened, and Clay wouldn't harm me. He'd be good for my soul, while bad for my heart.

I could love a man like him but that is a dangerous thought. I trust fast and fall hard, and I promised myself I'd do better. I'd steel myself against charm and good looks and falseness. Besides my life is too complicated for someone to love me in return, and I don't want to put anyone in a position where they feel led on. It wouldn't be fair. I'm free of Wesley, wherever he might be, but I'm still not in the right head space to open up to someone new. I might never be.

Because one thing I'd need is control. Of my future, my decisions, my sexuality. And I have yet to meet a man who is willing to let me be domineering in the bedroom and an equal outside of it.

"Good night, Clay."

"Night, mama bear."

6

———

[Clay]

I might have come on a little too strong, especially since being sick in bed isn't the most attractive position to be in. Thankfully, I didn't scare Mavis off, and she stayed the remainder of the week. I needed the time to fully recover from the horrible flu I'd had. I still felt a little shaky, even weak at moments, but I couldn't stay in bed another day. I was coming out of my skin and filled with concern for the Seed & Soil. I had to get back to work.

Dressed in my typical Seed & Soil button up, sleeves rolled to my elbows, and wearing a pair of faded jeans, I enter my kitchen where Mavis stands motionless near the stove. Those dark eyes are wide, doe-like, and watching me.

"Where do you think you're going?" she teases, but concern etches the angles of her cheek. She's hard in some places, soft in others. Delicate like a butterfly's wing while granite at the same time.

I haven't been out of my bedroom much, other than a late meal with Mavis two nights in a row. While we didn't talk much, more like exchanging details on my condition, there was something comforting about her presence in my home, in my kitchen, seated across from me at my table. In the typical quiet of my house, noises existed. Soft ones. Homey ones. Her smile was practically a sound. Her dark eyes a noise as well, and I liked it better when she looked at me rather than away from me.

"Work." As soon as I say the word, my gaze catches on her son sitting at the table. I haven't had much interaction with him. Dutton wasn't present during those late meals, being already in bed by then. Seems like an early sleeper but what do I know about kids. I don't have any. Haven't wanted any.

I'm happy as Uncle Clay to Adara, the sweetest toddler in the world. Recently, my brother Ford moved home, adding three more nieces to my roster with Zelle, Winnie, and June. My sister Vale has a boy, Hudson, who is going on eleven. Knox is now a stepfather to Tim and Violet. The second generation of Sylvers is growing but still small compared to my six siblings.

We could use some more boys in our crew, and I glance at Dutton again but then my forehead cinches once. His nails are painted light pink, and his T-shirt has a sparkling unicorn on it.

"Can you wear that to school?" I ask, uncertain if the kid attends. Mavis has hardly left my place. She explained how she paid for a service to bring the first round of groceries to my house. Which reminds me, I owe her money for the purchase.

"I'm homeschooled," he states, not looking up at me and sounding indifferent about his education. I was never a fan myself, thus deciding against college. Plus, someone needed to be in charge of the Seed & Soil as our dad certainly wasn't minding it properly.

"Huh." With my hands on the back of a kitchen chair, Mavis continues to watch me.

She clears her throat and lowers her gaze, then gives me her back as she moves eggs around in a skillet. "Dutton doesn't attend school because I don't know yet where we'll permanently plant."

"Meaning you aren't staying in Sterling Falls?" Surprise peppers the question.

Mavis glances over her shoulder and shrugs. "I have some unfinished business here and then Dutton and I can make a fresh start." She turns her head over her other shoulder and gives her son a warm smile. He smiles back at her, but his expression is more pensive.

We should probably talk about what that unfinished business includes, as I only know the tip of the iceberg about her, but right now is not the time.

Either way, a strange knock hits me in the sternum. I hold my breath, willing away a cough. The contracting of my lungs is getting to be a nuisance and I'm tired of it.

"Well, you're welcome to stay here as long as you'd like." The invitation is sincere.

It's been nice to have someone else in my space. *Two* people. I like hearing Mavis's softer tones directed toward her son as she flits around. The easy laughter shared between her and Dutton. The low hum of cartoons playing on the television. Mavis's distinctly floral scent lingers in my bedroom when she visits there. A faint strawberry fragrance wafts out of the guest bathroom on the rare occasions I've traveled down the hallway. The sounds and scents are warm, and Mavis and Dutton's presence make my place feel more than a house, more like a home.

Not going to lie, an added bonus is having someone cook for me. Too often, I eat on the fly, ordering from takeout places or finding myself at Milton's Roadhouse late at night, because the diner in town closes early. Mavis's homemade soup was just what I'd needed. Then her chicken and mashed potatoes were extra. The other night, she made me breaded pork chops and roasted potatoes. I could have asked her to marry me on the spot.

This morning she's making scrambled eggs and sausage links.

I really need to get to the Seed & Soil, but damn, that smells good, and watching her move easily around my kitchen has that strange knocking inside my chest happening again. Only, I don't think it is another cough coming on. Mavis is so stunning with that long hair, a hint of gray strands mixed here and there upon further inspection. And I've had lots of time to inspect her as she's waited on me the last five days. She didn't wear one of my T-shirts again. She didn't sleep in my bed again either. But she's circled around me enough her floral scent has taken up residence in my nose as my favorite fragrance, and her cheeks darken a bit when she catches me tracking her around a room.

I'm not afraid to admit I'm attracted to her, but I'm afraid admitting my attraction might scare her off. And I'm not ready for her to disappear again, especially after the news that she *will* be leaving at some point.

"Is there anything I can help you with, pertaining to that unfinished business?" I also don't want her to feel like I've taken advantage of their situation. She's here with no strings attached, and I'd hate for her to think I'm expecting anything in return. I'd be gutted if she thought there was a power imbalance between us. I want to respect her privacy while letting her know I'm here for her.

I give a quick glance to Dutton before meeting Mavis's eyes. We don't need to discuss her situation before the child, but I'd still like to know if I can help somehow.

She offers me a waning smile. "I've got it."

The answer doesn't settle well for me, but I let the topic rest for now. I have eggs and sausage to gobble up before getting back to my routine.

Work, work, work.

Sʏʟᴠᴇʀ Sᴇᴇᴅ & Soil has gone from one low building to a giant barn-like structure, complete with our home and garden merchandise in the front and our original feed and farm supplies sales department in the back. We aren't a garden center so much, but we do sell house plants and seasonal flowers. We also have a landscaping business and brick patio department, run by my brother Knox.

Who happens to be in my office when I arrive.

"Well, well, well. Look what the cat dragged in." He tips back in a spare desk chair that serves no purpose in my office.

"Did you bring him back?" Knox dips his head, purring in response to my office cat, Tillie, an orange tabby who keeps the mice at bay around here, and presently sits on his lap, having her chin rubbed. He coos at the feline. "Giving him one of your lives?"

"And to what do I owe the honor?" I interject over the cat lovefest, and arch a brow, implying his presence in my office. Knox has his own corner of our Seed & Soil world on the other side of the building.

"Heard you were coming in today. How are you feeling?"

"Better."

Our eyes meet. My brother, like all my younger siblings, took some hard knocks while growing up. Our Dad doled out abuse like one might toss out playing cards. You never knew what you'd get, and yet some seemed to be dealt a losing hand more often than others. Maybe the harshness came about because Stone and Judd were gone, and I was a man in Dad's eyes, so the younger set were thought to be weak when that's hardly been the case for any of my siblings. We each have strengths in varying forms.

Stone is fiercely protective and bears a burden of guilt he doesn't need to wear. Knox and Sebastian have always been scrappy; fighters in a sense. Vale is the lover, but her sweetness covers battle scars I'm worried she'll never address. Ford appears to have a tough outer shell, deflecting harsh words flung at him like weak arrows, bouncing off his thicker skin. Judd was not so fortunate as a child. He tucked hard words beneath his pillow and wrestled demons he didn't need to fight, but still his perseverance has carried him far.

As for me, I seemed to know how to play the game with our dad. How to dance around muddy water and duck the thunderclouds in his voice. Didn't mean he didn't hurt me emotionally or insult me verbally, but I never experienced his fist.

And I always felt a little sorry for him.

The love of his life died by a condition brought on by her final pregnancy.

The child—Vale—was spared, but our mother was gone.

Dad was left to raise seven children from ages twelve to newborn on his own.

His position, however, did not excuse his behavior. He needed help but refused to get it for himself or allow it for his children. He was a sad, lonely, pathetic man, but heartbroken, nonetheless. While child-rearing had been our mother's greatest joy, she had been his, and he simply did not know what he was doing without her. He chose bottles of Jack for comfort over his kids, drowning in depression and abuse that scarred each of us in our own way. Frustration and helplessness ate at me for what our father did to my siblings and me. Internally, I raged with anger when I was younger, and a need to save them all, especially Vale, our only sister.

Dad and I had our brand of conflict. A complicated relationship that involved strong differences of opinion on *how* to run this business. Harsh disagreements about *who* was doing the running. His name might have been on the title of this company, but I was the one working my ass off to keep it afloat, working against the tide of creditors he'd pissed off or owed. Our family was constantly poor until our father died when I was almost twenty-two. The debts were steep. The money nearly non-existent.

I rebuilt Sylver Seed & Soil. Stone raised our siblings.

Our positions were a strange marriage of brother and brother, trying to parent the younger set. Stone had the role of bad cop, although he was hardly a disciplinarian, and eventually did join the local sheriff's department. I was good cop, but I don't believe I deserve the title. I just had more patience, empathy maybe, for our family situation.

I didn't fault my father. I didn't hate him. I also didn't love him in the end.

"Heard you have a house guest." Knox continues, giving Tillie a good scratch behind her ears. Her enjoyment is so loud I can hear her purr from my own desk chair where I take a seat. I'm shakier than I thought I'd be after so many days of rest.

"You're so fucking nosy." I chuckle. Knox loves gossip, although he isn't one to feed into rumors. He's just curious by one resident saying this and another resident saying that. He's friendly with everyone and happy as a man can be having been reunited with his high school sweetheart a little over a year ago.

I don't have to ask who told him about Mavis. Stone most likely.

"You sure about her." He stops eagerly scratching Tillie and swipes a hand down her back before moving her off his lap to the floor. She gives him a sassy glare over her shoulder and saunters out of my office like it's his loss she isn't in his lap anymore.

"Mavis?" I counter. "She's been helping me while I've been sick."

"More like taking care of you." Knox arches his left brow, the one with a scar through it.

I scoff, but he's right. Mavis did take care of me.

"And you're used to being the one doing the caring," Knox states, reminding me of the family joke about that damsel in distress syndrome.

"I was the damsel." I flutter my lashes and press my hands together, bringing them beneath my chin in mocking jest.

Knox laughs but then his expression turns serious. "I'm worried about you."

"Me?" I chide, feeling my forehead furrow. "Or her?"

Knox purses his lips. "You know her story, right?"

I turn to my computer, turning it on, and waiting for it to boot up. "She hasn't told me anything."

Knox sighs. "But you know, right?"

My brother isn't only our company brick layer and patio expert, he's also a volunteer firefighter for Sterling Falls because he has a hero complex, complements of nearly twenty years in the Navy.

While leaning back in the desk chair, that moves with my position, I glance at Knox. "I think she should tell me her version."

I don't want hearsay, although Knox knows some hard facts about Mavis.

A little over a year ago, her house across the street from Knox's then girlfriend, now wife, caught on fire. Mavis and Dutton were both inside when the blaze began. The instant memory churns my stomach. The fact that Dutton wouldn't be here without Knox finding him, hiding in the house, and carrying him out of the burning house. The churning turns to bile, threatening to choke me, when I consider Knox rushed back into the home to assist a second firefighter who found Mavis. Collectively, they carried her unconscious body to safety only moments before an explosion occurred. Mavis and her son would have been horrifically lost to me forever, and I find myself clenching my hands into tight fists at the thought. A chill runs down my spine. I'd never have the chance I currently have with Mavis had it not been for Knox.

Rumor had it her husband might have sparked the flames, an arson job, and drugged his wife.

If I were a violent man, I'd light the match to burn *him* to the ground.

After cooperating with local authorities, Mavis and Dutton moved out of town. Her husband was officially considered missing.

But a lot can happen in a year, and those were the details I didn't have. And I wanted them from Mavis.

"I appreciate you being worried about me, little brother, but I think I can handle a woman and her child."

"Said Sebastian," Knox jokes. "Before he fell head over heels in love."

Our youngest brother was the definition of troubled teen and eventually became a menacing adult, but after time in prison, he is a reformed man. He opened a local bakery, appropriately named after his grumpy ass, Curmudgeon Bakery, and three years later a beautiful woman stumbled into his business. Or rather, fell before the shop during an autumn rainstorm.

I'd known Enya Calloway before Sebastian. Sylver Seed & Soil had been audited by the state and needed an outside accountant to review our financials. Enya had been around for months before she encountered Sebastian. For a while, I thought our brother Judd, also an accountant and our chief financial advisor, might win her over.

Enya fell for the reformed bad boy instead.

Mavis might have a thing for bad men as well. A man who was still potentially dangerous, possibly on the loose, and a lingering concern in the back of my head.

"Yeah, well, Sebastian is a sap, just like you with Halle," I tease.

Knox chuckles. "Gonna happen for you, too." He stands and claps me on the shoulder.

"Never," I counter before he exits my office.

I just don't see love in my future. I'm too busy. I like projects, not long-term investments.

But if I had time, I'd want to spend it with Mavis.

With that thought, I laugh at myself because my computer is awake and glaring brightly at me, and I dive into the longest, and biggest, investment I've ever had.

Work.

7

[Mavis]

"Honey. I'm home." The jovial sound of Clay's voice rings through his house when he enters his front door sometime after eight o'clock.

I'd finally given up on him returning for dinner and was putting the leftovers away in his fridge. Stepping into his living room, I pause just outside the entrance from the kitchen, opposite where he remains by the front door.

"That was weird, wasn't it?" He wrinkles his nose. "I just made it weird." His eyes light up and he chuckles, but the sound is rimmed with nerves. He swipes his thick hand over his salt-and-pepper colored hair.

Clay takes my breath away. He's so rugged and tall, while casual cool and friendly. His personality beams through the wrinkles near his eyes and the smirky grin on his face.

Slipping my hands into my back pockets, I rock on my bare toes. "Not weird." But it was a little strange. He's hours later than I expected him when he doesn't owe me his time. And I'm not his sweetheart, or his wife. I'm a nearly forty-year-old single mother squatting for a while because of his hospitality.

Shouldn't I have my life better pulled together by now?

"I've just always wanted to say that." His voice lowers as he dips his head, his gaze dropping from me. "Never had anyone here to say it to."

The confession feels like an admission of loneliness which is difficult to believe. Clay Sylver is a very good-looking man in his mid-forties. Those icy-colored eyes. The scruff on his jaw. Even his wrinkles add to the sexiness.

Then again, I've learned not to judge a book by its cover. Beneath a pretty image can be a dark tale and pages full of aggression.

I should tell him I'm honored he shared his thoughts and his greeting with me, but I don't want to make this moment any more awkward.

"I made you dinner," I state instead, and then decide I've made it awkward anyway. Announcing dinner sounds like an accusation, like I made it, waited for him, and he didn't tell me he'd be late. Or not present. When neither case is necessary. I'm a guest, nothing more. He doesn't owe me explanations. I owe him everything right now.

Clay's head lifts. His brows flinch. Confusion fills his cheeks. "You did?"

"I just thought . . . I assumed . . . I—" I take a deep breath, hating how I sound like I'm cowering. Removing my hands from my back pockets and rubbing them along the side seam of my jeans, I try again. "I thought it'd be nice for you. For letting us stay even though you're on the mend."

Although, I misjudged. He clearly doesn't come home for dinner, and I hate how I waited on him. Hate how I questioned where he was, who he was with, what he was doing.

He isn't Wesley.

Clay steps further into the room. "I don't typically eat at home." He glances around his living room, as if looking for something. Or someone. Or maybe he's simply reminding me of what he already admitted. There hasn't been anyone here to eat with him in the past.

"But I'll make more of an effort tomorrow." He takes another step closer to me. "Not that you need to cook for me. But if you were cookin' . . ."

He reaches for the back of his neck and tips back his head, blowing out a breath. "I'm making this fucking weirder, aren't I?"

I chuckle, hoping to ease the subtle tension between us. "Not used to someone in your home. I get it. I don't need to make you dinner if you prefer to eat out."

"No." He's suddenly in front of me. He smells like earth and fresh air and the misty fall rain. "I'm so used to just working and working, I don't stop half the time until the shop closes at eight. Taking dinner late."

"Did you eat?" I question, then worry at my lower lip with my teeth.

"I did. But I'm still curious what you made."

"Fried chicken and homestyle fries."

Clay closes his eyes and tips back his head again. He inhales and hums like he's tasting the meal. When his eyes flip open, he says, "How about a second dinner?"

I laugh. "You don't need to do that. I packaged it all up as leftovers. You can eat it tomorrow for lunch, maybe."

Placing his hand on my upper arm, he says, "I'm sorry you went through all the trouble. I'm a terrible host."

I shrug. "I don't want to be an overbearing guest. It wasn't any trouble."

He nods and we seem to agree to drop the dinner debate.

"Where is Dutton?"

"In bed."

"Already?" Clay's brows lift.

"It's after eight. And he was tuckered out. There's a saying about boys playing hard from *son* rise to *son* set. That's him. We explored your yard a bit more today." The outdoors was our science classroom, as approved by the homeschooling curriculum I'd been using.

"Sounds like a healthy boy to me." Clay chuckles.

I clear my throat, about to impart on a difficult discussion. Maybe it's more of a test, which doesn't feel fair, but a test nonetheless, for Clay's reaction, and I utter a silent prayer he'll pass. "You might have noticed how his nails are painted and he wears a lot of typically female-defined clothing."

Clay stays very still.

I take another deep breath. "Love is love, Clay. And I love Dutton more than anything in this world. He's discovering who he is. Who he wants to be, who he's destined to be, and I'm giving him the freedom he needs to define himself in a world that wants to label everything."

Clay swallows. "Is your boy gay?"

"I don't know that he understands what that means but he knows what he likes. He likes pink things and glittery unicorns. He likes to play with my makeup and nail polish and enjoys watching female-led animation programs like *Princess Power*."

I don't know if Clay is familiar with *Princess Power*, but now isn't the time for explaining a television show.

He nods, his expression pensive, thought-filled, like he's really listening to me and not judging Dutton.

"My point is, I don't use the constructs boy or girl with him yet. He's just Dutton. My adorable, sweet, loving six-year-old, who has had a rough go of life so far."

Within seconds, Clay responds, as if he didn't need time to choose his words carefully or respectfully. His thoughts are instantaneous. "I think *love* is all that matters, especially for a child. Loving Dutton as he is, for who he is, is all he needs. The best thing you can do for him is love him."

I could hug him.

Sadness fills his voice before he clears his throat. "About that rough life, though, . . ." His eyes meet mine, softening a little, but I predict what's coming next. He should know more about us. He deserves to know more if we're staying in his home. I'd simply hoped I could put off truth telling for a little longer.

"How about a beer?" Clay asks. "Then we can sit on the couch for a chat."

I lower my head like a chastised child, preparing for a lecture about bad behavior when I've been labeled a good girl most of my life. "I'll get you one."

Clay's fingers come to my chin, startling me and I flinch back from the sudden touch. His hand holds still a second before he flips it, palm up. "I'll get *you* one. Take a seat."

Anxiety spikes within me as we trade places. Him heading for the kitchen, me heading for his couch. With the nerves inside me rattling a little harder, I swipe my hands over my thighs again as I take a seat.

Clay quickly joins me, settling at the opposite end of the couch, placing his back in the corner. He hands me my beer and taps the neck of his against mine. "To chats."

I don't reply, watching as he lifts his beer and takes a long pull while I only take a hesitant sip of mine. I'm not much of a drinker, especially beer.

When Clay lowers his beer to his thigh, he watches me. With his other arm extended on the back of the couch and one leg hitched up on the cushions, he looks like a mature model, the essence of casualness, about to have a photo taken.

"I'm not going to push, but like telling me about Dutton, which I appreciate, I'd like to know whatever else you feel comfortable telling me."

I sigh, glancing down at my beer bottle and picking at the label with my thumbnail. "But you already know things about me." I was surprised he remembered my name. Surprised he recognized me after a year's absence from this town. But I shouldn't be surprised he'd recall a thing or two about me from when I'd lived here.

"I want to hear them from you."

Certain he'll kick me out after I spill my tale, I inhale. I don't have anything left to lose that I haven't already lost, so telling Clay a few things isn't going to hurt.

I glance up at him. "Wesley and I moved here about five years ago. He said it'd be a fresh start for us. A beginning. We hadn't been dating very long before Dutton came along."

I weakly smile, remembering how pretty Wesley's promises sounded. We'd get married. We'd raise a family in a small town. Life would be easier, better than it had been in Florida.

"We bought the house and started renovating." My head lowers. "I'd been worried from the beginning that the house was too much. Too much money, too much space, too many projects, but Wesley kept saying we'd fill it with more children. And we had the funds."

I turn my head and glance toward the now dark window panels, staring out into the night. "But we didn't have the money. The house had been expensive, and all the renovations added up."

Wesley tackled a few projects on his own, but eventually, he was fed up with DIY, and started hiring out the work. We needed functioning bathrooms and a serviceable kitchen. I didn't know anything about the contractors who took the jobs. But I quickly learned we owed more money than we had.

"I'd been lucky to find a nursing job at the local hospital. We hired an older person in the area to watch Dutton. Wesley was gone a lot."

At the time, I'd thought Wesley was a salesman. Poultry was

his business. He had customers all over the United States and some even overseas. He was gone for large chunks of time.

Turning back toward Clay, I see he continues to observe me. Eyes kind and patient. Forehead furrowed with concern. What I'm telling him is only surface level.

"Time passed. Wesley was gone more often than home. And when he was present, life was . . . unpleasant. He had these ideals of what a wife should be while not living up to husband-standards. He criticized me often." I swallow hard as Clay's eyes darken. His fingers once loosely holding his beer bottle tighten around the glass. "And he was cruel to Dutton."

"How?" Clay's voice cracks.

I shake my head and lower my gaze. "He wasn't as open to letting him be who he wanted to be. He called him names. Criticized him and his choices. And he accused me of babying him, making him weak."

I swallow around the bile in my throat. The sick sensation within my gut every time I think of what Wesley said, and how I'd defend Dutton. The insults turned from an unnecessary teasing of Dutton to venomous abuse toward me.

"Did he ever touch Dutton? Lay a hand on him?" The strain in Clay's voice rises. His knuckles whiten against the brown bottle in his hand.

"He went for him once. I got in the way." I don't close my eyes. Don't need to recall the way I threw myself between man and child and took the slap that sent me to the floor.

We'd been arguing about finances, about his absences, and about our relationship before that moment occurred.

"He ever lay a hand on you?"

I don't speak, but our eyes meet, and the watery appearance of mine answers his question. I swallow hard and blink back the tears. I refuse to waste any more on Wesley.

"Shit," Clay mutters before lifting his beer and tossing back the bitter crispness. His eyes snag away from me and stare at the opposite corner of the room, somewhere near his fireplace.

Maybe I've said more than I should. Maybe I've confessed too much, but once the flood gates have opened, the rest of the story pours out.

"There's no doubt you heard about the fire." The house irreparably torched. "It took forever for the insurance company to accept the claims because . . ." I swallow hard again. "Because there was suspicion of arson."

The investigation took six months before they finally processed the claims. Another three months passed, and constant nagging on my end before the claims moved through the chain of command. The final payout was expected in July, then August. The final days of September are upon us and still nothing.

I scrape at the label on my beer once more. "They eventually determined faulty wiring but that faulty wiring could have been on purpose." Those sketchy contractors. Or a contract on my life.

I lift my head again. "The night before, I'd told Wesley I was leaving him. I was putting the house on the market and taking Dutton back to Florida."

"You wanted a divorce." Clay states the obvious.

"I didn't need one. We weren't married."

"But—" His gaze drops to my left hand, looking for the ring I haven't worn in over a year.

"It was an act. We called ourselves Mr. and Mrs. Holland but we weren't legally a couple on paper. Wesley always said we'd get to it. We'd have a proper wedding. A grand affair." I weakly wave my hand through the air, like the magic wand he'd pretended to be, fulfilling my every wish.

"Only we never did. We didn't have the money and even though we could have had a civil service, we didn't do that either." And here's where the stab wound in my heart reopens.

My eyes prickle with tears once more. "He already had a wife. In Florida."

"What the fuck?" Clay snaps, leaning forward and staring at me. "He what?"

"A wife in Florida. Me in West Virginia. And, I suspect, a new girl in Kentucky."

"What a mother—" Clay cuts himself off, chewing hard at his lower lip to hold back a slew of terms I've used myself to label Wesley Holland. Whatever Clay is thinking, I'm certain I said it out loud at some point. For all the names Wesley called me, I have some choice ones for him as well.

"How did you find out?"

My laugh is bitter. "When Wesley went missing, it wasn't as hard as I thought to trace a few breadcrumbs in his history."

What did surprise me was my parents never had the foresight to investigate him. My dad thrived on fault with authority and suspicion of others outside his world. Maybe they had looked into Wesley, and hadn't wished to share the truth, waiting for me to discover it for myself. Waiting for me to fail and come home with my tail between my legs.

Hadn't I done that for a while?

I shake my head. "He's still married to his wife, as far as I know, but she reported him as missing as well. I don't know what happened to the girlfriend."

I'm not certain what I was considered. The other woman? Never his fiancée. Never his wife as we'd told this community.

"Did you know about his wife before you planned to leave him?"

I shake my head. "After."

"And the house?"

"Was in my name." I came into a bit of money. The upfront investment had been all mine. "So, when the bills came due, or creditors called, and the insurance needed to be claimed, it all fell back on me. The arson investigation started with me." As if I'd want to torch my own home.

"I had to prove I wasn't a flight risk, which was first implied with Wesley's disappearance, before I could leave the area."

For a few weeks, Dutton and I stayed with Meredith Mulligan.

"Do you think he did it?" Clay asks, then immediately sits back and swipes his hand down his face. "Is this more than you want to talk about?"

His concerned expression tells me he's giving me an out. I don't need to overshare, but it feels good to tell someone other than my parents my thoughts.

"Considering I had Rohypnol in my system and Dutton was in the house, I can't rule out that Wesley wanted to take everything from me. My home. My life. My son." Tears well once again.

I shouldn't be sitting here. I shouldn't be back in Sterling Falls.

I should be dead. And so should Dutton.

8
____

[Clay]

Holy fuck. Just holy fuckity fuck.

What a *mothertrucking*— I grunt. As if the silent words I'm trying to restrain are a punch to my gut.

This poor woman. This beautiful, strong survivor sitting on my couch, staring sheepishly at me like she'd done something wrong when her life had been a living hell.

Wesley Holland, if that even is his name, was a dick of immense magnitude. The fucking bastard is trotting all over this country, staking claims to innocent women, making babies, and building homes on bottomless pits of promises.

"I'm so sorry that happened to you." The words are weak in comparison to how I feel. My future sister-in-law had gone through something similar but still not half as bad as what had happened to Mavis. Men can just be worthless pieces of—

I exhale and swipe my hand down my face again. Then I

finish off my beer. I might need another to cool the volcanic acid bubbling inside me.

If I ever saw Wesley Holland— If he dared to return to this town—

"So now what?" I ask, a thousand times calmer than I feel.

"I took a loan from my parents to pay off the debts." Mavis shakes her head. Her eyes still glisten. "I don't even know if half the contractors were legitimate, but I had invoices and receipts."

"Give me their names. Contacts. Anything. I'll check them out." I have extensive connections within the surrounding area, and I'll know within days if someone Holland hired took advantage of Mavis. Or if the person has an association with the thief. Because that's what Wesley is. He stole this woman's soft heart and used it against her.

"I was stupid to trust him." Her voice lowers.

"Don't do that," I snap, then take a calming breath. "Do not take the blame for his . . . his . . . his asshole-ness. He's a crook. A liar *and a thief*. A con artist."

"Well, I was conned," she states, her head lifting. Her voice rises. Guilt is written on her stunning face. *She* feels guilty for falling for him, but I refuse to let her accept fault. Maybe she'd been duped. Maybe she believed in false words, but that didn't give him permission to insult her or her child. To lay his hands on her or that kid.

Hastily, I press myself up off the couch to pace. I want to throw my bottle against the brick fireplace. I want to shatter something, but I don't want to scare her. She's had enough violence in her life.

He drugged her. Did he plan to burn them alive in that house?

Had he hoped the fire would take them out along with the property?

A home in her name which meant she'd have nothing once it was ashes, as if they never existed in his life.

How could a man be so cruel? Even my own father hadn't been that conniving, that *hateful*. He'd turned into a mean-ass drunk, who went too far with my younger siblings, but I believe he had regret. I believe he'd lost himself and didn't know how to swim out of the bottle he'd chosen to drown in.

And I never, ever take the blame for my father's behavior.

And Mavis should not fault herself for another man's evil ways.

Suddenly, I push the coffee table out of the way and lower to my knees before her, clasping her hands in mine and lifting them to my mouth. My lips linger against the knuckles. An incessant need to touch her takes over me. A need to press my lips to her skin, and inhale her intoxicating scent into my lungs, reaffirming she's alive.

I flip her hands, opening them to see her palms, and place another kiss against each of them. She's a fucking warrior of epic proportions and I want her to know that I worship her strength and resilience.

"I'm so sorry for all that happened to you, beautiful." I shake my head, shattered by her past.

The entire night's confession was so much more than I thought she'd share, as if the moment she began, she couldn't hold back. The truth spilled forth like a river of relief. What was left now was a muddy, dried riverbed, one thirsty to be refreshed.

Mavis had a look in her eyes I recognized. One I couldn't quite explain but empathized with, knowing that *something* would restore her confidence. Revive her spirit.

Damsel in distress, be damned.

I think of the care she gave me when I was sick. Making me dinner, hopeful I'd be home. We would have eaten together like a family.

She doesn't appear all that stressed out to me.

She's a survivor, like me.

UNFORTUNATELY, try as I might, I don't make it back to my place for dinner as I'd anticipated each morning. There was always one more order to check on. One more project. One more this or that.

A gnawing twist churned my stomach every time I thought of Mavis waiting on me. I wanted to get home to her and Dutton. I really did.

But by the third night of missed dinners, Mavis wasn't waiting. The house was dark. Mavis locked inside my guest bedroom with Dutton. Her car in my drive was the only hint she was still present.

I stood outside her bedroom door, fist raised, prepared to knock, but what could I say to her? An apology for another missed meal felt fruitless. She didn't owe me anything so why was she putting forth the effort? And I didn't owe her an explanation, so why was I going to apologize?

Still, guilt chewed at my insides. This is why I didn't have a woman in my life. A family outside of my siblings and *their* offspring. Long ago I determined I was destined to be alone.

But I wanted more. Man, did I want more.

Deciding against a knock, a risk of disturbing Mavis and Dutton, I turn toward my room. Two nights in a row Mavis left a plate covered in the microwave, ready for me to reheat. Tonight, there wasn't even a leftover.

For some reason, the absence irked me when it had been my own damn fault. I should have called Mavis. Better yet, I should have been here. I have managers and assistants, and employees in different departments who could handle what I couldn't get to, and I was always feeling I had something to *get to.* My excuse was that I didn't have anywhere else to be or anyone waiting on me.

But Mavis was here, and I was blowing an opportunity to get to know her better. We'd hardly crossed paths since that deep confession the other evening. I didn't know what she did with her day. I didn't know if she was having trouble with her insurance. I was letting a virtual stranger live here and I needed to know more about her.

Because I had a feeling about Mavis. An over-all good vibe about her character. Mavis made some wrong turns in her life, but who hadn't?

After a quick shower to wash off the day, I slip on loose fitting pajama pants and head for the kitchen, wanting a beer to cap off my foul mood. The wind howls outside the windows. Another storm is brewing.

Within seconds, rain lashes at the panes. The glass covered with thick rivers so opaque I can't see outside them.

A rumble of thunder booms.

A flash of lightning snaps.

Then a scream. And the lights go out.

I set down my beer without thinking about the action and race for my guest room. Thankfully, Mavis hadn't locked the door and I push it open with enough force it swings inward and slams against the wall.

A muffled cry occurs. Mavis sits upright on the bed, both arms wrapped around Dutton like she can pull him into her chest. The position is all I can make out of the two of them in the pitch blackness.

"What happened?" I call out just as another bolt of lightning illuminates the room.

A whimper sounds.

"Dutton is afraid of storms." Mavis's voice carries to me, and I cautiously enter the room that contains a queen-sized bed and a dresser, and not a lot of additional floor space.

"I'm not much better." Her voice is small, quiet, but brave enough for her son.

Another clap of thunder happens. The storm is right above us.

"I'm approaching the bed," I warn her, so I don't further frighten her. Running my hand along the edge, I use the next flash of lightning to guide me onto the mattress.

Dutton is deeply tucked into Mavis, her arms protective like the mother bear she is. Something inside me snaps, and I slide my arm around her shoulders, tugging her toward me, Dutton between us.

Another crack of thunder. Dutton trembles so strongly that the vibration quivers against me.

"Hey, Dutton," I coo. "We've made an Oreo cookie out of you. A sandwich between your mama and me."

He doesn't respond but I sense Mavis shift.

"And you know what they say about an Oreo cookie." I pause for an answer, hoping to distract the kid but he doesn't respond. "The filling is the best part. Which means you're the best part of this cookie."

Without a thought, I lean forward and press a kiss to the top of his head. He smells fruity, like strawberries maybe.

Still no response from him, but Mavis relaxes beneath my arm. I wrap my other arm around them both cocooning them in and feeling comforted myself. I don't dislike storms. I rather admire them at times and appreciate the necessity of them. Right now, I'm thankful for this one.

Grateful that it's allowing me to sit on this bed and cradle Mavis and her kid.

I've never quite felt like this before. My need to protect in contrast with another person who is doing the protecting. Because there's one thing I'm certain of, Mavis wouldn't let a hair on Dutton's head be harmed. Calling her mama bear fits, as he is her cub.

I'm just wondering if they might have room for a papa bear somewhere.

The thought is ridiculous, and I tip back my head, closing my eyes since there's nothing else to do but wait out the storm. Slowly, Dutton slumps between us, falling back asleep as the thunder moves on and the lightning subsides. The rain is more of a steady shower, thudding on my roof in a rhythmic patter that has me nodding off as well.

With Mavis still tucked beneath my arms, holding her child while I hold her, I slip into a dream where they are mine.

IN THE MORNING, a loud annoying ringtone rouses me. My head lolls forward. My neck cracks from the awkward angle I slept in all night. At some point, Dutton burrowed back into his pillow. Mavis rests beside him but I remained upright, vigilant while asleep.

As the ringtone blares, Mavis sits upright, does a double take at my position, and then scrambles over both Dutton and me to reach her phone on the nightstand beside me. When she pauses to pick up the device, and turn off what I assume is an alarm, she straddles my outstretched legs.

"You're a lovely sight to see first thing, butterfly," I tease. Her jet-black hair sticks up on one side of her head. Her eyes are soft. Her mouth lush.

Her head lifts, eyes wide, brows deeply pinched. "Why would you call me that?"

I shrug, uncertain, but the name seems fitting.

Sleepily, she assesses her position over me. Those dark eyes do a quick scan of my bare chest and her legs split over my lap before she scrambles in a way that causes her to lean awkwardly off the bed and nearly tumble to the floor. Her foot lands on the hard wood and she wobbles. I catch her hip to steady her.

"You stayed?" Her question is one of surprise and my answer surprises me.

"I stayed." I didn't want them frightened again during the night. Nothing will get to them with me here. Which means I need to be more present.

"About dinner—"

Her raised hand cuts me off and I take a second to assess what she's wearing. She stole my shirt again. The thigh length tee exposes her legs, and my gaze drops to her light-pink polished toes. She's a vision in my T-shirt. Her nipples erect, evidence of no bra. I want to explore what else she has underneath the shirt, but when Dutton stirs beside me the desire drops.

"I need to get dressed."

"Where are you going?" The question comes out without a care to the accusation within it.

"I have an appointment with the insurance company today."

I straighten on the bed. My lower back is killing me from having slept at an upright angle. My neck is certain to have a crick in it. I glance down at the zonked out kid beside me. "What about Dutton?"

"Meredith Mulligen is going to watch him for me."

"Meredith Mulligen?" Everyone in this town knows Meredith's secret. The one not quite so well kept about the seventy-year-old woman selling sex toys out of the second-floor apartment over her yarn shop, The She Shed. Years ago, the shop had an additional -e and -p in the title, making it The Sheep Shed, a place specializing in yarn and knitting supplies. When Meredith took over the shop, she used her living space on the upper level to supplement her daytime business. With the -e and -p fallen from the original sign, she left the spaces empty. Called the absence, *character*. *She's* a character.

As Mavis nods, while checking her phone for the time, I ask, "Are you certain that's wise?"

I have nothing against sweet Meredith, who lost her husband young and has been preaching to the women of this community, behind closed doors of course, that self-pleasure is the preferred pleasure. I'd like to disagree. While I don't mind my hand on occasion, I prefer the touch of a woman on me. Her hands. Her mouth. Her inviting, open thighs.

But then again, Meredith isn't talking about *men* pleasuring themselves. She's all about female empowerment.

"Dutton adores her."

I glance down at him again, wearing a pink pajama set, recalling what Mavis told me the other night. He prefers feminine things. While I'd like to think the world is changing, open-minded and progressive, I'm reminded daily how archaic, even stepping-backward society remains, and this little guy might have a tough road ahead of him. What he needs to know is he isn't alone.

Looking back up at Mavis, I want her to know neither Dutton nor his mom are alone. I'm here for them.

"She's like the grandmother he doesn't have here." Mavis wrinkles her nose in a way that suggests she doesn't like the comparison, but she sets down her phone and glances up at me. "I need to get ready."

With her penetrating eyes on me, time stands still a second. I don't move even though I'm thinking that's what she subtly implies. *Get out.*

"I just need another day or two and then Dutton and I will be out of your hair." Her gaze lands on my lips and drops to my jaw covered in a mix of silver and gray, and thicker each morning.

"You aren't in my hair," I argue, keeping my focus on her.

Her puffy lips. Her high cheekbones. "And I already told you, you don't need to leave."

Watching Mavis, I realize her hard stare isn't a threat to leave. She's drinking me in, letting those piercing dark eyes skim along my collarbone like a soft caress and along my tattooed arms. Her sleepy gaze travels to my chest next, lingering over my pecs and the patch of hair between them before taking her time to scan lower and lower to another trail of hair that leads to the waistband of my pajama bottoms.

She swallows hard before her eyes flick upward and land on mine. "I think it's for the best."

"Why?" I swing my legs over the edge of the bed and stand right before her, ignoring that her perusal of me is affecting my body. Her floral scent invades my nose. Her breasts are mere inches from my chest. My hands twitch, wanting to touch her face and bring her mouth to mine.

"We're just taking up your space—"

"Take my space," I interject.

"And wasting your time."

"Waste my time." Then I tilt my head, realizing how that might have sounded. "How? How are you taking my time or my space?"

She shrugs, lowering her gaze. "It just doesn't feel right, us being here."

Unable to resist the urge to touch her, I cup her shoulders to gain her attention. "Tell me how to make it feel right." Because I don't want her fluttering away now that she's back.

While I can admit that permanence isn't something I foresee in my future, work being the only constant in my life, my gut tells me not to let Mavis go. At the same time my gut speaks, I hear warning bells, telling me not to jump into savior mode. Don't make her a damsel in distress when she's clearly explained how she's on her own path of survival and restoration. Which makes Mavis refreshing, puzzling even, and someone I'd like to explore more, get to know better. Be present for her.

"I'll be home for dinner."

Mavis closes her eyes and shakes her head. "Please don't give me false promises. It's a trigger for me."

"Trigger?"

Her eyes snap open, ignoring the word. "You don't need to be here or not be here. It's your house. You deserve to come home and not find us squatting here. Or stay away because that's your routine."

Routine? My life *has* become a little too repetitive.

"Plus, I don't want to cramp your style. Staying here you haven't brought anyone home with you because I'm here with my kid."

My brows rise at that argument and I softly chuckle. Mavis glances around me at Dutton and I turn my head to check on him as well before peering back at her.

"First, of all, you aren't squatting." I squeeze her shoulders to emphasize my words. "And secondly, I've never brought another woman to my home."

Her eyes widen.

"I want you here," I state, quieter, softer, vulnerable in the admission. For reasons I can't fully explain I don't want her to leave.

"But why? You don't come around when we are here, and after all I told you the other night, I figured you'd want us gone."

"Gone?" I choke, stroking over her shoulders. "You just came back. I don't want you going anywhere."

Her brows arch, one lifting higher than the other, questioning me and my adamant admission. Then, she shakes her head again, like an afterthought occurs. She takes a step back, slowly slipping out from underneath my hands. "I need to get ready for my meeting."

She turns for her suitcase, which isn't unpacked but open on the floor in the corner. She isn't making herself at home like I've asked. She's living like she's on the run, and I don't want her running.

"Is today the day I go to Miss Meredith's?" Dutton groggily asks.

"Sure is, little bear," she calls out, standing once she's found what she wants within her bag. "I need to shower quick and then I'll get us breakfast."

"I can do breakfast," I offer.

"Do you know how to make oatmeal with the right amount of cinnamon and some milk?" Dutton asks, his voice morning rough while he doesn't appear fazed that I'm in their room this early.

"I know my way around a microwave and a bowl of oatmeal, buddy," I counter, placing my hands on my hips to tease him while he assesses me, taking in the hip hugging pajama bottoms that I typically don't wear to sleep in. My hair might be a fright like Mavis's because of the way I slept.

Softly, Dutton smiles. The first real smile I've seen on the kid.

"Then let's go." He scrambles forward, crawling until he reaches the end of the bed, then swings his legs off it and stands ramrod straight, lifting his arms in the air like a practiced gymnast.

"How'd I do on the dismount?" Dutton asks, although I'm not certain if he's talking to me or Mavis.

"A perfect ten," she says at the same time I say, "Eight point seven-five-five."

Dutton glares at me, holding his position a second before lowering his arms with a slap to his thighs. "I'll work on that."

"You do that," I remark.

With that, he gives me a nod and exits the room.

"You could have given him a better score," Mavis chastises,

scowling at me. Even with a frown, she's still stunning. Somehow her expression only makes her edgier, bolder, fiercer. Her desire to fight only sparks my need to rescue.

"Not doing him any favors by making him think everything he does is perfect," I state, and instantly regret my answer. My mind flits back to Mavis's ex and the abuse poor Dutton must have experienced at the hands of his father. Mavis's encouragement might have initially sounded over-the-top, but it makes sense. She's his sole support system and number one cheerleader, and she's trying to erase every mean or disparaging word Dutton has endured.

Scratching at the back of my head, I apologize. "I shouldn't have said that."

Mavis's mouth pops open. Then claps shut. She shakes her head once more and then brushes past me and out the door.

And I'm left wondering if I can ever make things right with this woman.

9

———————

[Mavis]

Clay's words were triggering once more, reminding me of Wesley's constant criticism of how I parented Dutton. Also reminding me of my parents' comparison to how Cecilia would have done things differently.

On the other hand, Clay wasn't wrong. While I did want Dutton to think he was perfect just the way he is, I might overcompensate on the perfection-praise to make up for all he'd endured. All his losses. All his conflicts. All I'd put him through. And no one faulted me more than me, for the precarious position Dutton and I found ourselves in with Wesley.

My emotions were a mess because Clay Sylver held both Dutton and me through the night, offering comfort during a storm, and then woke looking too smug and sexy for his own good. That deep, rugged tenor. I'd have lady morning wood, if there was such a thing, from that voice alone, but then throw in a patch of hair on his chest, the tats on his arms, and the silvery scruff along his jaw. *Deep sigh.*

I need a cold shower but want the heat to wake me up and calm me down. I have no business getting sexually worked up over Clay. He was hospitable, if absent, and doing us a huge favor by letting us crash here for almost two weeks. But we needed to move on. I hated feeling like a charity case, and I'd learned my lesson the hard way by putting my faith in someone who had nothing to stand on but his own two feet. And even that was shaky at best after he drank too much.

But today, I wasn't thinking about my past. This morning, I was looking forward to my future. I had an appointment with the insurance company.

Day one of regaining some financial stability.

Rapidly, I finish my shower, shifting my concern to Clay's ability to make oatmeal. The man hasn't prepared a meal since I've been present. After quickly moisturizing, braiding my hair, and dressing in a casual skirt and sweater, I near the kitchen to find Clay seated across from Dutton.

The two dive into their breakfast like a synchronized pair of oatmeal connoisseurs. To my surprise, Clay isn't on his phone, which Wesley would have been, had he been present, and Dutton isn't on his tablet. Instead, the two are talking about Halloween.

"And you want to be a what?" Clay asks, confused by what Dutton first mentioned.

"I want to be a Power Princess. The pink one."

Clay pauses, his spoon suspended over his oatmeal. "And what exactly does that costume look like?" Distracting himself, he shovels up a large scoop of his warm breakfast while waiting for Dutton's answer.

"She wears a pink morph suit with a silver belt and a sparkling tiara. She also has a cool wand." Dutton wields his spoon like the magic tool, twirling it through the air.

Proudly, I smile at Dutton who doesn't appear to see me standing just outside the kitchen.

"Like a Power Ranger?" Clay looks up at Dutton, staring across the table at him.

"What's a Power Ranger?"

Clay chuckles to himself before scooping up another large spoonful of oatmeal. "And what kind of powers does this princess have that makes her special?"

My shoulders relax when I hadn't realized how tense I'd been, holding my breath over this conversation that could derail at any second. I remind myself once more that Clay isn't Wesley.

"She can outrun her enemies and cast a spell on them. Plus, she has the power to disappear."

"Like be invisible?" Clay's brows lift, like he's impressed by an animated character.

"More like she knows how to hide in all the best places. Like Mama taught me."

Clay slowly lowers his spoon, hovering it just over his bowl and now is the time for me to make my presence known.

"How is the oatmeal?" I ask with false cheer, a ripple of anxiety rushing up my belly. I wish I had the superpower to wipe away Dutton's memory. Chase away the ghosts and the past experiences that might haunt him forever.

Dutton shrugs. "Pretty good."

"Pretty good?" Clay counters. "You told me it was perfect."

Dutton lowers his head, scooping up a much smaller sample than Clay's portion. "I'd give it an eight point seven-five-five." A sheepish grin graces Dutton's face, his face pink from his own cheekiness.

I chuckle at Dutton's assessment while Clay's spoon clatters against the inside of his bowl.

Dutton flinches at the sound but Clay winks. "I guess I'll need to work on my presentation."

"You do that," Dutton softly commands, his voice light, relaxed, mimicking Clay's. His smile grows but he fights it, exploring his limits with this man offering us a safe place to stay. Dutton is extending an olive branch, a hint of his innocent six-year-old sass, and I don't want that twig to snap. He is fragile, hesitant when it comes to men, but I'd love for Clay to be a positive role model in his life. If only for the time being.

"Alrighty. Dutton, finish up. You need to get dressed and brush your teeth. Quick. Quick." I clap my hands emphasizing my haste, knowing he's about to turn into a sloth when I don't want to be late for the appointment.

"I can take him to Miss Meredith's."

The suggestion has me pausing mid-clap while Dutton sits taller in his chair. His legs swing beneath the table, another tell that he's comfortable sitting here. He isn't waiting for the proverbial other shoe to drop like I am. Like he's had to live his life for most of his six years.

"I can't ask you to do that."

"You aren't asking, I'm offering. I typically swing by Curmudgeon Bakery before heading to the Seed & Soil. The She Shed is right down the block."

While Clay had his reservations about Meredith's child-care abilities, something that wasn't his concern, I appreciated that he was uneasy, at least in theory. Meredith's extra-curricular income-related activities were common knowledge, although the community liked to pretend it was a secret. I didn't disapprove of her. In fact, she'd given me something to *ease the tension*, as she called it, knowing I was alone too often with Wesley out of town. Eventually, the Purple Pleaser became more stimulating than Wesley.

I hadn't lived in Sterling Falls very long before I was initiated into the Sterlets, like starlets, an exclusive group of the female population in town. Under the guise of a book club, the members met twice monthly, once to discuss a book, which typically involved more wine drinking than discussion, and once to peruse Meredith's new wares, which also involved copious amounts of wine.

I'd been honored to be included in the local tradition and secret society. Most women were welcoming and open to me joining their private group. As the club was held in Meredith's home once a month, various locations taking the other dates, she'd been the one to invite me into this inner circle of women. However, I'd emotionally kept my distance within the group, afraid someone could read in my eyes what happened behind the closed doors in my home. Cautious that they'd see the lie I was living with Wesley. At first, I even feared they'd detect my failure as a mother. Like real moms could smell the fake ones.

Six years into Dutton's life, I've grown more confident and comfortable with my role. And Meredith expressed an invitation to return to the Sterlets whenever I was ready, reminding me I deserve a night out to feel like a woman, not just a mother.

Calling Meredith was the first step of bravery I took returning here. Reaching out took courage because she knew my situation with Wesley. She'd once offered to help me move on.

It's not that bad, I'd argue. Telling myself someone else always had it worse. My sister certainly had.

With another glance at Dutton, I softly smile. His eager face staring at me as if he asked me a question.

"Well?" One tiny brow tweaks higher than the other.

"What's the question again?"

"Can Mr. Clay take me to Miss Meredith's?"

"Mr. Clay?" I smirk at the man I've been conditioning Dutton to call Mr. Sylver.

Clay sits taller, patting the Seed & Soil T-shirt covering his chest. He gives me a smile I'm certain wins over many ladies and helps him get his way on a most occasions.

"I don't know." Hesitating near the table, I wring my hands.

"You can trust me." Clay makes it sound so simple. I wanted to trust him. I didn't want to believe all men were the enemy, but this was Dutton.

"Maybe another day," I whisper, trying but failing to hide my cautious thoughts. Then I clear my throat.

"Okay, buddy. *Quick quick.*" I clap my hands again, signaling I need some speed this morning.

Dutton takes another bite of his oatmeal before sliding from his seat.

Sloth-mode detected, Clay intercedes. "I'll race you. First one to be dressed and ready wins."

This has Dutton's attention. "What do I win?"

"Hmm. I'll need to think about it." Clay taps his chin, but the gleam in his eye suggests he already has an idea.

"And if you win?"

"I'll watch an episode of *Princess Power* with you. I need to see what that's all about. My niece Adara might love it one day."

Dutton perks up at the promise. He rushes from the room, finding a companion for his television time a good enough excuse to hurry, which strangely makes both results a win for Dutton.

"That was sweet of you," I say once Dutton clears the room. I start picking up his bowl of oatmeal watching as Clay doesn't move to join in the competition.

"Leave it," Clay mumbles around another bite of his own warm cereal before he runs his palm lightly down my forearm to circle my wrist.

At the sudden movement, I flinch, and Clay doesn't miss my reaction. What he also doesn't do is drop his touch. Instead, he softens his grip and runs his thumb along the delicate skin on the inside of my wrist. He gently strokes, as if willing my pulse to settle, willing me to stay still. The tenderness speaks volumes. Like he's telling me he understands that I need time.

Like maybe I could get use to his touch. Like maybe I could trust him.

"I'll clean up in a minute."

I'm still stunned by the offer even though I shouldn't be. It's not that he isn't capable of cleaning up after himself, it's just that I'm not used to someone else picking up after us. Even at my parents' home, I waited on them, feeling like I needed to earn my keep as they allowed Dutton and me to stay with them for nearly a year. They'd never deny Dutton anything, but they had firm opinions about helping me. My parents were still resentful of decisions Cecilia and I had made.

"I'll see you tonight," Clay says.

Those soothing strokes on my wrist have worked their magic. I want to believe he'll be here tonight, but whether he's here or not, should not be my concern.

Today, my focus needs to be on the future for Dutton and me.

Freedom. *Finally*.

10

[Mavis]

"What do you mean you can't pay the claim?" I stare at the insurance agent seated behind a large metal desk. Her office is above a store in downtown Sterling Falls.

A turmoil of emotions collide within me. A contrast between punch-to-the-gut shock and numbness despite my heart hammering, anxiety hitting almost immediately before my brain catches up to what this might mean.

If there was one thing Wesley did right, he had us purchase homeowner's insurance. During the arson investigation, I learned that many people take out the fire policy then set their own house ablaze to make a claim, and thus receive the money.

I'd felt sick at the accusation that I would do something like that to my own home. And being that the mortgage was listed in my name, I'd been the first to be accused of the crime.

Thankfully, Stone Sylver came to my defense in his report

about the doping. When Wesley handed me a glass of orange juice that morning, I hadn't been suspicious. I'd considered it a peace offering after our explosive fight the night before, when I told him I wanted him out. When I'd suggested I'd sell the house and return to Florida, a place I loathed to consider living in again.

Wesley had threatened to burn the place to the ground before he let me leave him or sell our place. At the time, I'd thought his threat was one of many, often said in the heat of an argument. I never suspected he'd go so far as to literally start a fire with Dutton and me inside. Stone assumed Wesley slipped me the roofie to prevent me from saving Dutton and myself. Wesley's action would have burned us alive.

The irony was Wesley Holland had no claim to any insurance policy if he had set the blaze.

Also, there was now a warrant out for his arrest for attempted double homicide.

Wherever he was, I doubted he'd show his face again in Sterling Falls. He was stupid but not that foolish, which was another reason I felt safest here.

Still, I needed money to live anywhere and the insurance agent, with her perfectly polished red nails and professionally dyed blond hair, was telling me there would be no payout.

A bubble of laughter pops free. Disbelief gurgles inside me. Hysteria takes over.

The agent continues. "There was an investigative report in which the arson charge was inconclusive."

"The conclusion was that there wasn't an act of arson." Even if Wesley had started the fire, the house had been titled in my name, and as the official owner, I hadn't done anything to spark the blaze. I'd been cleared of suspicion.

Ignoring me, she continues. "A further investigation was done into the faulty wiring claim. You didn't have a legal permit with a licensed electrician for the work on file."

I'd been over this with the adjusters, sharing the records I have from various contractors. The work invoices often were missing a phone number or an email address. Many of them were without legitimate websites and asked us to pay in cash. As several came after me for the outstanding debts, I'd borrowed money from my parents, like I'd told Clay, to pay them off. *I* hadn't further inquired into the legitimacy of each of them. Still, I refused to take the blame here. Not fully.

"And finally, the last two checks written for the policy bounced."

"What?" *How much more bad news can I take?*

"Which means your insurance coverage was voided."

My breath catches. I almost worry I've blacked out as the room disappears for a moment.

Was she serious? "Why is this the first I'm hearing about this?" I'd been on the phone over and over again, transferred from department to department, and not one person ever mentioned that the insurance payments were not up to date nor that the coverage had lapsed.

"So, what exactly are you saying?" Although she'd already told me, I needed to hear it again, disbelief now firmly rooted in me.

"I'm sorry." She averts her gaze, embarrassed for me, maybe ashamed of herself. "There isn't any payout for you."

"What you're telling me is, my burned house is a total financial loss?" My heart hammers faster. The office is suddenly too warm. The agent grows fuzzy in my vision.

She swallows and fiddles with the pens on her desk. Ones I notice are red to match her nail polish. "Yes."

"Unbelievable," I whisper. As if I still don't hear her correctly, as if I can't comprehend what this means.

But fifteen minutes later, I'm outside in the alley behind the building, sliding down the side of the brick wall at my back and curling into myself while the truth vibrates through my body.

And I'm too stunned to cry. Too angry to think straight. I literally have no feeling in my limbs and no thoughts in my head. I'm numb when I should be sick to my stomach.

I can't ask my parents for more money.

I can't go back to their home.

I don't have a plan.

How did I get into such a mess?

With my head in my hands and my elbows on my raised knees, skirt tucked beneath my thighs, I stare toward my feet, willing them to carry me away and yet begging for a few more desperate minutes to wallow in this new betrayal.

No money from the insurance company. No house. No job. Nothing. Nothing. *Nothing.*

"Mavis?"

Oh God, no. This is the last thing I need, but when a body blocks out the sun, and a man squats before me, I can't fully ignore him.

Instead, I close my eyes, as if I can disappear inside myself and wish him away.

"What's going on, butterfly?" Clay's rough masculine voice is full of concern.

The nickname flips a switch inside me. Tears fill my eyes, reminding me of my grandmother. She'd know what to do. She'd hold me when I am desperately in need of a hug.

Leaning forward, I drop my forehead to my knees and let the tears fall, wanting Clay to go away and leave me to my self-pity party.

"Fuck," he whispers, scooting closer before settling next to me, his back against the wall as well, but he slips his arm around my shoulders and I fall into his side, much like I did last night during the storm.

His other arm wraps around my front, tucking me closer to him, cocooning me against him. I am nothing like the beautiful butterfly Nana once called me. The girl who was quiet and shy and needed to fly. My wings are clipped, pinned back, and holding me permanently in place like a spectacle. I'm not even a pretty butterfly but one that's ugly-brown and frightening, like a large-winged moth.

Clay's lips come to my hair, lingering there as he tries to soothe me. "I've got you."

No one has me. No one ever has. I had my sister when she was alive. Now I have Dutton, and I need to take care of him.

"I don't know what I'm going to do," I finally whimper.

"Don't think about that right now."

He doesn't know what he's saying. I need to figure out my next step. I need a job. Money. A home. How did I get so help-less? I'm nearly forty, educated, skilled yet lacking so much.

Tugging out of Clay's arms, I roughly swipe at my face with the heels of my palms. My makeup must be a fright. *Ugly-brown moth syndrome.* "My brain is spinning and yet all I can think about is the fact I have nothing."

"You don't have *nothing*," Clay admonishes.

Turning my head, I glare at him and snarl, "I. Have. Nothing."

"What happened?"

"There's no money." My voice rises as I explain what the insurance agent told me.

Clay intently listens, not offering advice or commentary. Eventually, he casually holds up a hand, his forearm draped over a singular bent knee, and he points one finger. "Five facts. You have Dutton."

I stare at him.

"You're healthy and young." He flicks another finger upward, then adds one more. "You're smart and beautiful."

I scoff, wiping underneath each of my eyes again.

"You're here." He holds up four fingers, and I'm not certain if this comment means I'm alive or simply that I'm present in Sterling Falls.

He hitches up his thumb. "And you have me."

I derisively chuckle. Now he's just mocking me.

"Look, there's no rush to leave my house. Stay as long as you need."

I tip my head against the brick wall. The day is surprisingly sunny after the overnight thunderstorm. I could really use a rainbow right now, with a pot of gold at the end of it. "I can't do that."

"Why not?" His tone is a bit defensive.

Rolling my head against the hard surface, I look at him again. "Because we've already imposed too long." Still holding his cool blue stare, I add. "I just thought it'd be so easy. For once, it would be simple." My voice cracks.

Claim the insurance. Cash the check.

Clay shrugs. "So you sell the property as is. You get a job. You start fresh."

"Not easy," I whisper. "Not simple."

"You stay with me, so you have no expenses."

"I can't do that," I repeat.

"You can." The corner of his mouth ticks up, like we are two kids playing that silly game of you-can't-I-can my sister and I played as kids.

God, I miss Cecilia. I miss my grandmother. I miss my nursing job, my house, and my life. *Who am I?* When did I become . . . this? I stare down at my bent knees, my skirt hitched up and tucked beneath the fold of my legs. I'm sitting in an alley with my back against a wall literally and figuratively, feeling sorry for myself. The choices I've made. The man I thought I loved and now hated.

"Butterfly, give yourself a break."

I turn my attention back to Clay who is still watching me. He sighs and swipes a hand over his silvery hair, cupping the back of his neck.

"When I was almost twenty-two, my dad died. Hung himself in the family barn."

I gasp.

"He ran our family business into the ground. Took the dream my mother had and drove a spade right into it." Clay fists the hand balanced over his knee, and thumps at the hard bone. "Stone and I did all we could to keep our family together. Keep our siblings in one home, fed and clothed. And I worked my ass off to prove that Sylver Seed & Soil wasn't the failure our father had been. That business is my life. And I had to start over with it because of all the bad choices my dad made."

Clay tosses an imaginary ball from one hand to the other. "He used the left hand to pay the right. He took money we didn't have for his drinking and gambling debts and dug us into the ground."

Clay pauses and licks his lips, staring out at the alley lot, vacant except for my Jetta and another car. "Ever hear of a phoenix?"

"The mythical bird rising up from the ashes." I am all too familiar with the symbol.

"You're a phoenix, Mavis. You got this."

"But *up* doesn't feel like a direction I'm going right now."

"Give yourself today. Tomorrow we can make a plan."

"We?" I choke. "I've already taken too much from you."

Clay tips his head back against the brick wall and stares at me. "Like my space and time?" The corner of his mouth slowly ticks upward. "You aren't taking anything. What I give to you, I do willingly, beautiful. Think about that."

Hastily, Clay pushes himself upright and stands, brushing off his backside. Then he holds out both his hands for me to take and he pulls me upward.

A broken-winged phoenix struggling to rise up from the ashes, flapping my wings in the wreckage without a flight plan.

"How did you even see me here?" I exited the insurance

office through the back stairwell and stumbled into this alley, falling against the wall once I was outside in the fresh air.

"Curmudgeon Bakery. I told you I stop by there before work. It's around the corner and I parked there." He points at a black truck on the side of the road within easy sight of my solitary position.

"I'm kind of pathetic." I lower my head, but Clay catches my chin, tipping up my face.

"You're not. And I've already told you, you are beautiful, but if you need to hear it every day, I'll say it again and again." He gives me another smirky grin. One that's flirty but sweet, and for a moment, I pretend it's special just for me.

"Now, how about coffee and a donut? I have it on good authority Curmudgeon Bakery makes the best of both."

"Caffeine and a bad-for-me pastry? Who can say no to that. But don't you need to get to work?" I remind him, having already taken up more of his time.

He shrugs, while chuckling. "I know the boss. I think I can handle him."

I weakly smile back at Clay and then he does something that completely catches me off guard.

He pulls me close and holds me tightly to his chest, a hug I desperately needed. A comfort I craved.

I shouldn't get comfortable, but I can allow myself the few moments of grace he suggested. The strength of his arms. The warmth of his breath near my ear. The solidness of his body wrapped around mine.

Being pressed up against Clay Sylver feels too good, too safe.

11

———————

[Clay]

After the day Mavis had, she deserves to be spoiled, so I do my best. I bring home a pizza, and we eat together before she checks Dutton's unofficial math homework.

Earlier, Mavis made a series of decisions.

Sell the property. Find a job. Send Dutton to school.

Her perseverance is admirable, and I sit back and marvel at her superpower. After a tough morning, she came home and taught her kid some math skills, checked his work, and then lined things up to do it all over again the next day.

In the simplest way, she reminds me of my mother.

As we sit on the couch after Dutton's homework, trying to concentrate on *Princess Power*, I don't miss how Mavis is nodding off, the day finally catching up to her. With Dutton between us on the couch, my arm is outstretched behind his head, and I nudge Mavis's shoulder. "Why don't you go take a bath? Relax."

I have a soaker tub in my guest bathroom that I don't think I've ever used.

Mavis stares at me, startled by the suggestion. "I'm alright. Just been a long day. Need to focus on the routine of things."

Tomorrow, Mavis returns to the hospital as an emergency room nurse. She had been talking to her old boss who told Mavis they were begging for nursing staff and offered her a job on the spot. With Dutton still so young and childcare slim and costly in the area, part-time was the most Mavis could do at the moment.

It was a start.

As for routines, I knew all about them. I also knew that they lead to ruts, like mechanically moving through your life on autopilot. I don't begrudge my position at Sylver Seed & Soil. I am honored my family trusts me to keep it afloat. I love my job, something not everyone can say, but it didn't mean I wasn't overwhelmed by the demands. Never having a day off. Never taking a vacation. Never slowing down.

Then again, keeping busy kept me out of trouble, not that I'd get into any regularly anyway. Still, a little reprieve might be nice occasionally.

And a bath sounded like exactly what Mavis needed.

I wish I could join her.

"Go." I nudge her shoulder once more. "We've got *Princess Power* here." I nod at the screen. Surprisingly, the show had more plot than I expected.

Mavis blinks at the brightness of the large monitor over a wooden mantel on the field stone fireplace. Then she glances down at Dutton, sitting closer to her than me.

"Are you sure?" She's looking at him while questioning me.

"How much trouble can I get in?" I tilt my head at the screen again. "The princess is watching me." I crack myself up, but Dutton doesn't blink, mesmerized by the girl in pink, doing a one-two punch, and yelling *hi-yah* before racing after a bad guy.

Mavis smiles, the slight curl not lighting up her eyes like I've seen before. Like the look she used to give me when she'd wander into the store, or I'd see her in town. I'd feel like a high school teen stumbling upon my crush, earning a prize with that smile. Like we shared a secret. Only Mavis never knew about my conflicting emotions. I was highly attracted to her, while I respected the hell out of her marriage vows or, rather, the ones I thought she had.

She leans to the side to kiss Dutton's head. "I'm going to take a bath. Then it's your turn," she warns him. Looking back up at me, her face softens as she mouths, *Thank you.*

When Mavis leaves the room, a weird tension remains. I wouldn't say I'm not good with kids, but I also can't say I am good with them. Up until recently, my interaction has primarily been with my nephew, Hudson, who loves all things traditionally boy. Or should I say stereotypically boy?

He's into baseball, video games, and dirt. He'd never watch *Princess Power* or wear pink or want to dress like a female superhero for Halloween. He also isn't six.

I'd been raised in a male-dominated home, one fraught with the arrogance of my father, thinking because he was labeled the patriarch of our family it meant he deserved honoring when not one of us respected him toward the end of his life. I'd always love him in some twisted way because he was my dad, a sad, lost man. But it didn't mean I valued or obeyed him.

He'd lost that privilege when he knocked my younger siblings around and tried to emotionally tear them down as they aged. He'd used damning words on me as well.

So stupid you flunked out of college before you got in.

I'd been confused at first, wondering where the supportive

man who loved his wife and family more than anything, had gone. A bottle of Jack stole him from me. But I wasn't one to place blame. My father made his own choices, and unfortunately, his decisions had not been in favor of his children or his business. The legacy my mother built with him through both a company and their offspring were a painful reminder of what he'd lost.

Love hurts. That's what I'd learned from my dad. And the long-term investment in it can be cut short within a moment's notice.

Dutton flinches beside me, then he giggles, laughing at his own startling.

"What'd I miss?" I ask, knowing my mind had wandered off and my body wants to follow Mavis to the bathroom, climb into my tub behind her, and hold her against me again. Last night had been nice despite the storm and loss of power which came back on at some point in the early hours of a new day. Holding Mavis felt right. Sandwiching Dutton between us felt strangely good.

And finding her sitting against a brick wall earlier, crying into her hands, nearly broke me. Hugging her on the public street was the least I could do for her.

"She just found a hiding spot." Dutton stiffens beside me, straightening his arms at his sides and tightening his outstretched legs like he's the one hidden behind an open door.

"She why you're good at finding hiding spaces?" I hadn't forgotten what he said earlier today. How his mama taught him how to hide. I'd been puzzled on and off throughout the day what he meant by the admission.

"Mama used to make a game of hide 'n' seek when Wesley was fired up."

"Fired up?"

"When he drank too much and got mean." Dutton's eyes don't leave the television screen, but I can't be certain if he's focusing on the hidden princess or falling into a memory. His body slowly slumps into the couch cushions. I shouldn't be prying into his history. I don't want to trigger him.

Still, I don't like that a child was conscious of what drinking too much alcohol can do to a person and how it can make him cruel.

This reminds me of my father.

"So you hid from your dad?"

Dutton shrugs, lowering his gaze and picking at the track pants covering his legs. "When I could."

I didn't like the sound of that. Not one bit. If his father was anything like my father, I shiver to think what was said, what was done, to frighten a child enough he tried to hide. And at his mama's request.

Then another question strikes. He'd called Wesley by his first name, not Dad. I'd started doing the same thing as I aged. Working in the family business, it seemed better to distinguish myself from Dad by calling him by his given name, Flint.

The irony of his hard name compared to the softness of our mother's—Violet—was never lost on me.

"I'm sorry Flint promised we could deliver by Friday. That's just not possible."

"No, we cannot honor the extension Flint allowed you."

"What do you mean Flint owes three months of payment for the feed shipment?"

"How is it Flint didn't cover taxes for the last two years?"

The last one had almost been the end of me and the Seed & Soil.

Deciding I shouldn't question a six-year-old about his past, my attention returns to *Princess Power*, finding my focus waning occasionally. Drifting to a woman taking a bath in the tub down the hall, imagining the water enveloping her body. Maybe bubbles covering her thighs, her breasts, her nipples rising above the suds. Just a peek to confirm they are dusky like her skin, or rosy and pink.

All I want to do is comfort her.

Shaking the thought, I drift back to why her son had to hide from his dad. From Wesley.

And what the man has done to Mavis.

ONCE THE PROGRAM finishes and Mavis exits the bathroom, I call for a celebration.

"Why?" Mavis chuckles, freshly fragrant in that floral scent of hers. Her cheeks are brighter, heated from the bath. Her dark hair is piled on top of her head in a wobbly twist. She looks younger, relaxed a little bit.

And sexy as hell wearing a ratty, peach colored robe with giant mint-green flowers here and there on the worn material. I'm one-thousand percent positive she's naked underneath it and I'm jealous of the material. She looks comfortable, plus confident enough to wear something so casual around my house, like it's her home.

I want her to stay here, and she hasn't given me an answer about whether she will or won't.

"For the winner of this morning's race," I announce.

Dutton sits upright on the couch, leaning forward a bit, and tilting his head, like he forgot about my promise only this morning. He'd win something if he picked up the pace, like Mavis asked.

"I won?" Dutton whispers, as if suddenly remembering our deal.

"I won," he says louder, with more confidence.

"I was the fastest." He shifts his body so he's facing me. His dark eyes are wide like his mother's. His face incandescent.

"What do I win?" The enthusiasm in his voice causes me to chuckle.

"Your choice of ice cream."

"Ice cream!" He practically yells. "We never get ice cream unless it's a special occasion."

My gaze lifts to Mavis who is standing behind the couch, waiting out this moment.

"Well," I begin. "Today feels special. Your mama made a bunch of important decisions. And you won the morning rush."

For an average Tuesday, the day feels surprisingly special.

"So, your choices are chocolate swirl, which has caramel and chunks of chocolate. Or pink surprise."

Dutton sits as tall as a six-year-old can. "What's pink surprise?"

"I think it's strawberry ice cream in disguise."

"I like disguises," Dutton admits. "Strawberries are my favorite." He's nodding emphatically. "And I love pink."

"Somehow, I guessed that." I meet Mavis's eyes once more, only I'm not prepared for what I see in them. A storm of emotion swirls within the darkness. Sparkles crackling like fireflies in the night amid a depth too black to decipher. She anxiously runs her hands down the length of the robe-belt, then releases the sash.

"Why don't you head to the kitchen and grab some spoons? And your mama and I will be right there."

Dutton flies from the couch, literally springing himself forward and leaping over the ottoman where we'd had our legs outstretched.

As he rounds the couch, running for my kitchen, I cry out. "Seven point nine-nine for the dismount."

His laughter carries back to the living room, and I turn toward Mavis. "What's wrong, butterfly?"

Without thinking, I reach out for the end of the sash around her waist, holding her robe closed. A peek of her skin where the material slips open leads to a hint of her breasts.

"Don't do that," she whispers, dropping her gaze and running her fingertips along the top edge of the couch.

"What? What'd I do?"

"Don't spoil him."

Feeling strangely chastised, I shift on the couch, climbing up to my knees and leaning the front of my thighs into the back cushions to face her. I spread my arms, bracing myself on the top of the couch, leaning slightly toward her. "And how am I spoiling him? It's ice cream."

"It's pink, and you know it." Her eyes lock on mine.

"So?" I shrug, lowering my gaze to the belt around her waist. "I took a gamble."

"You didn't need to even buy it."

"It's dessert, not a crime." I don't understand where she's going with this. Why she seems equally worked up and worn down.

Glancing up at her again, I tug at the knot of the robe-sash, and keeping my tone playful, demand, "Talk to me."

"Don't be nice to us."

The words are like a blow to my chest. A straight up round-house kick with a *hi-yah* to the sternum.

"Why not?" My brows cinch, hard and deep.

"Because he can't get attached. I won't let him be hurt again." Her eyes flit between mine and the kitchen, then back, cautious, almost frightened. Vulnerable.

"I'm not going to hurt him. It's ice cream," I repeat. My hand grasping the robe knot tightens in the soft material and I gently jiggle her once again.

"Don't hurt me either," she whispers, dipping her lids.

"Mavis," I groan, slipping my hand to her hip, causing our upper bodies to draw closer to each other. "How could I hurt you?"

Her eyes leap up to mine once more. "By being kind. Then stripping that kindness away from us."

Wesley. Fucking false promises. Masked compassion.

"I'm not him." I struggle to keep any irritation from my voice. I don't want to be compared to that asshole. She doesn't know me. Not enough to understand I'd never be like him. I would never offer compassion then tug it away.

"You haven't told me whether you'll stay or not. But I want to be clear that my offer stands. I want you here. I want you and Dutton to stay as long as you need."

Mavis closes her eyes and leans forward just the slightest bit. The couch is a barrier between us, but I sense her wanting to lean into me.

I didn't miss the way she clung to me earlier, when I surprised her with a hug in the parking lot. Her holding me tight in response to my embrace did something to me. This wasn't damsel in distress syndrome. She was turning the tide on me. Doing something to me I couldn't explain yet.

Presently, I risk running my hand around her lower back, pinning her in place. The warmth from her bath seeps through the threadbare material of her robe. Or maybe that's just how she naturally feels, and I want to further investigate that heat. I want to feel her skin.

And I want to reassure her she's safe with me. "We might not know one another well, but I promise you I won't intentionally hurt you. Or Dutton. I realize that a promise might not be something you can take from me. You don't trust them. But I'm asking you to trust me. Have faith in me, at least."

She slowly nods, her eyes still closed, her head bowed.

"Look at me, butterfly."

Her lids flit open. "Why do you keep calling me that?"

I glance between us, my sight catching on the hint of cleavage easier to see from this vantage point. *Definitely naked beneath the robe.*

"Earlier, I mentioned a phoenix, but you're softer than that mythical bird. Butterflies mean transformation, too. And a change is coming for you, Mavis."

Dutton claimed he'd been taught to hide. Maybe Mavis has been hiding, too. Buried inside a cocoon of sorts. "You're free now. Free of Wesley. Free to be you. Whoever that might be."

Because I was certain Mavis didn't know herself, didn't fully recognize her strength. Not yet.

And for some unknown reason, I wanted to be beside her as the discovery happened. As she unfolded from the cocoon around her heart, a chrysalis liberated herself from slumber, to emerge stronger and more stunningly beautiful, if that was even possible. And simply be Mavis.

Tears well in her eyes and she rapidly blinks them away, touching her finger to the corner of one eye to capture the drop before it escapes. "You're too sweet, Clay Sylver."

"You ain't seen nothing yet, baby." I wink at her, and she chuckles, giving in to the pull between us and resting her forehead against mine.

I breathe her in again. Floral. Fresh. *One day mine?* I don't dare to dream. Not when she had to be hers first before she could give herself to me.

"Are we eating ice cream or what?" Dutton calls from the kitchen.

I'd like to answer *or what*. Want to take this woman to my room, remove this ratty robe, and show her how precious she is. How beautiful. How sexy. How liberated she could be.

Instead, I pull back and yell over her shoulder. "Eating ice cream."

The pink surprise kind.

Dutton and Mavis fit the flavor. They're surprising me.

12

[Mavis]

"Clay?" His name comes out as a breathless surprise as I'd been in a rush to pick up Dutton. Running late from the hospital sounds silly considering I work a shift schedule but getting back into the groove of working is taking a toll.

My part-time gig at the hospital includes three days on for eight hours, followed by four days off. I was fortunate my former director of nurses had an immediate opening. The hospital has been desperate for nursing staff.

My next steps toward a better future are to sell the property and put Dutton in school, but I can only address one thing at a time.

Day one was done.

Entering The She Shed with a flourish, Clay's presence in front of the customer counter shocks me. Not only am I attracted to his appearance, but his sweetness has taken my libido from zero to sixty-nine.

"Do you have a lunch?" Earlier this morning, the question surprised me.

Clay then stood from the table and opened his fridge. Quickly scanning the contents, he pulled out a jar of jelly and set it on the countertop. "How do you feel about peanut butter and jelly?"

"Who isn't a fan?" I'd countered, although it wasn't my first choice for a midday meal.

But who can deny a man offering to make you a sandwich for your first day of work?

Peanut butter and jelly it was.

And when my lunch break rolled around, nothing had ever tasted so good.

"Hi, butterfly." His slow smile unfurls like a flower, and I can't help my own lips from mirroring his.

"What are you doing here?" I'm doubtful he's shopping for specialty yarn. Hopefully, he isn't here for a novelty toy from Meredith's other business.

My gracious childcare provider is standing behind the counter watching the interaction between a town favorite and me.

"Thought I'd get off work early and take you and Dutton somewhere." Clay glances down at Dutton and I notice how close they stand to one another.

"Where?" The question comes out quick and terse, almost accusatory instead of gracious. My hackles rise despite knowing Clay is not my enemy. He isn't trying to hide Dutton and I away somewhere, and he proves it by what he says next.

"Sylver Seed & Soil sponsors the Harvest Fest each year. The entire town is invited out to the property where farmers sell their final stock and winter wares, and artisans share their crafts. We have pumpkin decorating contests, pumpkins for sale, Halloween-themed games and prizes for kids. Children are encouraged to dress in their costumes to get more than one use out of them. It's a real family affair."

Clay glances down at Dutton and winks, like they've already discussed this tradition. I'd taken Dutton to the fest when he was younger as a way to pass a beautiful autumn day, but I'd stopped going when Wesley attended once and accused me of having an affair with Clay Sylver because we innocently smiled at one another.

I didn't want to bring unwarranted attention to Clay because of Wesley's nonsense.

"Also, my sister-in-law, Halle and brother Knox host a Halloween party at their house. It's a new tradition for them."

My lips firmly press together as I recall who Knox and Halle are. Halle Reynolds inherited the house across the street from mine when I lived here before, and while we'd never officially met, she was always polite, waving at me from across the boulevard. Her mother, who'd died last summer, had been friendly enough, but a bit nosy as a neighbor. Knox had been the firefighter who rescued Dutton and me from the flames that eventually engulfed my home and burned the house and my relationship beyond repair.

"I'd like to invite you and Dutton to come to the Fest as my special guests, and the party."

"Like a date?" Dutton asks, his question innocent enough. However, it wouldn't be a date with the three of us. Just a generous offer.

"I don't know," I admit, as my gaze drifts to Meredith a second. The seventy-year-old woman's solid white hair is cut in a short, sharp bob, and a teasing gleam exists in her eyes as she glances back at me. An unmistakable curiosity about Clay's connection to me glitters in her gaze.

However, other than Meredith, I'm skittish about seeing people who might recall my story. Returning to the hospital had been difficult enough. The nurses who remembered me had questions.

Where had I been? Was I okay? What happened to Wesley?

I'd had to plaster on a smile and pretend I was doing well, which wasn't much of a stretch, but explaining Wesley had been the harder part. To keep things simple, I told people we'd divorced, and I'd gone to stay with my parents for a while. Too often people praised my mother and father for their generosity because they didn't know the whole story. So many lies I told, and half the time, I believed them myself.

"Can we, Mama?" Dutton turns toward me. His eyes are eager, wide, and pleading. His shaggy hair needs a cut.

Saying no to him is difficult when he rarely asks for anything. The only thing he'd wanted was for us to leave Wesley, and I hadn't done it until it was almost too late.

"Okay." The answer was half-hearted at best. I didn't understand why Clay would consider us special guests at a public event or why he'd want to bring us to a private family affair. But Dutton was suddenly beaming up at Clay with a smile I hadn't seen in a long time. My heart cracked a little, like a chip chinked into a favorite bowl. One you won't part with despite the imperfection because the item has too much sentimental value.

"Yes." Dutton pumps his arm at his side before Clay holds out his fist to bump it against Dutton's smaller hand.

"So back to answering your question," Clay continues. "We're headed to a pop-up Halloween shop in Huntington." The larger city was roughly forty minutes away and had all the superstores and popular chain merchandisers that Sterling Falls lacked.

"I thought we'd ride together. Grab dinner." Clay's smile continues, one side of his mouth curling higher than the other and that damn dimple peeks out.

With the hopeful grin on Dutton's face, how could I say no?

AN HOUR LATER, Dutton's frustration hits a new level.

Inside the Halloween pop-up store, we quickly found the spot where a pink Power Princess costume should have been but was sold out. I was slightly relieved as the sixty-dollar price tag was much more than my meager budget allowed for a one-time use costume. For years, we'd made do with things around the house for the autumn holiday. Dutton's first year he was a pumpkin, something easily made with an orange sweatshirt and some black felt cutouts sewn on to create a jack-o-lantern face. Another year, he was a cow. Not necessarily his favorite costume, but he was still adorable in a white sweatsuit covered in hand-drawn fabric paint spots and some makeup on his face.

Last year at my parents' place, my father refused to let Dutton dress in anything feminine, so Dutton was an unhappy turtle made by wearing all green attire and a brown backpack on his back that I tried to doctor up by drawing what looked like the outer shell of a turtle on the canvas.

This year, Dutton had it in his head that he'd be his beloved princess and he didn't want a homemade costume but the real deal. Only, with the item sold out, Dutton pouts.

"It's been one of our most popular items this year," the salesclerk told us. Then added the final kicker. "We don't anticipate receiving more before Halloween with it only being a couple weeks away."

Clay tried to help. "How about a pirate? Or a football player? Maybe Batman?"

Dutton shook his head at every suggestion, his irritation growing with each recommendation that had a traditionally male connotation to them.

On Dutton's behalf, I'm equally frustrated and disappointed. I'd thought Clay accepted Dutton when he bought pink ice cream and watched *Princess Power* with him. But I'd clearly been wrong in assuming Clay was cool with Dutton being who he is. He wanted the pink Power Princess outfit and wasn't going to settle for something considered boyish. He wasn't going to conform to constructs because of his biology. He wanted what he wanted, and I was trying to honor that.

I reminded myself it's what Cecilia would have wanted. My sister refused to follow the ideals of my parents. The misogynistic beliefs of the culture we'd been raised in. She wanted more for herself. More for me. More for our future children. Unfortunately, her strong independence cost her in the end.

However, my own agitation with Dutton grew when he refused to accept *any* alternative costume.

"How about Moana?" He'd wanted to be the Hawaiian princess last year.

"No." With an added foot stomp from Dutton, I turned to Clay.

"We're done here." I wasn't going to let Dutton have a public tantrum over a Halloween costume.

Clay looked bewildered.

And sensing I couldn't handle an argument with Dutton, he shifted his attention to me. "We need a costume for you."

I shook my head. "I have something." Amid my meager belongings was something special that I brought out each year to wear for Halloween, knowing I didn't have any other occasion to wear such a treasured item. My grandmother had given it to me with sage advice.

Be who you want to be, my Mavis. Not a mold of others, but unique. Colorful. Beautiful. Carefree.

She delicately waved her hand through the air, emphasizing the freedom of floating about in a breeze, like a butterfly.

The irony of Clay suddenly calling me such a beautiful creature was not lost on me, and startling, as he didn't know the love I had for my wonderful grandmother. Nor that she called me the same nickname.

"Let's just go have dinner." The anticipation of the surprise evening was now dampened a bit by Dutton's behavior. However, I hadn't wanted to spoil anything for Clay, who looked a little crestfallen when no costumes were purchased.

Dinner was at a local eatery, popular in the mountains around us, and a quick meal which had us back on the road for a silent return journey to Clay's home.

Once we return to the house, Dutton instantly heads for the front door, but I am not letting his sourpuss exit the night without a final request. "What do you say to Clay for taking us out to dinner?"

"Thank you," Dutton mumbles, not offering his eyes to Clay, and lacking sincerity in his gratitude.

"Anytime, buddy," Clay answers, the response stilted. He presses in the code to open his home and pushes at the door to swing inward for us to enter. Once inside, I tell Dutton it's time for a bath and he heads to the guest room without a glance back at us.

"I failed, didn't I?" Clay says from behind me.

I spin to face him. "It's the thought that counts. Besides, you couldn't help that the store was sold out."

Clay shakes his head, cupping the back of his neck. "It wasn't that. I'd been making all those suggestions. Coming up with things I thought a boy would like but he . . ."

My lips tighten, twisting a bit, before I fill in the blank. "He doesn't like those things."

"Gotta respect a kid who knows what he wants," Clay sheepishly adds. "I've just had a different upbringing."

I stare at him, understanding what he means.

"My dad was a man's man, so to speak." Clay narrows his eyes and turns his gaze toward the wall of windows. "But how much of a man are you if you belittle your kids and knock around a few of them?"

My mouth falls open, shock running through me. *Not Clay.*

Not his family. They seem so well-adjusted, so loyal to one another. But no one knows better than me, ghosts can live in everyone's history. Specters we don't openly admit haunt more than our dreams.

"What happened to you?" I whisper.

Clay shakes his head. "Another day. I want to make sure Dutton is okay."

I sigh, hanging my head. "I just want him to be accepted for who he is. No matter who that is."

"Don't we all want that?" Clay counters, not really questioning the thought but stating a fact.

And who are you, Clay Sylver? Because there's certainly more than meets the eye about him. And maybe he understands us a little better than I think.

The following day, when a package is delivered for Dutton, my faith in Clay is fully restored with the arrival of a pink Power Princess costume.

13

———

[Clay]

With the Harvest Fest looming, I'd been busy once more, although we have an entire committee which handles vendors and distributors. This year, my sister-in-law Halle is involved as she'd proven quite the party planner. She'd helped the local art studio, appropriately named Art's Studio, host a fundraiser last fall. The event garnered the attention of our mayor, who requested Halle's assistance on two town festivals: Founder's Day and Spring Fling. Now, we've hired her to oversee the fest.

I arrive at Sylver Seed & Soil early on Saturday, pitching in wherever help is needed. The last forty-eight hours with Mavis have been strained and the busyness of the fest is a good distraction from my thoughts.

I want to understand her. I want to know her better.

The beauty of her soul seeps out of her, like a hazy aura, and I want to capture a sliver of that warmth. Bottle it up like a firefly in a jar, only I'd never trap such an innocent creature. I don't want to stifle Mavis. I just want her to relax a little, but amid the wavering vibe is constant tension. Like she is one flap from flying away from me.

I'd hoped to bring Mavis and Dutton to the event with me, but the lead up to the fest was just too chaotic. Mavis agreed to meet me at Sylver Seed & Soil around noon. As I'm standing behind a table where we are passing out miniature pumpkins for the decorating contest, I do a double take at a woman dressed from head to toe in black. The sleek outfit outlines all her curves. Her dark hair is parted and twisted into two tight buns on the top of her head, like bound antennas. A vibrant orange material with black edging and white dots drapes over her shoulders and along her arms.

"Butterfly," I breathe out as Mavis approaches with a mini pink Power Princess beside her. However, I can hardly take my eyes off Mavis. She looks mystical, like a butterfly queen, especially when she spreads out her arms to emphasize the delicacy and beauty of the material.

"That's gorgeous," Violet says beside me. Halle's sixteen-year-old daughter has been recruited to pass out the small gourds for the decorating contest and manage the entries.

Mavis smiles. A true radiant beam lights her eyes and stuns me. "Thank you. My grandmother gave this to me before she passed away." She smooths her hands down the flimsy, sheer material, pressing it over her belly.

I'm transfixed by the shimmery black outfit she wears beneath the whimsical drape. The body-hugging costume gives away all her hills and valleys. She's a glorious landscape for everyone to appreciate. But I want to pull her aside, hide us both from prying eyes, and discover first-hand the tantalizing scope of all those dips and curves myself.

"Thank you," Dutton says, drawing my attention to him for

a second, noticing his gratitude extends to Violet who just handed him a small pumpkin.

"You can decorate it any way you want," Violet reminds him.

"I'm going to make it a mini Power Princess."

"I love *Princess Power*." The enthusiastic female voice comes from my niece, Winnie, my brother Ford's second daughter who is the same age as Dutton.

"Hey. You guys made it." I round the table and hug Ford. He'd never been to a Harvest Fest until last year, because he was a professional baseball player and living in Chicago. Now, he lives in Sterling Falls with his family of three little girls, awaiting the arrival of his girlfriend, Cadence, a world renown country singer who is on tour until November.

"Looks like quite a party," Ford states, his tall, lean demeanor relaxed after years of coming across as uptight. He glances at each of his girls—Zelle, Winnie, and June—dressed respectively as Belle from *Beauty and the Beast*, a baseball player, and a bright blue bug of sorts.

"June Bug, are you a June bug?" I tease the four-year-old in her glittering, iridescent blue costume.

"Me Bug," she repeats, proudly.

"I like your costume," Winnie addresses Dutton, who shyly steps closer to his mother.

"Girls, this is Dutton. He's been staying at my house," I address them before pointing out each of my nieces to Dutton. "Dutton, this is Zelle, Winnie, and June."

Ford clears his throat.

"And this guy." I clap his shoulder and look at Mavis. "Is my younger brother, Ford." I leave off that he used to be the center-fielder for the Chicago Anchors.

"Nice to meet you." Ford extends a hand for Mavis. "I've heard a few things about you."

Mavis stiffens, and Ford senses the shift. "Keeping this guy out of trouble, right?" He tips his head toward me, attempting to tease me.

Mavis's shoulders relax and she releases Ford's hand. "He's not trouble." But her eyes light up again as she speaks about me.

"Daddy, can Dutton sit with us?" Winnie offers, and I want to hug my niece for her kindness. The boy needs some friends other than his mama.

Dutton glances up at Mavis like he isn't certain how he should respond.

"Go ahead." The hesitation in Mavis's tone might stall the kid from making his own decision, but when he glances back at Winnie, who has an eager expression on her face, Dutton returns her smile. Before we know it, the superhero princess is running after the baseball player to find seats at the tables provided for pumpkin decorating. Zelle leads June to the table as well.

Mavis keeps her eyes on Dutton a minute, before turning back to Ford. "How old is she?"

While they discuss ages and the local school, I check on Violet and her assistants who are tackling the pumpkin decorating activity like future teachers. Her stepdad, my brother Knox, is around here somewhere.

And a sudden wave of gratitude rushes over me. Our family has been spread out for years. Knox in the Navy. Ford playing professional ball. Sebastian serving time in prison. But slowly we've come back to this place. Not necessarily the Seed & Soil, but Sterling Falls, and I'm a little overwhelmed by how happy that makes me.

"You okay?" Mavis's hand on my forearm has me turning my head.

"Yeah. Just . . ." I blow out a breath catching a glimpse of Ford helping his girls, having stepped over to them, and even pointing out something for Dutton seated beside Winnie. "My family."

Mavis glances in the same direction as me. "It must be nice to have so many siblings, living so close."

"We weren't always living this close," I chuckle, having just recalled such a thing. I move us to the side, away from the registration. "Do you have siblings?"

"A sister." Mavis's voice softens. "She's no longer with me."

"I'm so sorry." I run my hand up and down Mavis's arm, relieved she doesn't flinch away from the unannounced touch.

"It happened a little over five years ago." Mavis chews her lower lip, not offering more, and once again I want to pull Mavis to me. I want to tell her she isn't alone. She has me. She can have my family. They'd welcome her with open arms.

She takes a deep breath, lets it out, and offers me a weak smile. "I should check on Dutton."

"He looks good in his costume." He tried it on the other night, but I wasn't home. Mavis told me he wanted to sleep in it, but she told him no. She didn't want to risk anything happening to the costume before the event. She also promised to pay me back when she got her first paycheck.

I'd been insulted at the thought. The costume was a gift. One I gladly gave for the smile on that kid's face.

He and Winnie look like they'd become fast friends. Her chattering away at him and him answering her with a quieter voice. His face turning pink, and him getting that hooded look when he says something snarky, like he's spoken a private joke.

He's a good kid. And Winnie could be the friend he needs.

"Speaking of costumes." I turn to Mavis. "This. Wow." I do nothing to hide my appraisal of her and she tosses her arms out to the side again to expand the material, showing off its brilliance.

"My nana was special to me. This is a treasured gift from her." Mavis swallows. "I was fortunate it wasn't lost in the fire."

She doesn't speak about her loss. We haven't discussed further the sale of her property, and today I don't want to mar the pleasantness of the Harvest Fest by asking about her sad history.

"You're a beautiful butterfly."

Her dark eyes widen and catch on mine. She chews her lower lip but in a coquettish way. Mavis Grant needs compliments and I'm willing to give her anything else she desires.

"And what exactly are you?" Her eyes appraise me as well, roaming down my body, taking in the weathered boots, worn jeans, and a flannel shirt, plus a straw cowboy hat on my head.

"I'm thinking I need to find a giant net and be a butterfly catcher," I tease.

Mavis chuckles. "I might be too big for your net."

"Too beautiful to capture." I smile.

"You might not have to chase too hard."

Both our eyes light up. Hers perhaps because she's surprised she suggested such a thing, and mine because I'm shocked as well. It's the first hint I've had that Mavis might be interested in me.

Could she reciprocate my crush on her?

If this woman wants me to chase, I'll be happy to try and catch her.

14

[Mavis]

When I finally approach Dutton, he's smiling and relaxed, swinging his feet beneath the table which mirrors Winnie Sylver's movement, while painting his miniature pumpkin hot pink. My position leaves me close enough to Clay that I can watch him check on the girls staffing the decorating contest before he turns toward me and takes a step that has me believing he's coming to where I stand.

Only he's intercepted by a beautiful blonde.

"Glady?" Surprise laces his voice while his gaze leaps up and over her shoulder to me.

Quickly, I divert my eyes, concentrating on Dutton, but I can't help but overhear the conversation behind me between Clay and a *friend*.

"Hey, Clay." Her voice is sugary sweet.

"What are you doing here?" The question isn't accusatory, but simply stated out of curiosity.

"It's a festival, silly." Pause. "Plus, I haven't seen you in weeks. Thought I'd come check on you."

Clay clears his throat. "But you never come to the Seed & Soil." His voice tightens only a pinch.

I imagine her lips pouting when she drags out, "I missed you. And you were so sick when I last saw you."

Sick? Had Clay been out with this Glady person when his truck broke down? He told me he was picking up a mechanical part for a friend.

How well I know these kinds of lies, and I want to kick myself.

"Dutton, honey. Mama needs to use the bathroom."

He looks up at me with deep, dark eyes, staring at me like I've suggested something completely unnatural. While watching me, I tip my head, implying he needs to follow. I'm not leaving my six-year-old alone amid this festival.

"We can come right back," I assure him. *Mama just needs a minute to mentally scold herself.*

"He can stay with us," Ford offers. He's taller than his brother. His hair is jet-black compared to the silver weave in Clay's. He's also edgier than his older brother, but the resemblance is still remarkable.

We haven't spoken in the few minutes I've been standing here, as he's concentrating on helping his youngest paint her pumpkin to look like a duck.

I smile at Ford and glance back at Dutton, widening my eyes in a silent command. *Come with me.*

Dutton doesn't move. Instead, he drops his gaze and continues painting, defying my request. But I need to move away from the conversation behind my back. The one with a woman still cooing over Clay and him engaging her in conversation when I've been staying in his home for three weeks. And this is the first I've learned of a woman in his life.

"Dutton." I clench my teeth while holding back any hostile tone.

"I'm good here," he states.

My gaze flips up to Ford, concern hitting me hard that he can see I'm not a candidate for mother of the year.

"Honestly. He's welcome to stay. I'll keep my eyes on him. We aren't moving from this spot."

I could play off the bathroom lie I told. I don't really need to go, but now I feel trapped into walking away for a few minutes.

"If you're sure?"

"Go." Ford grins.

I hesitate before saying, "Thank you. I'll be quick." But the last thing I want to do is be fast, so I take my time to find the indoor facility down a hallway near the back of the main building. I'm grateful there isn't a line and do my business when I didn't think I had any to do.

Afterward, I run my hands under warm water to calm myself, refusing to look in the mirror to compare myself to a stunning blonde who'd gravitated toward Clay. I'm better than the comparison game, and I've come a long way in recognizing my self-worth. But Clay's omission still stings. The truth has taken me by surprise and rattled me. Of course, Clay has a woman-friend even if he told me no one has ever been to his house.

The moment is more of a trigger from Wesley and his behavior. *Lies and deceit.* I'm only minutely relieved that I'm not the shaky mess I would have been shattered if Clay had been Wesley. *If Clay were mine.* With Wesley, I never knew fact from fiction. My inquiries into where he'd been, what he'd been doing, or *who* he'd been with would lead to insults or injury. I could never predict when my ex would be reactive. Never knew what was truth versus what was a placating tale.

My infidelity suspicions with Wesley didn't happen until the final year or so we were together. When something in him flipped, like the toss of sunny side eggs to over easy. Life was no longer bright and cheery. I'd been painfully aware things between Wesley and me had been dimming for years, and I became brutally cognizant of how foggy my eyesight had once been when looking at a man like Wesley.

When I exhale deeply, I double check my tightly wound hair before exiting the restroom. My head is held high, but my mind is still a bit muddled. Clay doesn't owe me explanations, but finding out he has a woman in his life seems like something I should have learned by now. Amid all I'd shared of myself with him, he could have told me he had someone waiting for him.

Not paying attention, I'm jarred by the assertive and forceful bump into my shoulder from a large man passing a little too close to me for the restroom. The startling movement is aggressive enough that I spin and stumble into the wall lining the narrow passage.

"Mavis."

Holding my shoulder, I twist, certain I heard my name, but the darkly dressed man continues speedily toward the men's room without a second glance at me or an apology. With his back to me, his tall form moves away as if we didn't just collide, and he didn't say my name. Maybe he simply called me *ma'am*. But a fragrance lingers behind him, like the exhaust behind a moving vehicle. *That scent.* Worn leather, cigarettes, and cheap cologne is all too familiar to me.

I'm frozen in place, like a picture nailed to the wall behind me.

"Mavis?" My name is spoken from somewhere to my left but all I hear is a garbled sound, like someone trying to speak through water.

When a hand comes to my elbow, I tug it so sharply away

from the unexpected grasp I knock it into the wall at my back. Pain radiates up my left arm, matching the sharp twinge lingering in my right shoulder. I can't seem to catch my breath. An imaginary vise is squeezing my chest, constricting my airway. My nose is clogged with the recognizable stench, and I gag on the reminiscence of such a fragrance.

"Butterfly?" Clay stands before me, hands in the air in surrender, eyes wide with concern. He quiets his voice. "You okay?"

"Clay." The anxiety clogging my throat makes his name come out as a croak. My ears ring from the rush of my blood pumping. My pulse races.

"Butterfly." He slowly exhales, almost purposefully exaggerating the breath. "Focus on me. Look at me. Talk to me."

His wide icy-blue eyes. His sun-kissed skin. His white scruff.

A deep inhale from him.

Sweat beads along my forehead and trickles down my spine. *Clay is not my enemy.*

Following his lead, I copy his exhale.

"Clay," I gag on relief and do the unexpected. I leap for him, wrapping my arms around his neck and holding onto him like he's a buoy in deep water.

I inhale his earthy scent, the fragrance a cleansing smell and calming balm.

Just as quickly, I release him and step back, colliding with the wall once more.

"Dutton." I need to get to him. I need to get my son.

"He's safe with Ford." Clay remains stone still, shocked by the sudden embrace and retreat. His hands raise again, keeping his distance, like he's talking to a caged animal. "Let's get you some air. Some space."

Slowly, I roll my head against the wall behind me, staring in the direction of the men's room. Did I imagine that man? Why isn't someone coming out of the bathroom? Is something wrong with me?

"Dutton," I whisper again, lifting a trembling hand to my upper lip and swiping at the dampened skin.

Clay pulls his phone from his back pocket, presses a contact, and speaks. "Hey. I'm taking Mavis to my office for a second. Need to show her something. Can you keep an eye on Dutton another minute for us?"

Clay scowls at whatever reply his brother gives him, but his eyes meet mine when he says, "It's not like that."

We aren't like that is what 'that' implies, and I'm drawn back to my initial upset, learning Clay has a girlfriend.

I press off the wall and brush a shaking hand around one bun on the top of my head. My hair suddenly feels pulled too tight, and I want to remove both twists. I glance over my shoulder one more time. Clay looks in the same direction before offering me a pinched stare and clicks off his phone.

"Let's get you away from the crowd for a minute." He holds out his hand. "Come with me."

His request is more like a suggestion. He's asking me to trust him, and I want to, I really do. As the panic inside me slowly subsides, washing down my body like a too-cold shower, I begin to shiver. However, deciding my mind has played a trick on me and I'm making a scene, I place my hand in Clay's, finding it warm and comforting.

With his fingers curled securely around mine, he leads me to a door behind the cash wrap station, and we head up a flight of metal stairs. We don't speak until we enter his office which has a surprising view of the entire property and the festival. Clay releases my hand and walks to a small fridge to remove a bottle of water.

"I'm sorry," I whisper, uncertain why I overreacted to either the woman in his life or the man in the hallway.

"Something tells me this isn't about Glady."

"It's not my business who you—"

"We're friends." He stops a foot from me, pausing to open the bottle of water before holding it out to me. "Here, drink this."

"Thank you." My voice quivers, my hand trembles as I take the cool container from him and sip.

"What happened down there?" He tips his head toward the door.

I shrug, not nearly as nonplussed as when I'll say, "Someone bumped into me." I pinch my brows. "Or so I thought." I glance in the direction of the stairwell.

"Are you hurt?" Suddenly, Clay is before me, filling my space and forcing me to focus on him. With his hands on my shoulders, he visually inspects me.

"It was nothing. Just passing too close to each other in the hall." However, the bump felt more purposeful, intentional. And how do I explain the man speaking my name? I deflect. "But since you mentioned Glady. Why didn't you tell me you have a girlfriend?"

"Because I don't." Clay drops his hands from my shoulders.

"But you omitted you have a woman in your life."

"Because she's just . . . a friend."

Right? And now I know more than I need to know about their situation.

"Wesley was the king of omission," I state, taking another sip of water from the bottle in my hand.

"Fuck." Clay turns his head, twisting his lips. "I didn't omit." His head swings back to face me. "There's nothing to *admit*. Glady and I are friends." His emphasis clarifies their status. Friends with benefits.

"It's not my business—"

"And I haven't seen her in weeks," he interjects, waving between us. "Since you moved in."

"Well, we can go." I snap, still rattled by what happened in the hallway plus discovering a woman in Clay's life. "I never meant to stop you living your life."

"You aren't stopping me from living," he grinds out, irritation in his tone. Upset, not that I've discovered Glady, but from what I've just said.

"And I don't know how long it had been before stopping by her place weeks ago." Clay continues as if wanting to continue his thought before I interrupted him. "When nothing happened between us."

"Because you were sick," I remind him, reminding us both of his condition the night we connected on the side of the road. Then, I scoff. "You don't owe me—"

"But I want you to know." His words are softly spoken but no less intense than telling me he hasn't stopped living. He steps forward, filling the distance that existed between us. His eyes blaze, like he's communicating without speaking. His hands clench at his sides, as if he's restraining himself from touching me again, when all he might want is to grab me, maybe gently shake me to enforce his thoughts. Tension mingles with passion and emotion emanating off him, sealing the sliver of space between us.

Taking a deep breath, I hold my ground. I have a choice.

Maybe he *is* telling me the truth. Maybe he hasn't been with someone in a while. Maybe he wants me as much as I want him.

"Now, tell me what happened downstairs. Something or someone spooked you." He exhales heavily again, swiping a hand down his face as if he can strip the tension off him. "Fuck Wesley. Tell me what to do so I don't frighten you."

"You don't scare me," I counter.

"But downstairs you looked ready to dart. You also looked like you'd seen a ghost."

"It was nothing," I state again, hoping to convince myself. The man wasn't Wesley, or anyone else from my past. Just a man, and maybe even not that as no one came back out of the bathroom while we stood in the hallway. I might have imagined the entire interaction. I definitely overreacted.

"I think too many things collided in my head. Thoughts about you and . . ." I don't speak her name.

Clay tilts his head, a sexy smirk curling his mouth. The fists at his sides relax into flexed fingers. His shoulders lower a little. "Were you jealous?" Then he reads something in my face and his expression falls, straightens. His eyes fill with surprise. "You *were* jealous."

"I was not," I defend, and take another drink of water to dispel the lie on my tongue.

Clay is suddenly so close I can feel the warmth of his flannel from being outside in the fall sunshine.

"What if I tell you I was *always* jealous of Wesley." His eyes are bright, sincerity in every word. "Jealous that he got to look at you and be with you. Touch you and hold you. Even when I shouldn't have thought those things, shouldn't have wanted them for myself, I was always jealous of him."

I shake my head. He can't mean it. No one should ever be envious of Wesley. But Clay's admission is more about me. He wanted to look at me and be with me. He wanted to touch me and hold me. And the thought of this kind, generous, accepting, and fun-loving man wanting those things with me has my eyes filling once more with a new level of tears. Tears for all that I've missed out on and all I want. All I've ever desired in a man.

"We weren't like that." Wesley was hardly affectionate and never patient.

"What are my limits?"

Confusion strikes. "What do you mean?"

"How do I approach you? How do I get close to you?"

If he stood any closer, we'd be wearing each other's clothing, but what he's really asking hits me hard. Understanding blossoms like a spring flower. Clay wants to touch me, but he's afraid he'll frighten me away.

"I need to be in control," I tell him, finding strength in my voice while the rest of me trembles with a new set of nerves. Unfiltered desire. "Be in charge."

"No element of surprise?" Clay asks like he honestly wants to know how to make me comfortable. "Got it. What else?"

"I don't know." How do I explain that I'm not certain I can be intimate with someone else without knowing what will happen. Expectation. I don't trust intimacy because I fell for the lies of it before. I believed in Wesley's soft touch before it became harsh words and broken promises. Then pinches and slaps. And eventually, an attempt on my life.

Clay's eyes remain on mine. "What if I gave you the power?"

"What do you mean?" I ask again, as my heart rate accelerates. My insides heat.

"Tell me what you want. What you need. *Take it* from me."

"Clay, I don't know what you—"

"Yes, you do." His voice is sharper, but steady as his eyes darken. A layer of promise glides through them. A sense of protection. I'm safe with him. I can make all the decisions between us. I can do nothing, or I can make demands.

"Kiss me," I whisper, uncertain the words have even left my mouth.

Clay slices that thin layer of distance between us in a slow, measured movement that includes cupping my jaw with one hand and placing his other lightly on my hip. He leans forward and the softest brush of his lips paints mine. A whisper of a kiss.

Somehow, I'm turned on more than I ever expected to be. A rush zings up my belly and my throat dries, desperate for more than a sip of him. I'm a parched woman in a desert of stifled desire and imprisoned passion. I've crushed on Clay Sylver too long not to take my chance with him. I want him.

He leans away but I'm quick to capture the back of his head, halting his retreat. Our eyes lock. He's holding back. His desire is to dive in but his strength to protect me by staying distant remains steady. Patient. Waiting.

"Kiss me like you'd kiss her." The request comes from somewhere deep within me. A place I've kept under lock and key for too long. I don't care that I'm not his *friend*. We don't have a situationship. But I want to know what it would feel like if we did. How does a good man kiss a woman? How does Clay's mouth feel?

"I'd never kiss you like I kiss someone else, butterfly. A kiss between us would be unique. Special and beautiful, like you."

"Smooth," I murmur.

"I'll kiss you any way you want, but I want to remind you, you have all the power. Take more if you need it. Pull away if you don't. Just don't hurt me, Mavis."

The vulnerability in his tone has me leaning forward and offering him what we both want in this moment. A connection. A comfort. When our mouths meet, I melt into him, wrapping my arm around his neck and tugging myself closer to him. His hand on my hip slips behind my back, pinning me in place against the strength of his body. Our mouths seek solace and more. Something I don't want to define because I've lived without it for so long and I can't be certain it could ever be more with Clay.

"Keep holding me," I whisper against his mouth, relishing how he's given me the power I want to take. Allowing me to instruct him.

"Not letting go," he murmurs along my lips, the vibration heightening the moment. Or maybe it's his response. He'll follow my lead.

"Kiss me . . . slowly."

Clay hums, drawing out his movements. Taking his time to suck at my lower lip before re-capturing both of them, savoring them, tugging at them. Possibly struggling to hold himself back while letting me claim dominance.

"Give me your tongue," I quietly demand, still shy and unsure, but as Clay slips his tongue forward, another rush of confidence rips through me. The fire in Clay's kiss sets off a blaze inside me.

I don't want to take advantage of him. He's sacrificing himself for me. Still, I can't seem to stop. The kiss grows from the initial soft sips to eager pulls. Lost in one another, I'm no longer certain who holds the reigns, but we're racing toward something.

My wings are emerging, stretching, breaking free from containment, like the butterfly he calls me. The transformation he claims awaits me. I'm ready to spread those wings wide and lift off . . . when a knock startles us apart.

Breaking away from one another, we stare at each other, our breaths coming quick and shallow. His eyes are bright, full of laughter and longing. We both wanted more in the moment. Unfinished business rolls between us. One kiss won't be enough.

And I'm never going to be the same after that kiss, after that kind of control. The power to make this man as desperate for me as I suddenly am for him.

"Clay," someone calls out before opening his office door.

I take an exaggerated step back and turn to face a person I recognize.

"Mavis." The broad man with silver at his temples and a scar through one eyebrow doesn't sound surprised to see me.

"Knox." My throat clogs on his name. He's one of the two firefighters who rescued me from the flames that took my home. The man who saved my son.

Reality douses the fire inside me. Knox is a harsh reminder of what happened to me, where I'd been and how much further I need to go to fix my life.

"Nice to see you again." He steps forward, placing a friendly kiss to my cheek, like we're old friends instead of acquaintances from a harrowing incident.

"Sorry to interrupt," Knox says, a tease in his voice as he addresses his brother. "But you're needed downstairs. The festival." He raises that scarred brow in reminder, as if somehow Clay has forgotten the party in the yard of Sylver Seed & Soil.

For a few seconds, I certainly had, but everything crashes back to me. "Dutton." I step toward the door, preparing to exit when my elbow is gently cupped by Clay. This time, I don't flinch away. His eyes catch on mine, concern suddenly filling that icy-blue gaze.

"He's good," Knox says, interrupting the silent moment Clay and I need. "Ford has him. He took the kids to see the newly hatched chickens."

I nod once, tightly smiling as if I know where that is, and I hadn't just gotten caught kissing his brother. Guilt is written on both our faces.

"Thank you. I'll go find them." Without a glance back at Clay, I exit the office, thundering down the metal stairs. The sound matches the clanging of my heart.

I just kissed Clay Sylver.

And I liked it more than I should have.

15

[Clay]

"**W**as I interrupting something?" Knox teases and wiggles his large brows, implying he knows damn well he did.

"Don't be obtuse."

Knox chuckles while I swipe a hand over my mouth, desperate to contain the kiss, while simultaneously wiping it away as if Knox can see it on my lips. As if he senses that the kiss I shared with Mavis was exactly as I said it would be. Unique. Special. Beautiful.

I'll never be the same.

Even her whispered plea to kiss her had me jolting to life. Like I hadn't known I needed someone to tell me to do such a thing before. Like I hadn't found it hot as hell that she was claiming what she wanted, moments after acting afraid of me.

Then she offered additional instruction. Soft demands and hesitant commands.

Give me your tongue. Fuck, I'm still hard just thinking about her requesting such a thing from me.

If she wants control, if she needs to be the lead, I'm not going to fight her. Especially not after the buzzing sensation that still vibrates within me. As I told her earlier, I'd chase her, no net required.

I feel exalted, elated, like I'm high on something. My dick is hard as a rock. My heart hammers excitedly within my chest. The desire to race after Mavis and beg her to command me again grips my throat.

What the fuck is happening to me?

She's like a fine wine you only get to sample, but I want a full glass.

"Powerful stuff, huh?"

My head swings upward and I glare at my brother. "What?"

"Must have been some kiss."

"I don't know what you're talking about." I give him my back and take a seat at my desk, needing a moment to calm down.

Knox chuckles. "Dude. Festival."

Right. Yes. The fest. "I'll be down in a minute."

My brother laughs harder. "I get it. I want to whisk Halle off as well but—"

"It's not like that." I spin in my desk chair, using the desk to shield my hard dick like I'm some randy school-aged kid, while I glare at Knox. My voice is sharp and direct. I clutch the edge of my desk as if holding myself back from pouncing on him. I clear my throat. "We aren't like that."

I hate how I said the same thing earlier to Ford when he teased me on the phone. When I said I wanted to show Mavis something in my office and he asked me if that was a sexual euphemism.

Mavis and I *aren't* like that. She's coming off a bad relationship. I don't do them period.

Case in point, my brother standing in front of me,

reminding me of a festival I run every year, where I attend to every detail, making certain it's perfect. It's profitable. It goes off without a hitch or scratch or dent that would soil what I've rebuilt in our family business. I'm in control.

And yet, I'm off-kilter. Mavis has unraveled me. And deep down I'm afraid to admit what I really want. What I know I need. Someone for me. Not my siblings or the Seed & Soil or a festival of people, but that one person who is all mine. Who wants me as me, not brother or boss or community leader.

Hell, I don't want to lead anything. I want Mavis to be the driver, take the wheel and guide our journey. She's the one I'm afraid to be close to, because someone like her could break me.

Because before, she was someone unobtainable. I could smile and be kind, offer a compliment, maybe a little flirt, and it was all innocent because it had to be. She was married, or so I thought.

But now? Mavis Grant is within my reach, and I can do all the things I told her I was envious of with her ex. I can look at her and be with her. Touch her and hold her, with her permission. With her guidance. With the power firmly in her hands.

Could she want more? Could she offer me more?

"Be careful here, Clay." Knox interjects over my rambling thoughts.

"You think I'm trying to save her, don't you?" I demand, still on edge. Still shaky, with the energy I can't contain.

"Aren't you?" He arches a brow again.

I shake my head because it would never occur to anyone that I'm not doing the saving.

She might save me.

～

FOLLOWING Knox out of my office and back to the festival, I reflect on Glady's sudden appearance. How it must have looked to Mavis. As small-town rumors bleed into other small towns, Glady must have heard about my housemates. It was the only explanation for her sudden appearance at the Seed & Soil because we didn't see one another outside of our rare hookups.

When Mavis disappeared, I was quick to follow her, rushing to excuse myself from Glady after telling her I'd met someone. I was no longer available. *No feelings, hard or soft*, Glady and I once promised each other.

And right now, my emotions are in turmoil as I struggle to find Mavis and Dutton in the crowd and fight the urge to take them back to my home. I don't buy the excuse Mavis was selling about an accidental collision in the hallway. Something, or rather someone, spooked her, and the last thing I want is Mavis frightened of living in Sterling Falls. Or afraid of me.

That kiss proved she didn't fear me.

Fifteen minutes of searching here and there pass before I find Mavis and Dutton, who were not in the area with the newly hatched chicks or in any of the other animal petting experiences provided by local farmers.

Instead, Mavis and Dutton are doing some kind of dance to kid-friendly music on the temporary dance floor where a group singing children's songs performs. Zelle and Winnie join them.

Later tonight, there will be a band for adults. I should have asked Mavis to hang out. I hadn't considered childcare. Haven't ever been with a woman who has a kid. Now, I'm certain I'm too late to find someone to watch Dutton.

Someone bumps into my arm, and I turn toward Ford, who is holding June against his chest, her head on his shoulder. His hand gently rubs up and down her back.

"Someone tired?"

"Yeah, she needs a nap."

"No nap," she mutters around the thumb in her mouth.

"When's she going to give that up?" I chuckle, noting her thumb's position.

"Probably not until she's sixteen." Ford presses a kiss to her downy blond curls. Then he tips his chin toward Mavis and the girls dancing. "What's her story?"

"Still trying to figure it all out myself," I admit.

"And Dutton." Ford means the costume.

"He likes pink and princesses." I hold my breath recalling how I first reacted. A bit stunned but not offput by the behavior.

"Winnie wants to have him over tonight for a while."

I spin to fully face my brother. Was the Universe just listening to me? "How would you feel about that?"

"What?" Ford shifts only his head to glance at me. "Winnie making a new friend?"

I smile, knowing Ford's deflecting any issue with a boy liking stereotypical girl things, as in, Ford isn't bothered by it, as he shouldn't be.

"He isn't in the local school. Mavis is homeschooling him right now."

"So I heard. Now Winnie's trying to convince me she shouldn't have to go to a physical school, and I should be her teacher." Ford chokes. "Put me out of my misery. Kudos to the parents who homeschool, but I can't educate from home. And I know teachers aren't paid enough to deal with my rascals, but I'm still not interested in homeschooling."

"Might help Dutton if he had a friend as well. He's been through a lot, but he's a good kid."

Ford nods, not needing all the details.

The silly song finishes, and the kids rush Ford with Mavis laughing as she follows them.

"Daddy, can Dutton please come over?"

Mavis and Ford catch a look before Ford speaks, "I really don't mind."

Dutton has his hands folded together like he's praying, bouncing on his toes, pleading with his mom.

"If you're really sure." Apparently, the invitation must have already been offered.

"Got a call with my girl later. That's my only plan tonight."

My brother is newly in love and his world-famous country-music girlfriend will be home from her tour in a few weeks. Until then, he's doing lots of Facetime and hand jobs to get him through the absence.

I don't think I could ever have a long-distance relationship. *If* I had a woman, a wife, I'd want her present all the time, working with me, beside me, like I remember my parents before everything fell apart. I'll never understand how my father loved my mother before her death, and then seemed to forget all that love after she was gone.

My gaze lands on Mavis.

"Let me swing back to Clay's place so Dutton can change and then I'll bring him over to your house."

"Sounds like a plan," Ford agrees.

Dutton and Winnie face one another and scream, jumping up and down like bouncing beans and teetering with excitement.

As for me, I'm thrilled for Dutton. Then, I step over to Mavis.

"Hey, you think you might want to come back here after you drop off Dutton? There'll be a grown-up band playing later tonight."

Mavis's dark eyes open wide, whether surprised by the invitation or something else, I'm not certain, but I'm not interested in brushing off that kiss and I don't want her avoiding me until we can talk about it.

"Let me get Dutton settled." She glances back at him, brows furrowing. "I'll think about it."

"Think yes, butterfly. You deserve a night off."

She offers me a cautious smile and I want to reach out for

her, tug her to me, and give her another kiss right here to ease her troubled mind. But I promised to let her lead.

For the first time in my life, I'm relinquishing control, and the sensation is both frightening and thrilling.

I watch as they all walk away. Ford and his girls. Mavis and Dutton. Then Ford turns around, walking backward a few paces. He points at his eyes with two fingers then swivels his hand toward me.

You owe me, he mouths. Then he laughs and spins back around.

Apparently, I'm not fooling anyone about my attraction to Mavis.

Not even myself.

16

[Mavis]

I'm anxious. Nervous about leaving Dutton at Ford's home. Nervous about returning to the Harvest Festival. Nervous to see Clay after that kiss.

Still, I talk myself into accepting that Dutton needs a friend his own age and I do deserve at least one night that's kid-free for a little while.

Wearing a denim dress and cowboy boots, I walk amid the people gathered around the wooden dance floor, now lit by strings of Edison bulb lights and a few spotlights on a new band.

Clay sent me a text earlier, telling me where to find him, and I slowly approach where he's standing with his brother, Knox, and the woman I recognize as my old neighbor, Halle. My anxiety creeps up another notch. I might not know these people, but they know about me.

"Hi." My voice cracks as I near and Clay turns.

His eyes light up underneath the warm bulbs overhanging the dance floor, and he smiles wide.

"You made it." Relief washes through his words. He didn't think I'd come. I wasn't certain I would either, but here I am. And he's looking at me like I hung the stars.

Quickly, he steps up to me, rubs my arm and leans in to kiss my cheek. I'm startled by the sudden rush of affection, but I don't flinch away. Clay is a physical man and holding back his desire to touch must be difficult for him. I appreciate that earlier he wanted to understand and respect my boundaries. He wanted to know what he could do to make me comfortable.

Embarrassment lingers over the way I asked him to kiss me. Still, that kiss. I felt it from the ends of my hair to the tips of my toes. And for a few blissful minutes, I forgot everything. Wesley. My parents. Florida. The past didn't matter.

Clay's hand slides down my arm, distracting me, until he wraps his fingers around mine. Then, he seems to think better of the connection and releases my hand. With the warmth of his touch missing, I shiver under the fall, mountain air.

"Mavis, you met Knox earlier." Clay points to his brother. "And this is his wife, Halle."

Surprise hits me. If I recall correctly, her mother, Mrs. Reynolds, was praising Halle's apparently now-ex shortly before she passed away over a year ago. It's a reminder that a lot can change in twelve months.

"Nice to officially meet you." I hold out a hand for Halle but Halle steps forward to hug me.

My, they are a friendly bunch.

"So great to finally meet you," she says, pressing me back by the shoulders. "I'm sorry we were never properly introduced before." When I lived across the street from her.

"Clay tells me you'll be coming to our party next weekend."

"I . . . I haven't decided yet." But I catch Knox watching me, and he winks like he already knows I'll be there.

Love floats around this couple in a thick cloud, and my heart flutters. Could this happen for me one day? Would it be better than my previously misguided relationship?

"Shall we dance?" Clay asks, and I'm grateful for the distraction from my thoughts. He takes my hand again and tugs me toward the dance floor.

"How do you feel about two-stepping?"

I laugh. "I don't exactly know how to do that kind of dancing." I'd grown up on hard rock and heavy metal.

"Just follow my lead," he prompts before spinning me to face him. Our hands are clasped together at waist height, and he keeps some space between us. Then, he's guiding me to twirl away from him before tugging me back to his chest. He's a fine teacher and I'm laughing my head off when I step on his foot a time or two. Clay isn't fazed as he dips me left and right before pressing me away and pulling me back as the band covers Brad Paisley's song "Wrapped Around".

Breathless, I continue to giggle when the song ends, and another begins at a slower pace. Clay pulls me back to his chest, wrapping one arm around my lower back, keeping me close.

"Having fun?" The smile on his face fills his voice.

"I can't remember the last time I did anything like this." My returning smile conveys every emotion. I can't recall the last time I was without Dutton, didn't feel like a mom, and acted like a woman.

As Clay draws me closer to him, my heart gallops. I'm certain he can feel the rhythm pounding beneath my chest. He holds me in a way we fit, like we've been together for longer than a few weeks, and I don't want to get caught up in how good it feels. To be held. To feel cherished. To want more.

He leans forward, dipping his nose near my ear. "You smell pretty."

Such a simple statement, and yet I giggle like a schoolgirl. I don't think anyone has ever said that to me.

"Honeysuckle?" He pauses. "Violets?"

"A combination of the two, I guess." A floral concoction my grandmother once made and shared the recipe with me. Wearing it reminds me of her, with fond memories of being young and happy.

Clay inhales deeper along my neck and my skin pebbles.

"Ticklish?"

I hadn't ever thought so but the way he runs the tip of his nose against the column of my throat, I suddenly am. And I want him to do it again. I want him to sniff and nibble at me everywhere.

The thought surprises me, but also doesn't. Two years without tenderness has been a long drought and I yearn deep inside for the connection. The sensual touch of another. The intimacy of two bodies coming together.

Thankfully, the song about a girl not knowing what she does for the man singing ends, and the band breaks into "Boot Scootin' Boogie" by Brooks & Dunn. The crowd goes crazy and those who exited the dance floor due to the slower beat return in large groups of giddy women and men with moves.

Clay is among those men who can dance as the line begins. He points out how he moves his feet so I can follow half a beat behind, but I'm a fast study and within seconds, I'm dancing like a pro. Clay tips his head back, laughing at the sky with a gleam in his eye as we rock forward and back, hopping here and there, and lasso the air. When the song eventually ends, we fall into one another, laughing once more.

"Thirsty?" Clay asks with his arm around me.

"I'd love a drink."

Clay leads me toward the bar, then continues past it.

"Where are we going?" I chuckle as he gently tugs me behind him.

"My office is where I keep the good stuff. Plus, it's free up there." He winks at me over his shoulder. "At the bar, I'd only be paying myself."

The reasoning makes sense. I'm not ready to leave the fresh air, but inside Sylver Seed & Soil, the main store is quiet, the lights dim. A man working security nods at Clay as he leads me deeper into the store and then to the door leading to the stairs to his office.

Once inside his private space, blinds closed on the window block out the party down below. Clay turns on a small desk lamp, the illumination low in such a large space. Beneath the desk is a set of drawers, and Clay pulls out a bottle of Tennessee's finest.

"I'm not much of a drinker," I state.

Clay sets the bottle down, stares at it a moment, and then rounds the desk again. Leaning against it with his backside, his hands clasp the edge of the surface. "Sorry about that." He tips his head in the direction of the alcohol behind him. "I'm not much of one either, knowing what it did to my father."

"What did it do to him?"

Clay shakes his head. "Not tonight, butterfly." The look in his eye ends the discussion.

Watching me, the air around us shifts. The tension builds, like the charge before a storm.

"I want to kiss you again," Clay blurts. "But I'm keeping my promise to let you lead. You tell me when you're ready."

I nod once, lick my lower lip, and then chew at it. "What if I want more?"

"More than a kiss?" His brows rise. His voice deepens. His knuckles tighten against the desk.

I nod again.

"Like what?"

My gaze drops to the desk behind him. The surface flat and

clear. Clay shifts, twisting his upper body just the slightest to follow my stare.

Turning back to me, his voice roughens, ragged and raw. "Tell me exactly what you want, butterfly. Be specific."

I shake my head. I can't do it. I can't—

"Say it," he commands, the sound almost pleading, begging me to tell him.

"I want you to kiss me."

His eyes roam down my body. "Where?"

"Clay," I whisper.

"Tell me."

"Everywhere."

Clay lowers to his knees, surprising me with the slow folding of his body to the floor. On his knees with his thighs spread, he gazes up at me. "Be specific," he repeats, locking on my eyes.

With boldness I don't recognize in myself, I tug at the first few snaps on my denim dress, popping them open to reveal a little more cleavage.

Clay swallows hard, peering up at me. "Let me."

I still my hands and Clay crawls toward me, actually crawls the short distance on all fours, before kneeling at my feet. Then, he rises up on his knees and tugs at my dress, popping several more snaps open at once.

He hums while I moan a sigh of relief. Like I've been buttoned up tight and now I can breathe.

His hands come to my belly and travel upward, digging into my skin before he reaches my breasts. He cups the heavy swells and squeezes.

"Oh God," I whimper, my nipples instantly erect. My breasts ache for more from him. Clay doesn't disappoint. He tugs down my bra, trussing up my cleavage. His gaze fixes on my breasts, exposed for his pleasure. For my pleasure.

"So pretty," he murmurs before massaging them once more. "Tell me more of what you want."

My gaze travels to the desk once more before dropping to him, on his knees in front of me, working my breasts in his large, strong hands.

"Suck one," I quietly order, surprising myself at how easily I give the command.

Clay stills, glancing up at me. Then holding my gaze with his, he leans forward, and takes one swell into the warmth of his mouth, sucking hard until his lips circle the taut peak. His teeth graze along my nipple, the sting causing me to flinch.

But I also like it.

I cup the back of his head, stroking his thick hair as he moves to the other breast repeating the sweet torture. With my nipples erect and breasts damp, he pulls back and admires them once more.

"Perfection."

He lowers to kiss my belly and work his way down until my dress restricts him from lowering.

"Open the rest of my dress," I demand.

Clay rips at the edges so fast the snaps pop with a collective gasp. Brushing the material to the side, Clay leans back on his haunches and stares at my skin. His hands move over my belly once more, coasting lower to cover my hips, but his eyes don't leave the apex of my legs.

"Kiss me," I say quietly.

Clay obliges like a starving man. Quickly, his face is between my thighs, spreading my legs wide and kissing me over my panties. Then he pushes the silky, damp material aside and kisses me like that first kiss. A brush of his lips like a whisper of air. I whimper with need for more, and he latches on, startling me once more. I grip his head for balance.

"Holy . . ." The invasion of his tongue has me seeing stars

and I cling to him as his lips suck and his teeth nip before his tongue swirls once more. His hands clasp on the back of my thighs, inside my open dress. The warmth of his palms heats my skin, and he hangs onto me like I'm holding onto him. With his desperate mouth against me, in places that haven't been devoured in so long, I rock against him and moan.

"That feels so good," I encourage, needing more, reaching for that special edge. As he swipes his tongue forward, he hits my clit, and I jolt. Knowing he's hit the spot, Clay concentrates on the sensitive nub until I'm out of control.

My hips move like I'm choreographing a new kind of two-step, one private between me and this man. I'll never be the same again, and with a quick strum against tender folds, I crack.

"Clay." I cry out his name, grip the back of his head, and curl forward as if I can draw him into me. The release washes out of me, coasting along with the call of his name, and rushing to one central place on my body.

My pulse thumps. *I'm free. I'm free. I'm free.* My mind floats with the mantra as I flutter against Clay's mouth while he draws out every drop of my essence.

"Oh, my God," I mutter, eventually pressing at the sides of his head, needing him to give me a moment.

Clay pulls back but tips his forehead against my lower belly and inhales again. "Your scent is intoxicating."

He rights my underwear and leans back, looking up at me with innocent eyes, but also ones full of mischief. Like he knows what he's just done to me, and he's damn proud of himself.

"What else?" he demands, wanting more of me. More of me telling him what to do.

My gaze flits to the desk once more. I imagine Clay and me, joined as one on the surface. The two of us moving in unison together, connected together. I want to feel all of him. The weight of his body on mine. The feel of him inside me. Not his fingers. Not his tongue, but the clearly impressive-sized cock straining at the front of his jeans. I want to take pleasure from him, as well as give it in return. To relish in this newfound power of sexual expression. To explore this exciting strength within me. The freedom to ask for what I want and receive it.

"You want it there, don't you? Say it and I'll do it." He's almost taunting me, goading me into admission.

"I want to have sex with you on the desk."

His brows lift, perhaps surprised I confessed so easily. Maybe too easily. I step back, fixing my bra, ready to concede that what he did was enough. I don't want to appear selfish or desperate, eager for more of him.

Slowly, Clay rises, like a stalk unfurling toward the rising sun. He stands tall but not imposing before me.

"To be clear, you want me to bend you over my desk and fuck you."

I glance around him once more, staring at the surface because I'm not certain I can look him in the eye when I speak.

"To be clear, I want you to lay back on the desk and let me fuck you."

"Hot damn, Mavis," he groans, swiping his hand around his mouth and choking. Then he steps back, and back again, until he hits the edge of his desk.

"Do I undress myself or do you take over?"

Goading me once more, I stiffen my spine and close the distance between us, popping the button on his jeans before lowering the zipper. Clay leans back, letting me take control in lowering his jeans over his hips. Then I tug at his shirt, pushing the flannel down his arms. He's got too many articles of clothing on him, and I decide to skip ahead. I push at his shoulders and Clay hops up on the desk, leaning back to his elbows and watching me as I tug at his denims and his boxer briefs, removing them only enough to free him from the confines.

I stare at the heavy length, erect and protruding from his lower belly.

"Butterfly," he chokes again, and I wrap my hand around the stiff shaft, tug once and then lower for a lick.

"Jesus," Clay hisses as I take him to the back of my throat before pulling up the length and circling the tip with my tongue. He falls to his back, slings an arm over his face. His exhale is shaky. "You do that again and we aren't going to get to you riding me."

I release him and Clay moves his arm, lifting only his head to watch me tug down my underwear and step out of it. I leave my boots on, my dress open.

"Whatcha doin' to me, beautiful?" He groans, not suggesting I stop, not concerned for himself, just questioning the Universe.

Then, as if sensing I'm not certain how to climb up and over him, he holds out his hand. With his assistance, I set my knee on one side of him and then swing my other knee over his other hip. Straddling him, I stare down at where he's big, and thick, and I'm suddenly nervous.

"I don't have a condom on me," he warns, his tone suddenly anxious. "Don't keep them in my office." The admission suggests he's never done this here before. "But I'm clean."

"Me too." Pregnancy won't be an issue either. I should tell him the truth about me, but I don't. Now isn't the time.

I hitch his lengthy dick upright and tease the tip through my sensitive folds. Clay watches every motion, enraptured by the torment until I still, and my body opens for him.

"Mavis." His deep voice cracks as he glides easily into me, filling me until he can't go any further.

Sitting on top of him, I lean forward, hands on his desk on either side of his biceps and take a deep breath.

"I've never been so full," I admit, wheezing out the words.

"Fuck, sweetheart," Clay grunts, dropping back his head and staring up at the ceiling.

Then, I move, drawing up his thick dick and watching Clay's abs flinch. His upper body moves the slightest bit, like a jolt of electricity shocked him. When he falls back, his hands cup my hips, squeezing at my flesh, but letting me lead.

And I begin the slow ride up and down, and circling round and round, until my clit hits him in such a way, I'm losing control once again.

"Clay," I whimper.

"Take it, baby. Take everything."

I'm slipping up and down his length, and riding back and forth, the friction building, teasing, taunting me.

"I never . . ." I gasp, surprised at how quickly another orgasm is going to shatter me.

"Yes," Clay demands, his fingertips tightening into my skin.

"Clay." I groan. "Honey." The word contains my shock. The sheer incredulity that this could happen to me. That I could come a second time. That I am riding this man. That he let me take what I wanted from him.

I'm in control. The thought has me crashing once again. I slam down on his dick, my channel clenching around him, milking him, as wave after wave crests and falls. I tip my head back then drop it forward, spellbound by the release.

Instantly, Clay takes over, moving me up and down his length, once, twice, . . . "I'm going to come," he warns.

"Yes," I cry out before he abruptly tugs me off him. I whimper with disappointment, immediately missing the connection with him.

He pulls me down so tender folds cover his thick balls and slicked length, still wet from entering me. He pulses beneath me, and I clench in response, glancing down at where he spills on his lower abdomen, washing himself in ropey, white substance. His head tips back. A vein stands along his neck. His fingers grind into my hips, and he holds still.

I collapse forward, catching myself on my hands on either side of his shoulders, bracing myself upright with shaky arms when all I want is to fall over him, lay on his chest and hear his heartbeat, wondering if it matches the chaotic rhythm of mine.

When the lids of his eyes pop open, he stares up at me. With ragged breaths, he says, "I didn't want to go off inside you without your permission." An anxious chuckle fills his throat next. "But you felt so good, baby. That was close."

I bite my inner cheek to prevent from spilling any confessions. The truth doesn't matter. "It's okay," I say, fighting my disappointment again that he hadn't released within me, but admiring him all the more for respecting me.

We remain like this—me straddling him, him awash in the sticky substance—for several seconds as our heart rates settle and our breathing regulates.

Pressing myself upright, I peer down at him again. "Should I get you something?"

Clay easily chuckles, the motion jostling me over him, and I feel an aftershock jolt from him against a swollen, sensitive area. "I think that's my line."

Hesitantly, I laugh as reality catches up to me. I asked him to touch me. I told him to suck me. I begged him to kiss me down low, and then I admitted I wanted to have sex with him on his desk.

Who am I?

I scramble to remove myself from Clay, moving gingerly in an attempt to gracefully climb off both him and his desk. Clay easily sits upright and reaches for me, but I step out of his grasp.

"Butterfly?"

With shaky hands, I try to reattach each snap on my dress. Clay hops off his desk, tugs up his pants, but leaves them loose around his hips as he stands before me. Uncertainty is etched in his brows and the stillness of his jaw.

"Mavis."

My name is strongly stated, and I glance up at him, my own concerns written on my face.

Without more words, Clay tugs me to him and holds me tightly against him. "I enjoyed every second of what just happened, and I'll never be able to look at my desk again without thinking about it. About you. About us." He squeezes me. "No regrets, beautiful."

His words ease me. "No regrets," I whisper, then struggle to pull back, causing him to release me. "But I should really pick up Dutton."

His name is like a thunderclap between us. A reminder that I'm a mother and have responsibilities. I shouldn't have done what we just did but I meant what I said. I won't regret it. I'll hold onto this moment like a treasured gift. Like I kept my grandmother's butterfly shawl and the recipe for her home-made perfume.

Clay's brows pinch but he doesn't argue with me as I scoop up my underwear and ball it in my hand.

"I'll see you later. At your house." A reminder that his place isn't *my* home.

"If I leave my bedroom door open, will you come in?" He already knows the answer.

I can't spend the night with him. This needs to be a one-time thing. A fantasy acted upon. A dream fulfilled but nothing more.

"Clay," I whisper, the answer in his name. *I can't.* And it's one more reason to move on. I've made things awkward between us.

He looks away from me, the side of his jaw clenching. "Yeah, I'll see you later."

Slinking away from him, my shoulders are heavy. My heart

hurts while my body still pulses with what we just did. However, my retreat is for the best. I can't involve Clay in the mess of my life. He's already done so much for me.

More than he'll ever know.

Especially tonight.

17

[Clay]

Dammit.

The word plays on repeat as I watch Mavis leave my office, then realize I should have walked her to her car. It's dark outside. The crowd rowdy out there. Only, once I right clothing and get a grip on my emotions, she's gone.

Dammit. The word resounds like a broken record as I shut down the festival around midnight and crawl home, exhausted while exhilarated.

Mavis is amazing. The look in her eyes. The innocence in her voice yet the confidence in her demands. With a little prodding, she told me exactly what she wanted, and I've never been so eager to please. What I liked best—she took control. The sheer power of *not* having to make a decision by letting her lead, was such a turn-on.

And I wanted to feel that way again.

Only when I reach my house, the guest room door is closed,

and while I leave my bedroom door open, I'll be sleeping alone, like I always do.

Dammit.

~

THE WEEKEND FOLLOWING the Harvest Festival is Halle and Knox's Halloween party. Essentially, it's an open house where neighbors come and go. Halle felt terrible a year ago this summer when she hadn't known Mavis and all that she'd been through. So, Halle wanted to make certain she knew everyone on her block and then some, including family and the new friends she'd made when she'd returned to Sterling Falls.

I still wasn't certain I knew everything there was to know about Mavis yet, but I wasn't giving up on her.

Mavis had to work earlier in the day, but she had plenty of time to prepare for the party. She wanted to bring a dish to share although Halle told her it wasn't necessary. Mavis insisted but her movements were rushed, her aura edgy as she mixed ingredients in my kitchen. Fifteen minutes before leaving the house, her nerves were getting the better of her.

"Hey, Dutton, I need to see your mama in my room a second. Help with my costume." I was a terrible liar, but Dutton seemed content on the couch watching a Halloween special involving his beloved *Princess Power* girls. And I needed a minute with Mavis.

From her position at the counter, she glances up at me, startled by the request. "I need to put the cheese on this function dip."

The term is a fancy name for taco dip, I think.

"It can wait," I suggest, holding out my hand which she eventually takes and allows me to lead her to my bedroom. Once inside, I close the door until there is just a sliver of a crack.

"What do you need?" I ask.

Her eyes widen, shoulders stiff. "I don't know what you—"

Holding up my hand, I stop her. "I know what I need." I run my gaze up and down her body in that damn formfitting, black body suit, outlining every curve and dip. Her hair is pinned up again in those two tight buns. She doesn't have the butterfly shawl on yet, but I've had visions all week of her riding me again wearing nothing but that gauzy material.

"Clay," she whispers, glancing toward the door.

"Ask me. Command me." Maybe if I give her permission, she'll take away this damn pressure between us. Between her job and mine, plus Dutton, it's been a week of circling each other. I'm desperate to reclaim the connection we had on my desk a week ago.

Clasping my hand, she tugs me toward my bathroom, shuts the door behind us and locks it. Turning to face the mirror over the sink, she meets my eyes through the reflection.

"Get me off." Her expression remains tight. "Don't remove my costume."

Her demand is like a starting gun. The stopwatch clicking as my heart races from zero to sixty in less than a minute. My dick is on board just as fast. Her sultry voice, her fierce command. She has no idea what it does for me. How it surprisingly calms me while the rest of my body is jacked up.

With her dressed like Catwoman, the material skintight over her body, touching her will be easy enough, and I take my time to coast my hands over the curve of her hips and the dip of her waist. Standing behind her, I cup her breasts and tug her back to my chest.

"Want me to get you off," I repeat her demand, nuzzling into her neck. "Want to get wet on this suit. Feel the dampness all night. Know my fingers have touched you there."

My hand rushes down her body and between her legs. Her

hips jolt backward, crashing her ass into my cock, already stiff and standing erect with need.

"I've missed you, butterfly." *Can I say that to her?* She's in control but I still want her to know how much she's made me crave her.

"Tell me what to do," I whisper against her neck.

"Touch me. Make me come." Her boldness is like an electric current straight to my dick and I nudge my hips forward, letting her feel what she does to me. She presses back, taunting with that ass, with every inch of her body outlined in this costume.

With my hand between her legs, I easily find her clit and rub hard in tight circles. She spreads her thighs and purrs. Arching her back, she leans forward, grinding her backside harder against me.

"Fuck, Mavis," I hiss. "I want to be inside you again."

"Yes."

"I want to lick your pretty pussy."

"Oh God."

"I want to feel your heat and—"

Mavis clutches my wrist on the hand working her clit and uses her other hand to cover her mouth. She arches her back deeper and cries into her own palm.

"Fuck yeah," I whisper, nipping at her neck as she comes apart in record time.

Her head lolls forward as she drops her hand from her mouth to the edge of the sink. With my hand still on her chest, I can feel her sporadic breaths. In the reflection of the mirror, I watch her blink. Stunned by how quickly she came.

She spins and slithers downward before me.

"Butterfly," I choke, watching her descend to the floor and pop open my jeans. "We don't have—"

I'm cut off when her hand slides over my boxer briefs and cups my balls. Then she has my underwear and jeans tugged down to my knees.

"I need to taste you," she groans.

And my lungs stop working as she sucks me to the back of her throat. Leaning forward, I place one hand on the edge of the sink to steady myself as I watch her head bob. Her mouth circles my cock, and she sucks up and down my shaft, tugging, teasing before twirling her tongue around the crown and dipping along the slit of my tip. Then she draws me deep within her warm mouth and cups my balls again.

I stroke my hand over the back of her head. Then I palm the nape of her neck and squeeze.

Mavis drops her hand from my balls, spreads her thighs, and I watch as her hand disappears between them. She slurps and sucks at me while touching herself.

"Is it getting you off that you're getting me off?"

She hums around me.

Fuck. This woman is going to be the death of me. My hips begin to rock until I'm fucking her sweet mouth, and she's stroking herself like she can't get there fast enough. The frantic rhythm of her own movements increases the intense way she devours me until I'm giving her a singular warning. "Butterfly."

I thrust forward and Mavis rises up on her knees, swallowing me down as I go off inside her. Her shoulders collapse as she reaches a release herself.

Clutching at the sink behind her head, I raggedly breathe as she slips up my shaft and presses a final kiss to the tip. Then she looks up at me from her knees, all innocent dark eyes, sweet and trusting from her position below me. She swipes over her lips with a fingertip, not missing a drop.

"You little minx," I tease her, reaching underneath her armpits and hoisting her upward. She lets out a squeak as I set her on the sink.

"Let me see the stain." I glance toward her legs, and she spreads them the slightest bit. "No need to be shy now."

I force her knees apart and then lower my face between her

thighs, inhaling her intoxicating scent. Her hand swipes over my hair before she tugs at the short strands.

Lifting my head, I meet her gaze.

"Thank you," she whispers.

I chuckle, deep and rough. "Thank *you*." I don't know where any of that came from, but I feel refreshed, relieved. The week without touching her has been torture. And I'm not going to last another week without more of her.

"We should probably go." Her voice is quiet. Her lids lowered.

"Are you okay?" I tip up her chin. "Are we okay?"

She nods but doesn't answer me with words. Then she kisses my nose and hops off the counter, forcing me to move back.

I right my jeans while she checks her hair in my mirror, like it's natural for us to share this tight space. Doing our own things but still being close to one another.

"I need a minute," I tell her. Time to settle my heart and cool my thoughts. Because there are things I want to say to Mavis that she might not want to hear.

She opens the door and I smack her ass, liking how the sound resonates in the confined space.

Mavis turns only her head, chewing her lip and fighting a smile before walking away.

And I'm overcome with fear that one day she'll walk out of my house and out of my life when she might be the one person I need more than she needs me.

18

[Mavis]

othing surprises me more than when Clay exits his bedroom, wearing the VillainMan costume from *Princess Power*.

"Dutton, look!" I choke, as he has his back to the hallway when Clay enters the living room. From his position on the couch, Dutton does a double take, then jumps up on the cushions and squeals, shocking me. I thought he might shriek in fright.

Instead, he leaps over the back of the couch, like he's the actual Pink Princess and intends to tackle Clay. Only Clay catches Dutton and brings him to his chest, holding my son like he's a gift. Like he's his.

I shake the thought. It's too much to consider.

"What do you think?" Clay holds Dutton on his hip while glancing down at himself, cool as a cucumber, and not displaying one bit of emotion about the sexy time that just happened in his bathroom.

As for me, I am still wet between my thighs and feeling the imprint of his fingers touching me. It's going to be a long evening.

And yet, Clay looks even sexier, holding Dutton and dressed in a costume that complements my son's.

"This looks amazing." Dutton squeals again, running his hand over Clay's chest and the padded pieces that exaggerate his size.

Clay sets Dutton on his feet. "I was going for scary." He jumps into a karate pose.

Dutton only laughs, and the sound tickles my insides. "I'll give you a nine point two."

"What?" Clay straightens and his expression stills. "I'm at least a nine point eight six."

Dutton bites his lip and shakes his head. "Nope."

"Oh, man," Clay drones like a child. "I'll work on it."

"You do that," Dutton admonishes, attempting to sound stern but giggling afterwards.

"Okay, people." Clay claps his hands once. "Ready for a party?"

"Yeah," Dutton raises his arms in the air and wiggles his hips side to side before rushing to the front door.

"Jacket," I holler as the temperature has dropped in the final days of October. "Let me just grab the function dip and—"

I'm cut off as Clay follows closely behind me, practically shoving me into his kitchen. He checks over his shoulder as if he can see the front door from our position then turns toward me. "You didn't kiss me."

"I certainly did." I keep my voice low reminding him with a glare that I had him deep down my throat only minutes ago.

"No, a kiss." He taps his mouth, and I chew my lip. He glances around the corner of the kitchen again. Then he sneakily dives for my mouth with his, the kiss fast but direct, sucking on my lower lip before swiping his tongue into my mouth. When he pulls back, he steps away from me like he didn't just take my final ounce of energy. I fall against the refrigerator and nervously laugh, covering my lips with my fingers as I can still feel the kiss on my lips.

And the kiss is the last thing I need to officially calm my nerves and face this party, where his family will be present in one place and old neighbors will gather and speculate about me.

And wonder what Clay Sylver is doing with me.

A question I've been trying to avoid answering.

Because the truth is, I'm growing too comfortable around him. Too attached. I'm falling for him.

Like I always do; fast and easy, like his kiss.

WHEN WE ARRIVE at Halle and Knox's place, my function dip— your basic seven layers of bean dip goodness—is whisked out of my hands by Halle, who takes it upon herself to re-introduce me to my former neighbors. With polite smiles and pitying eyes, they greet me like an old friend even though I hadn't interacted with most of them. One thing I liked about Sterling Falls was how everyone knew one another, but I could somehow keep to myself. Just under the radar, like I'd been raised.

I also see people I remember from the Sterlets, especially Trinity Haven.

"Oh, my gosh, girl. Where the hell have you been?" Trinity is a short, blond powerhouse and she hugs me tight. "I heard you're back at General."

Trinity is also a nurse there, although we work in different departments, but news certainly travels fast in the hospital. It's only been a few weeks.

"Only part-time." My gaze finds Dutton across the room, giggling with Winnie Sylver near a popcorn station Halle set up in her dining room.

"How is he?" Trinity follows my gaze before turning back to me. "How are you?" Her eyes narrow, sincerity in them.

"I'm good." Out the side of my eye I see Clay lingering nearby. "Really good." I can't suppress the smile curling my lips and Trinity glances to my left, slowly nodding her head.

"Ah. The Sylver effect." Trinity chuckles. "It's like a pandemic lately."

I laugh. "What do you mean?"

"First Sebastian. Then Knox. Ford, and now Clay." She smiles kindly and rubs her hand over my arm. "I'm so happy for him."

"Clay?" My brows lift.

"He needs someone like you."

My brows crease, certain that's a compliment but not certain how. "What do you mean?"

"He needs someone to take care of. That savior complex of his needs saving." She chuckles like we're together on an inside joke, but I have no idea what she's talking about.

Savior complex? I glance at Clay, noticing him watching me. He lifts his beer in salute from his place chatting with his brothers, and I nod, but my smile is tight.

Attempting to relax my pinched lips, I offer Trinity an easier grin. "We should have lunch soon at the hospital, if we work a similar shift." I grip her arm, giving it a squeeze. "I better check on Dutton."

But after heading toward him and Winnie, I veer right, and step out the front door to the expansive porch, needing some air. Taking a standing position in the corner near one of the columns holding up the roof, I'm hidden in the shadows and have a clear view of the ruin that was my former home across the street.

The day I found out there was no insurance payout I stopped by the place after coffee with Clay.

Standing before the chain link fences, the privacy tarp ripped here and there, and the fence panels falling over like a haunted mansion once existed behind them, I stared at where my home once stood. The house certainly was haunted with the fear of never knowing how Wesley would act. The tension his drinking caused. The verbal attacks. The small physical assaults. Saving Dutton became the priority. I'd almost been too late to save us both and I shiver at the reminder.

With that tremor comes a familiar scent. Worn leather, cigarettes, and cheap cologne.

Standing straighter, I fold my arms over my midsection and scan the side yard. Narrowing my eyes, I slowly inspect the dark space, continuing to gaze over the front yard and then glancing across the street once more.

The scent is stronger than a week ago at the Harvest Fest, but I shake my head when I don't see anyone, deciding once again I'm imagining it.

Stress. Anxiety triggers suppressed feelings. Reminders of Florida and when I first met Wesley hit me hard when I'm worked up, and thinking Clay sees me as a project, someone to be saved, has kicked up my fight or flight response.

Flight wants to take control. Not the bold phoenix Clay referenced or the graceful butterfly he calls me, but the woman inside me, angry and hurt that he might think I'm weak and desperate. That I need to be picked up and coddled when what I want is someone to stand beside me and cherish me instead.

"Hey."

I flinch at the deep tenor of his voice and spin to find Clay standing close behind me. "You okay?"

With my arms crossed around me, protecting myself, I stare

back at him, uncertain how to respond. Am I okay? Will I ever be okay?

"I think it's time I move on."

"Whoa." Clay lifts his hands in surprise, eyes wide and blinking like I've just socked him in the gut. "Where is this coming from?"

"I don't need you to save me, Clay. And while I'll be eternally grateful for you giving Dutton and me a place to stay, I have my job now and we should find our own space." I grimace. "Plus, I can't keep sleeping next to a flailing six-year-old."

Dutton and I need our own space within our own home.

Clay's brows crease deeply. "I'm not trying to save you. Where the hell did you hear that?"

"Savior complex." I smirk.

Clay sighs heavily, lowering his shoulders, but his gaze remains on me, eyes firm. "That is not what's happening here."

"Yeah, well, I don't know what is happening here," I mock his tone, dropping my arms and reaching for the railing behind me.

Clay steps closer to me, filling the space between us. "What's happening is a beautiful woman saved me in a storm one night. She took care of *me*. She helped me get better when I was sick. She cooked me dinner because she's kind. And I asked her to stay with me because I want to keep her near me."

My eyes widen, hands tightening on the porch rail to hold me steady.

Clay runs a hand over his hair. "Since I was in my twenties, I've done nothing but work. Save my siblings. Save the Seed & Soil. Feed a stray cat. Give a man a job. Save, save, save, Mavis. And for once . . ." He holds up a finger. "It feels like someone is saving me."

"How?" I whisper.

"Do you have any idea what you do to me? How I crave what happened last weekend? Earlier tonight? You telling me what to do?" He exhales. "I don't have to make a decision. You take the lead and I fall in line, and it's blissfully mind-numbing to only concentrate on pleasing you."

My shoulders relax, hands loosen on the railing. "Clay. Honey."

"And that." He points at my face. "That look in those dark eyes. That sigh in your voice. And when you call me honey." He swallows. "Jesus, Mavis. It takes all my strength not to blurt three little words at you and scare the fuck out of you. And the last thing I want you to do is disappear again."

"I didn't disappear," I whisper, but I had been gone.

"Do you know how long I've wanted you?" Clay continues like he's on a roll he can't stop. He places both hands on the back of his head. "I've crushed on you since the first day you walked through the doors of the Seed & Soil. How fucked up is that? Wanting a married woman."

"I wasn't married," I remind him.

"I know that now," he blurts louder. "And now you're back and it takes all my willpower not to touch you all the time and kiss you in front of your kid because I know you don't want any of that. You need time, Mavis, and I'm standing here, willing to give it to you." He drops his arms. "Just, please, don't run. Don't move out."

I stare at him, absorbing all he said. Laying out his feelings, both past and present.

"I wanted you, too. It didn't feel right, but the moment you smiled at me the first time I saw you, something lit up inside me." I clench my fist to my chest. "But I knew my place. I was in a relationship, for good or bad. I was with Wesley. And Dutton . . ." I swallow around his name. "We thought we needed Wesley. But I don't want to feel that need for someone again. I don't want to feel like I have to be saved."

"I'm not saving you, butterfly. You're saving me." Clay's voice strains, his plea desperate while reassuring. His hands wrap around my upper arms, and I sense him fighting himself. He wants to pull me close, but he's respectful that I need space.

I need to call the shots.

And I don't want distance between us.

"Dammit, Clay. Kiss me."

His mouth crashes on mine so quickly, I bend backward over the railing from the force. Then he's maneuvering us so my back hits the column of the porch. His mouth melds to mine, leading me, teasing me. His tongue slips against mine before his teeth nip my lower lip. Then he opens wide again, drinking me in while I'm equally thirsty for him. I know what he means about mind-numbing pleasure. The kind that makes you focus on him and me, and us together. Nothing else matters. Nothing.

"I only want you thinking about earlier." He mutters against my mouth. "The way I touched you. The way you sucked me. How we feel good together. We feel right."

"Yes," I whisper before our lips collide again. Clay's hands cup my backside, tugging me tighter to him. My hands wrap around the back of his head holding him to me. If it were possible for him to lift me against this column at my back and enter me without making a public display of things, I'd beg him to do it.

Instead, the screech of the screen door and the familiar cry of "May-May" in a frightened voice has Clay and I breaking apart.

Within seconds, Dutton crashes into me, face burrowing into my belly. I cup the sides of his head, gently pushing him back so I can look at him. A new sensation rips through my body. *Fear.* "What happened? Why is your head wet?"

Dutton is sobbing hysterically, his face soaked with more than tears. Water saturates his hair. He refuses to look up at me, leaning his head for my stomach again. I wrap my arms around his head tucking him tight to me and glance up at Clay, who looks equally concerned.

Glancing toward the door, I see Winnie stands a few feet away, Ford behind her with his hands on her shoulders. Winnie looks like she's crying as well. Behind him, Knox is pushing a man through the screen door and toward the porch steps.

"What the fuck, man?" The guy counters Knox's aggressive shoving. I cover Dutton's ears as if hearing a swear word compares to whatever has him so worked up.

"Talk to me, baby," I beg of him, curling my body forward, around him, like I can protect him from everything evil in this world.

"What's going on?" Clay asks. I sense him stalking down the porch. Ford moves Winnie backward while Clay thunders down the stairs behind his brother, Knox.

"Just helping the little princess bob for apples." A male voice smirks.

"What?" Clay yells.

At the same time, another man walks through the screen door. He chuckles as he stumbles down the steps to Clay.

"Clay, dude. Relax."

Clay spins on him. "Perry, what the fuck? Who is this guy?"

Despite the darkness in the yard, I can see the person Clay addresses as Perry shrug. "A new friend."

"Pick better ones," Clay demands, pointing at Perry, a stocky man with a mullet, wearing jeans cut off at the knees and a flannel shirt missing the sleeves while open and exposing a white tank beneath it.

"And you." Clay turns back to the other guy still standing but leaning a bit like a listing tree. "What the fuck did you say about a princess and bobbing for apples?" Clay's face is so close to the man dressed as a poor impression of a biker, he could kiss him. Instead, the angry energy vibrating off Clay reaches me all the way up on the porch.

The porch door opens once more and another man exits the house, and rushes down the stairs. I recognize Sebastian Sylver from his bakery and being more formally introduced to him earlier tonight. He's at Clay's side in a blink. From the street comes another man, equal in size to Sebastian, and for a second, I worry a brawl is about to start in the front yard. It's three against three, or so I think until the newly arrived man steps up to the other side of Clay.

I tuck Dutton closer to me, knowing I should remove him from this scene. Knowing I need to hear what happened.

"The *boy* just needed a little help being a man."

"What the fuck did you say?" Clay growls, raising his hand into a fist.

But a sharp hook goes to the fake biker's face in a flash from the new man on the lawn. The other guy goes down, both from the impact and the surprise. He folds to his back in a way I've seen too often in my life. Curled into himself on the ground, holding his face, he whimpers and kicks out his leg, making contact with the tough new guy. Who kicks the man back before Sebastian is in front of the new man, pushing him away.

Knox is next, standing before Clay, telling him to step back.

Only Clay isn't letting this end. He waves his arm around his bulky brother. "Can you believe this guy?" He glances down at the man on the grass wreathing in pain. "He's a fucking child." Clay points blindly behind him toward the porch, implying Dutton.

I squeeze him tighter to me. His head has shifted and he's watching the display in the yard. My hands still cover his ears, and I should shield his face. He doesn't need to witness this type of scene. This is exactly what I wanted to protect him from by leaving Florida.

"Clay, just calm down," Perry says, sensing Clay is on the edge of losing control.

"Fuck you, Perry." Clay snaps at his friend. Then, he turns

to the man slowly sitting upright, but still cupping his nose. "And you. You fucking come near my kid again and I'll run you into the ground."

"Clay, man." Knox bitterly chuckles. "Chill." He works on pressing his brother backward. Over his shoulder, he hollers at Perry. "Get yourself and this piece of trash out of my yard."

As Perry bends to help up his *friend*, the two stumble toward the street, and my gaze falls to the collection of men huddled near one another at the bottom of the porch stairs.

Knox claps the new guy on the shoulder. "Judd, where did you come from?" He laughs good naturedly, jostling whom I now realize is another brother of theirs. Clay has mentioned the accountant brother for Sylver Seed & Soil.

"And *where* did that come from?" Knox continues to chuckle. "Nice left hook."

Judd doesn't even flinch. He doesn't shake out his hand. The tall man who looks a little more billionaire in a suit than badass simply shakes his head. "It was nothing." His voice is deep but quiet, almost shy or embarrassed by the sudden display of aggression. An act done for my son.

"And you . . ." Teasing fills Knox's voice as he addresses Clay. "Did you just say 'my kid'?"

Sebastian claps his hand on Clay's shoulder. "That's how it starts, man." He pats him twice more before walking up the porch stairs.

I'd forgotten about Ford, who holds Winnie to his chest, her head tucked away from the scene, but he didn't leave Dutton or me alone up here.

Sebastian enters the house. Ford follows.

Knox exchanges a word with Clay and Judd, and then follows his other brothers into his house, giving me a wink before he does.

As I slowly straighten, knowing Dutton has stopped crying and I have a better sense of what's happened, my body trembles with my own brand of anger. How ignorant. How disgusting. How cruel. Dutton is a child, like Clay defended, and that man is a man although the label hardly fits him. He's a weak person, and I can't even call him human.

Clay and Judd follow Knox up to the porch, and Dutton wiggles out of my hold, rushing Clay who catches him with a start, not expecting the sudden launch toward him. Still, Clay tucks Dutton to him, rubbing a hand down his back before combing his fingers into Dutton's longer hair and tugging his head back so he faces Clay.

"You okay, buddy?" Clay's voice is calmer than moments ago, soothing while I'm certain he's fighting for control.

Dutton nods his head and hugs Clay around the neck again. Clay's eyes meet mine over Dutton's thin shoulder and then they widen at something Dutton must have said to him. He pats Dutton's back before setting him on the porch and guiding him back to me.

"Mavis, this is my brother, Judd."

Judd nods, hands on his hips, but I want more than a cautious greeting. Stepping forward, I hug him, startling Judd. He stiffens under my impulsive embrace. Maybe I'm the one who needs a hug. "Thank you," I whisper to him.

I absolutely do not condone violence, but the way Judd reacted, out of nowhere, hints that hit came not only because of what was said or done to my son, but from something deeper within him. I don't have time to analyze him, though, as I step back and watch his bearded face turn pink.

"Nice to meet you, Mavis."

He runs a hand over Dutton's head and lowers to squat before him. On Dutton's level, he's more personable and sticks out his hand. "Nice to meet you. I'm Judd."

"Dutton." Dutton says, shaking the offered hand.

"Are you a superhero?" Judd asks.

"I'm the pink Power Princess."

Judd nods as if he's familiar with the character. "Well, if you ever need a sidekick, you let me know." He holds out a fist and Dutton bumps it. Then Judd stands, nods at me once more, and heads into the house.

With only the three of us remaining on the porch, I reach for Clay next. Holding him like I don't ever want to let go. The way he defended my son. The way he is with Dutton. The way he cares for us.

"Thank you." I squeeze him tighter while only one of his arms comes around my back. When I release him, Dutton is holding Clay's other hand.

"Think we should call it a night?" Clay addresses Dutton.

Dutton sheepishly nods and Clay reaches for him, picking him up again. Maybe he needs another hug from Dutton. I'll be taking more hugs from both of them, once we are at Clay's place again.

When we cross the yard for Clay's truck, I don't have the overwhelming scent of worn leather and cheap cologne in my nose but I also don't miss the outline of a lone figure near the collapsed fence around my property and the soft glow of a lit cigarette in the dark.

However, my adrenaline is depleted, leaving behind exhaustion and bone-deep weariness; so much so that the fear coursing through my body at the sight of the disturbing silhouette barely registers. Whoever he is, I don't draw attention to him. I can't handle anymore. I've had enough drama for one night.

19

———

[Clay]

The drive to my home is quiet. Once inside the house, Mavis runs a bath for Dutton and after, tucks him into bed, allowing him to read something on his own while she showers. I keep my distance, giving them time together. Letting Mavis work her magic with her son.

As for me, after stripping out of my VillainMan costume and putting on a fresh tee and gray sweatpants, I lay on my bed. I'd ordered the getup when I ordered Dutton's pink Power Princess, thinking the contrasting costumes would be a fun surprise for the kid.

The night had certainly not turned out how I'd hoped to surprise him.

I'm not sure how long I lay in the dark on my bed, my hands folded over my lower belly, images from throughout the evening colliding in my head.

Fucking Perry. And fuck that new friend of his. And why

did Dutton call his dad Wesley? And why did he call Mavis May-May?

I know I don't know everything about Mavis, allowing for time to further discover one another, but if I thought Wesley and the harrowing house fire were her only secrets, I was wrong. I don't want to accuse her of omitting important details about her life, like she felt I'd done about Glady, but I'm suddenly a bit leery about Mavis's past.

With too many rambling thoughts, and too many unanswered questions, my body still vibrates with the need to fight, although I'm the least likely to raise a fist in our family. It's one reason Dad and I didn't go knuckles to knuckles. He'd be confrontational and I'd try to reason with him. Or ignore him.

My ankles are crossed, and my eyes are aimed at the ceiling when Mavis enters my room. Her scent precedes her entrance. She's freshly showered with that floral fragrance wafting around her. She's wearing a Sylver Seed & Soil tee again with a pair of dark leggings.

I close my eyes for half a second. "How is Dutton?"

"He's sleeping." Mavis exhales. "I don't want to leave him alone tonight, but I wanted to check on you."

"I'm fine." But my voice is hollow, giving away the lie.

Mavis rounds my bed and helps herself to the other side, laying on her back, mirroring my position. I turn only my head for a second before facing the ceiling once more.

"Dutton isn't biologically my son."

This has my head swinging back in her direction.

"He's my nephew. My sister Cecilia's child." Mavis swallows and licks her lips, keeping her gaze focused on the ceiling dancing with shadows. "Before she was killed, we'd agreed that Dutton would come to me, if anything happened to her."

Mavis rolls her head to meet my shocked gaze. "My family is part of a motorcycle club. Not a riding club, but the real deal. They aren't bad people. They loved me and my sister, and God knows I owe my parents for lending me money and giving me a place to live for a year." She turns her face away from me.

"But all I'd ever wanted was a simpler life. I dove into nursing school and dedicated myself to helping others heal their aches and wounds. I didn't want to be part of the club and I'd walked away roughly twenty years ago."

She sighs.

"Cecilia was younger than me and got wrapped up with one of the club members. I don't know what she ever saw in him. When she found out she was pregnant, he didn't want to believe Dutton was his kid. When she died only a few months after Dutton's birth, I took Dutton in. My parents were upset. They wanted him with them, but them as guardians didn't follow Cecilia's wishes."

She rolls her head on the pillow again to look at me. Her dark eyes reflect the moonlight streaming into my room through the windows.

Mavis's situation is rather similar to my own, which hits me hard. Vale was only a baby when our mother passed away and our father checked out, leaving Sebastian, Ford, and Judd each under eight years old and in desperate need of parenting. Stone and I did the best we could to educate ourselves with the help of Trudy Wallace and Mary Haven, our mother's friends, and to raise children when we were kids ourselves.

"I have tried *so hard* to honor Cecilia's wishes and her memory. I taught Dutton to call me May-May because Mavis is a hard name for a toddler to say. But May-May is so close to mama, and my mama told me I *was* Dutton's mom now. My sister was his mother, but I would be raising him. We were sharing Dutton as our son."

Mavis is a savior in her own right. A saint in many aspects, and she's doing a fucking great job as Dutton's mother. No other term honors her position. She *is* Dutton's mom, and she should be proud of everything she's done for that sweet boy.

"I never pictured my future with a child. It wasn't that I didn't want one, but I hadn't given it much thought. I worked so much, devoting my all to the hospital, and I didn't have a man in my life." She scoffs, rolling her head to face the ceiling again. "I had dreams of a family, but I couldn't envision one with the reality of my life."

I can so strongly relate. In many ways, I'd done my time raising children, but it didn't mean I didn't want a family of my own. And similar once more to Mavis, work had taken precedence in my life.

"I'm on the pill. Went on it shortly after getting with Wesley, and he insisted on wearing a condom whenever we were together." She snorts, disgruntled. "At least he did one kind act for me."

What a fucking wanker. If I ever see him around here—

"Anyway." She licks her lips. "Everything happened so fast. I had Dutton in my care and Wesley came along. I collected the inheritance my sister had from our grandmother, as everything was set up in a trust fund. That's how I had the money for the house. I thought I was doing the right thing. Being with Wesley gave Dutton the semblance of a normal family structure, but what's normal really mean?" Her brows pinch, the question rhetorical but also one of deep concern for her.

Rolling my head, I face the ceiling again as well. I'm not one to define a normal family. *Our* normal was two brothers raising our younger siblings.

"Over time, Wesley changed toward me. He wasn't connected to Dutton. He'd taken all my money, lost most of it, or sunk it into the house we couldn't afford."

Mavis pauses a second. "Going back to Florida, with my tail between my legs, was exactly what my dad wanted. He always thought I'd be back for the life. For *their* lifestyle. But I couldn't stay. It wasn't what Cecilia, nor I, wanted for Dutton. Still, I needed that time away. I needed space from Sterling Falls, and I needed a place to live. My mother wouldn't let my dad push Dutton away, and my dad did what he could with Dutton. But he doesn't understand him. He doesn't appreciate the amazing, wonderful, special kid he is."

Out of the corner of my eye, I see her chest lift and lower. "I had to come back here."

"And now you feel like you should leave." It isn't a question.

She shifts her entire body to her side, and I feel her looking at me. "Do you want us to go?"

"No." My head rolls so fast on the pillow, my neck cracks, but I don't sound as convicted as I feel. I'm too wound up. The highs and lows of the night, and the special moments in-between. Mavis met my entire family tonight. She fit into the town dynamics. She fits with me.

Still, her and Dutton's story is a lot to take in on top of everything else that happened this evening.

"Thank you, Clay. For defending Dutton. For protecting us. You *are* helping us, and that's not a bad thing. I just don't want to take advantage of you."

"You're not." The response is edgy and rough, and I look at the ceiling once more. She isn't taking something I'm freely giving her, and I don't know how many times I need to tell her or how to reassure her that I don't feel taken advantage of. If anything, I feel like she's been doing me a favor by being here.

Mavis remains quiet. Her history swirls through the air. I don't need to know the details of the club or her upbringing. I only want to know Mavis now. Who she is. Dutton's mother. Part-time nurse. A woman I want to give more of herself to me.

Slowly, she sits up on the edge of my bed. "Can I get you something? Do you need anything tonight?"

I don't know what she might mean, but the only thought that comes to mind is her not leaving this bed. I just want to hold her, but more selfishly, I want her to hold me. I want her to tell me she won't leave.

Instead, I shake my head. "Good night, butterfly."

"Good night, honey." She presses off the bed, and I close my eyes at the sting suddenly burning them. Hearing defeat in her voice and feeling the distance between us.

I only last five minutes before I'm hoisting myself off my bed and opening her bedroom door. She's curled around Dutton, protecting him as best she can from the evils of this world. Violence. Ignorance. Hatred.

Saving the world starts with loving your child.

Mavis lifts her head and watches me round the bed until I'm behind her on her side. Climbing onto the mattress, I cuddle up behind her, wrapping my arm over her and around Dutton, who is nestled into her chest with his back.

Mama bear and her cub in one bed.

Dutton asked me earlier if I could be his dad. He must have heard me call him my kid by mistake.

But somehow, it doesn't feel entirely wrong. He's never had a positive father figure in his life, and my desire to be papa bear returns.

I close my eyes and squeeze mama and her baby tighter to me.

Because this feels just right.

20

––––––––––

[Clay]

"Weekly family dinner today," I announce during breakfast the next morning.

Mavis has been with me for more than a month, and I've only been to one Sylver Sunday meal in all that time. I missed the rest because I was sick, she was present, and the festival happened.

Stone will surely have words for me after last night, and Vale's been harping on me in the family group text about my absence. She only met Mavis for a few seconds at the festival and then again last night, and my sister wants to give her stamp of approval on the woman in my life, as she calls Mavis.

"I don't know," Mavis hedges, adding another pile of pancakes to the stack already on my plate. I pick up her plate which hasn't been filled yet and dump half my pile onto the dish.

"Mavis. Sit." I catch her wrist as she turns back to the griddle on the stove.

"I still have more batter."

"Eat these while they're hot."

Dutton has a stack of pancakes large enough for a lumberjack, and I'm sensing Mavis is cooking because she's still upset and anxious. Holding her breath on Dutton's emotions today.

"Will Winnie be there?" he quietly asks, his personality somber this morning as he pokes at the pancakes with his fork.

"She will. And I bet she'd like to see you." I don't know what my niece witnessed last night. I still don't know all the particulars of what happened, but my imagination holds visions that will haunt me for the rest of my days. A grown ass man holding a child's head face down in the water of an apple-bobbing barrel.

My phone blew up overnight with apologies from Halle and messages from Knox. Sebastian checked in, and I checked on Ford and the girls. Judd was his quiet self, not explaining where he came from or where he learned to punch like that. Out of all of us, he might have taken the insults from our dad to heart the most.

"So. Sylver Sunday around noon," I confirm, not letting either Mavis or Dutton out of today.

My family wants to know more about this family, and I'm looking to bring Mavis and Dutton into the Sylver fold.

WHEN WE ARRIVE at the house I grew up in, Winnie rushes Dutton, hugging him gleefully, as if relieved to see her new friend. She coos over him, asking if he's okay, and then quickly distracts him from last night's incident by tugging him to a low table covered with coloring sheets.

In a household of mostly men, Vale is thrilled to have

another woman around in addition to Enya and Halle. Soon enough Cadence, Ford's girlfriend will be home. For now, Vale loops her arm through Mavis's and leads her toward the kitchen.

Typically, these Sunday meals are a cookout, hosting the family in the backyard as long as the weather holds out, especially as the family expands. But today is gloomy and dull, kind of like my mood, so we gather inside the house that's had a huge makeover since I lived here.

When Stone went off to college, I didn't last much longer in this place, deciding I needed my own space somewhere else if I was going to face our father every day at the Seed & Soil. Unfortunately, that left Judd next in command of our younger siblings as our father grew worse and worse in his drunken insults and physical abuse. For years, I'd bounced around in apartments, which I found too confining, and then rental houses before finally finding my plot of land and building my small dream home.

As for this house, it still looks like something out of a classic television program with its white clapboard siding and green roof filled with dormers, plus a wide front porch. A few years ago, the once weather-beaten exterior was brightened by fresh paint and the roof was replaced, restoring the place to its original glory. Perhaps even making the house better. The inside has been remodeled in stages as well, especially the kitchen which is rather open and airy now.

As the kids remain in the living room coloring, and most adults converge in the kitchen around the large island or the newish table, I need a minute with Stone. He isn't surprised by the nod of my head signaling a former bedroom off the kitchen that's been converted to an office for him, nor does he hesitate to follow me.

"I'm assuming you heard about last night," I begin when he closes the door behind him. The dark paneling in the space adds to the dimness of the day and the shadow of yesterday evening's happenings.

"Halle called me. She was worried Knox would get into it with that man. More worried Sebastian would, and then be arrested again." Stone runs a hand over his head and softly chuckles. "Who'd a thought Judd would be the one to clock a man?"

I chuckle as well, although it isn't funny ha-ha. "He was defending Dutton."

Stone peers at me with eyes a shade deeper than mine. A little kinder, I imagine. The color of his matches our mother's while I have the icier shade of our dad's.

Stone leans on the edge of his desk while I take a seat in a leather chair that's seen better days.

"You know a little bit about Mavis, don't you?" Concern fills my voice. I hardly slept last night considering what she told me. How she came about Dutton. How her family has some sketchy connections.

"What all are you worried about?" Stone casually asks, crossing his ankles and his arms, rubbing his forefinger and thumb around the thicker hairs at the corner of his mouth.

"What should I be concerned about?"

"If it's Wesley, I doubt he'll show his face around here again. There is a warrant out for his arrest. Attempted double homicide."

The words alone send a shiver down my spine.

I don't want to expose too much of what Mavis shared with me, but she admitted she told Stone about Wesley's wife and the suspected other girlfriend.

"Plus, his wife wants to file for divorce." Stone continues. "Abandonment. He had a year to show, and it's about time that petition will be granted with or without him present. As for any girlfriends, only one was found. She hadn't dated him long and hadn't seen him since a week before the fire."

Stone and I exchange a look before he speaks, "Speaking of. The rubble has sat there long enough."

"She's going to sell the property."

Stone's brows lift. "She should talk to Trudy Wallace."

I don't know why I hadn't thought of Trudy myself. She handles most of the real estate deals around the county. Hopefully she could get Mavis at least a little money for the loss of her place.

"Good idea." I hoist myself upright to stand and Stone presses off the desk at the same time, stopping me from exiting.

"You know what you're doing with her?"

It isn't like my brother to pry into any of our lives, but concern is etched in the fine lines of his forty-four-year-old face. He's worried about *me*.

"I got her." I'm keeping her, I just don't know how to convince her to stay yet.

Stone nods once, not exactly liking my answer but he doesn't have to like it. We're both grown men, who have been alone for a long, long time. I want him to be happy for me, but if he can't, or won't, that's on him.

He moves around his desk and pulls forward a stuffed animal.

"What's that?"

"We're calling them bravery bears." Stone chuckles at the brown animal in his hands with a star near its heart. "I thought Dutton might like one. I heard about his costume." Stone tips up one brow but doesn't expand. "Thought he might appreciate being recognized for his bravery, especially after what happened to him last night."

"Marcie come up with this idea?" The dispatcher in the sheriff's department was always coming up with new concepts to soften the gruff officers.

"Actually, Emerson did."

"*Oh*. Emerson, huh?" The town's mayor and my brother the

sheriff's on-again, off-again, publicly acknowledged, friends with benefits situation. While her mother makes it her mission to broadcast that Emerson and Stone intend to marry someday, I'm not certain Stone has gotten the memo. Personally, I don't see Stone ever settling down. He was burned by love once before and carries the branding of that failed relationship like the badge he wears to work.

Plus, Emerson has never attended a Sylver Sunday meal. The fact comes to me only now as I've brought Mavis. Stone's rule has always been no outsiders. Only family. Very rarely has a friend been included, but as Sylvers keep falling in love lately, the number of attendees grows.

Does that mean I love Mavis? I almost admitted such a thing last night, confessing how those three words fight for release when I'm around her. Because I feel rather passionate about Mavis and Dutton, and this isn't some savior complex happening. Like I told Mavis, she's doing more for me than I might be doing for her.

Stone doesn't answer me about Emerson but holds out the bear for me to give to Dutton. "Thanks, man. I'll give it to him later. For now, I just want him to forget about last night and hang with Winnie."

"They've become fast friends," Stone chuckles. "Like Hudson and Zelle." My eleven-year-old nephew has been teaching a thing or two to my nine-year-old niece, and the pair have turned into double trouble especially when it comes to collecting money for their swear jars from their uncles.

Stone and I grin. We didn't know any of our cousins. Our mother was an only child. Our father's family moved away from Sterling Falls. As far as we knew, he didn't have contact with them as an adult. Or maybe he let any relationship he had dissolve like he did with his kids. As for the next generation of Sylvers, the cousins are close and an extension of their own families.

The grin Stone and I share is full of pride. Sometimes, we marvel at the fact we pulled it off. Sometimes, we still question how the fuck we did it. Only one of us got into trouble, that person being Sebastian, but even he's had a turnaround. He's definitely a reformed bad boy, and with his new wife and daughter, and another child on the way, he's transforming into a great dad and husband.

"Think Judd will be here," I ask as Stone and I step into the hallway leading to the kitchen.

"I should probably talk to him." Stone, still playing father-figure even though we're crossing into our forties.

"Let me," I offer as we enter the kitchen. I have questions and I can relay the answers to Stone later.

He claps me once on the shoulder like tagging me to be it, and we separate in the kitchen. He'll still play grill master for today's meal.

As for me, I need a beer.

21

[Mavis]

"What's this?" Dutton asks, his eyes sparkling at the item Clay offers him once we are home.

When we returned to Clay's house after a long but surprisingly pleasant afternoon at his brother's place, Clay carried a large bag with him and asked Dutton to take a seat on the couch. Sitting across from him on the ottoman, Clay holds up a stuffed teddy bear with a star-like badge in the corner of his chest.

"My brother Stone is the town sheriff." Clay begins. "And this is called a bravery bear."

Dutton glances at me, clearly remembering Stone before we were re-introduced today.

Clay wiggles the fluffy animal in his hand. "He thought you deserved one for a number of reasons. And every superhero needs a sidekick, right?"

Dutton stares at the bear.

"Stone also thought you were very brave as a Power Princess and that this bear might bring you extra courage."

Dutton's eyes are wide, his head nodding as though agreeing with every assessment Clay makes of him. As for me, I'm holding my breath. Not out of anticipation but in wonder. How sweet is this gift? And how amazing is Clay in this presentation to Dutton? Both Dutton and I were so easily welcomed to the Sylver family weekly tradition, and my heart is still swollen from their acceptance of me and my son.

Alone.

"I'm hoping the bravery bear will help you," Clay continues. "He'll be there to protect you during the night, from storms, from the dark, from everything, and keep you company. Maybe he can ward off bad dreams, too." Clay shrugs, like he knows the bear isn't a miracle worker, but has the possibility to be a comforting companion.

Seeing that bear, hearing Clay's explanation, and watching Dutton's reaction, gives me an idea.

Clay holds the bear toward Dutton, who eagerly takes it and gives the thing a tight squeeze. Dutton glances at me first and then back at Clay. "Thank you."

Clay smiles so wide and bright, I almost think Dutton's gratitude is greater than the gift Clay gave my son. Clay himself has certainly been a gift to both of us and I'll be forever thankful he's let us stay with him.

For now, Dutton continues to hug the bear and requests *Princess Power* time.

Clay looks up at me. "Uhm. I was kind of hoping to watch a baseball game."

I'd learned that Ford Sylver used to play for the Chicago Anchors and the team made the championship playoffs without him as their star centerfielder. Still, Ford is a proud supporter of his former team and will be heading back to

Chicago to watch a few rounds of the playoffs. Clay is a big fan of the sport.

"That's fine. Dutton, you can watch *Princess Power* on your tablet." We have access through a streaming app.

After Dutton takes a bath and settles into his room with the tablet, I join Clay on the couch.

"There's something I'd like to ask you," I begin, plucking at the hem of my T-shirt, unable to look Clay in the eyes. Asking this kind of question makes me feel extra vulnerable. "I was wondering if I could sleep with you."

Clay turns his head so fast I swear I hear his neck crack.

"I mean, in your bed. In your room. Like we could sleep together." I'm stammering and messing up my presentation when I'd hoped to appear smooth and casual about my suggestion. Like I've told Clay, I'm tired of sleeping beside a flailing six-year-old and the gift of the bravery bear feels like an opportune time to give Dutton some independence.

"I mean . . . this isn't coming out very well." I swallow hard while Clay tips his head back on the couch cushion.

"Mavis, it'd be my honor to have you sleep in my bed with me." He chuckles, curling up one side of his lips higher than the other, giving me a flirty wink. "*I'm* tired of sleeping alone with no one to flail around me."

Slowly, I match his smile.

"Plus, then you could boss me around and tell me where to touch you, and how." His eyes playfully flirt.

"Clayton Sylver," I snap, teasing him for his suggestion.

He grabs my hand and lifts to his mouth, pressing a kiss to the center of my palm before chuckling. "Scolding would be more effective if you tossed in my middle name."

"I don't know your middle name."

"And I don't know yours. We should change that." He leans toward me and kisses my nose. "Because I want to know everything about you."

I don't know what's gotten into him, but he's been very *handsy* today. Touching the small of my back. Running his palm down my arm. Tickling his fingers around my neck. It's as if he can't stop touching me, and I'm not complaining, I'm just anxious about what this means. And *if* it will abruptly end.

"What are we doing?" I whisper, my voice lowering to a more serious tone.

Clay mutes the game and glances back at me. "First, we're gonna hang out and watch the game. Then, we're going to bed, in my room, together. Whether we do more than snuggle is up to you, but having mama bear in my bed would be *just right*." Clay purses his lips, flirty in his response. Perhaps he feels the weight of my question. *Who are we to each other?*

I quietly chuckle, playing along with his avoidance tactic. "Oh, do you need a bravery bear, too?"

Clay pouts like he's vying for a forbidden toy. "I do."

"And what are you afraid of?"

Clay tips his head back on the couch cushion again and his playful expression shifts to something more sober. He looks me directly in the eyes.

"I'm afraid you will decide I'm not enough for you and leave. That you'll leave town and disappear again, and I've only gotten to know a sliver of who you are, butterfly, when I want the whole tree. The house." He waves around him. "Dutton. Us."

I stare at him, searching for any internal warning that he's only voicing pretty promises. I find no glaring threat. Nothing screams to proceed with caution, only care. To care for this man. To give him a chance.

"It's Shania."

Clay's brows deeply crease.

"My middle name. It's Shania."

One corner of his mouth slowly curls higher than the other side before a full grin graces his face.

"Everett." Clay pats his chest. "After a grandfather I never met."

I match his smile. "Mavis was my grandmother's name." The one who called me butterfly. The one who gave me the shawl. The one whose perfume I try to replicate.

"Well, Mavis Shania Grant, can we watch this baseball game together?"

I chew my lip before settling into his side when he extends an arm on the back of the couch.

"As long as we can go to bed together later," I joke.

"Sounds like a plan." He leans over and kisses me again, short and quick before settling into the cushions once more.

While I cuddle up against Clayton Everett Sylver, which feels *just right* to me.

LATER, I speak with Dutton about my sleeping in Clay's bedroom, and the conversation goes surprisingly easier than I expected. Dutton bravely states that he can sleep alone with his new friend whom he named Violet.

As Clay and I are tucking Dutton in together, Clay chokes at the suggestion, and I prepare to defend Dutton's choice.

"She's one of the other princesses," Dutton clarifies of the four girls who work together as Power Princesses. Pink. Violet. Azure. Chartreuse.

Clay swallows hard, leaning over Dutton. "Violet was my mother's name."

A moment passes between Clay and Dutton, as if some secret understanding occurs. "She was the best woman I knew, next to your mama. And with this special name, I bet this brave bear will have extra powers to keep you brave."

Dutton's smile proves he likes that explanation, and he hugs the bear tighter. "Maybe you could read *The Sandcastle Princess* to me tonight," Dutton asks Clay.

The book is the same one Dutton and I started when we first arrived at Clay's home. While I'm slightly stung Dutton wants Clay more than me, I also see the moment for what it is. Dutton trusts Clay. His request is a special offering.

Clay gives me a quick glance, confirming I'm good with the suggestion. When I nod, he says, "Absolutely."

He takes a seat on the edge of the bed, picks up the book, and flips the bookmark signaling where we stopped. I settle at the foot of the bed and listen as Clay reads, dropping in voice for the dragon or king parts, hitching his voice higher for the princess ones.

After a few pages, Dutton nods off, and Clay glances up at me. I squeeze Dutton's foot, which flings his lids open. Then, I warn him, "One more page."

Clay finishes on a cliffhanger-ish spot and marks the page before speaking like an old television announcer. "Tune in next time."

"That's what they say on *Princess Power*." Dutton shifts his head and glances up at Clay, love emanating from his sleepy gaze.

"Do they?" Clay teases as if he didn't know. "So how was my reading?"

"I'd give it an eight point seven nine."

Clay juts out his lower lip. "Sounds like a B-plus."

"What's a B-plus?" Dutton's comment reminds me I need to get him in the local school.

Clay chuckles and shakes his head. "I'll need to work on my skills."

"You do that," Dutton whispers back, his voice sassy but tired.

Clay twists off the bed, sets the book on the nightstand, and then leans over Dutton, running his hand over my little one's hair that desperately needs a cut. "Sleep tight, buddy."

Dutton lazily smiles before rolling to his side, his back to Clay.

When Clay steps away, I wrap Dutton in an awkward snuggle with him already on his side, drifting off to sleep.

"I love you, little bear."

"Love you, mama bear."

I press a kiss to his head and send up a silent prayer to Cecilia, thanking her again for the blessing of Dutton. As I stand upright, Dutton's eyes close and then he says, "Love you, too, papa bear."

I suck in air and turn toward Clay whose eyes go wide before softening. He clears his throat while watching Dutton. "Love you, too, cub."

We step outside Dutton's door, leaving it open just a sliver for him, while a nightlight is plugged into a wall outlet as well. We've barely made it past the door jamb when I turn toward Clay, pushing him awkwardly up against the wall.

"What the—"

My mouth on his cuts him off. While the transition was rough, we quickly melt into one another, sharing a kiss that's hotter than any I've ever experienced. I press into Clay's chest, hands fisted in his shirt, and lift one leg to his hip. His hands clasp my backside, and he squeezes tight, tugging me harder against him, like he did last night. Standing here in his hallway, I can't get close enough to him.

Watching him interact with Dutton, with patience, kindness, and compassion, is the sexiest thing I've ever seen. And knowing Dutton does not tell anyone he loves them except for me, I'm at a loss for words. The only way I can tell Clay what he means to me is to show him.

When I pull back, I remember the baseball game still has a few more innings.

"Baseball or bedroom?" I ask, prepared to wait for the end of the game.

"What's baseball?" Clay teases, setting his hands on my hips and guiding me backward into his bedroom.

With a gentle kick of his foot, his bedroom door closes, but doesn't click shut, leaving space to hear Dutton if he needs us.

He won't. *Son* up to *son* down. He was probably zonked out before we hit the hallway.

Still clutching Clay's shirt, I spin us and push him, releasing his flannel and watching him fall to the bed. Realistically, I don't have the strength to move him around as I have, which means Clay is allowing it to happen. Letting me take control. *Giving* it to me.

With him on his back, I climb over his body and straddle him, then lean forward for another toe-curling kiss. I never knew it could be like this. A man loving my son. A man adoring me.

"Make love to me," I murmur against his mouth. "Take your time with me."

As if Clay reads my mind, he flips us so I'm on my back. His hand coasts down my neck, over my breasts to the hem of my shirt. From that first lift of clothing, he savors each removal, placing lingering kisses on each part of me revealed, like I'm a treasured gift. He kisses my belly, sucks at my hip, and hums between my thighs when he takes off my jeans, pulling down my underwear at the same time. Eventually, I'm naked while he's still dressed, and he coasts his palms over my skin. He massages some places, explores others, as if discovering parts of me he hadn't before.

The backs of my knees are ticklish. The spot where my neck meets my shoulder is sensitive. The nape of my neck receives extra attention and I'm a squirming mess of desire once he's kissed every inch of me.

"Clay." I breathe out his name. "I need you, honey." I don't think I've ever needed anyone more. Not for him to save me but for him to give me this moment. To show me what being loved might feel like.

"You're stunning." Clay slides off the edge of the bed, his hand trailing along my midsection before he stands. "I don't know that I've ever used that word to describe someone. But you define the term, butterfly."

Giddy tears threaten my eyes. I've never been so happy that I could cry until this, until Clay.

I watch, unabashedly, as he strips, taking his time to tease me with the removal of each article of his clothing. Once he's naked, he climbs over me again. He knows I want control, which means I should ride him, but I want him to cover me. I want to feel him surround me, so I reach for his hips and gently tug him down.

"You're still in control," he reassures me. "But I'll take the lead on this one."

"You do that," I softly tease and chew my lower lip. The sass earns me another kiss while he slides his lower half between my spread thighs. The tip of his dick rests at my entrance but still we kiss for another minute.

Clay brings his hand to my chest, covering my racing heart. "There's this moment. When I'm just outside of you. And my heart hammers with anticipation." He presses up on his other arm, his tip still lined up with where I'm sensitive and eager for him.

"And then, I enter you." He nudges forward, spreading me, opening me, taking his time to glide into me. "And my chest nearly bursts. I'm so full from how I feel about you."

As he fills me to the hilt, he pauses and slides his hand down my arm, snugging his fingers between mine, until we are holding onto each other. He brings our collective hands above my head, and moves his hips, dragging out to the edge before gliding in again. Back and forth he moves, the rhythm slow.

My opening stretches around him. His body blankets mine. We are one in the way only two people can be, and the transformation he predicted for me happens.

I'm awakened in a new way. I feel Clay's emotions for me in every move, every measured thrust, every teasing drag. I've never felt anything like this before. Him. Me. Us. This lazy pull to follow his lead, to hold him tight, to never let go. My skin prickles. My body heats. My limbs wrap around Clay in every way I can, like a caterpillar clings to a twig.

Only Clay is stronger than flimsy wood. He's solid. Salt of the earth. Sexy in ways other than the physical. And I'm attracted to him on every level. His body. His mind. His heart.

My staggered moans turn to desperate groans as Clay slowly picks up the pace, dipping harder into me, moving faster with me. Our hips tap, pull back, then like magnets come together again. With my ankles over his calves, and one arm around his neck, our hands are still clasped above my head. I cling to him.

And then it happens. That fluttering sensation. That ripple effect. The gentle tear through my body, opening me wide and blazing through my center.

"Clay," I whimper as I come apart, ripped like a seam, and then sewn back together into something new, something beautiful. I *feel* beautiful in this moment. Stunning. Like the sunshine seen for the first time. Or the glow of moonlight across inky waters.

I have hope.

Clay is hope.

"Mavis." My name is said with wonder. He watches where he enters me. His dick slick. My body willingly taking him into me. His hips thrust harder.

"Come inside me," I whisper. He knows I'm on the pill now.

He glances up at me, double checking for certainty. Then,

he surges once, deep and sharp, and stills. His eyes close, while he goes off. His expression strained yet strangely peaceful.

Like I'm the place where he wants to be most.

As he comes down from the high, his eyes pop open, bright and light. He releases my hand and lowers his forehead, pressing it against mine, as he cups the sides of my face, resting all his weight on me a second.

"I never want to lose you, beautiful."

"I'm not going anywhere," I whisper, tipping up my nose to rub his.

While I struggle to accept promises, this is one I'm giving to him.

And hope I can keep it.

22

[Clay]

My night with Mavis is over too soon, but I'm hopeful we'll have more evenings like last night. Dutton sleeping safely through the night in his bed; Mavis remaining in mine.

Waking up to her was exactly as I told her a few weeks ago. She's a lovely sight to see first thing. Every new day, I want to open my eyes to the way she looks beside me in bed. Rumpled hair. A crease on her cheek from the pillows. And a sweet smile to greet me.

We didn't have time to come together again as the day calls for work and Dutton's schooling, but I leave her with promises.

"Tonight, butterfly." There is no question. She'll be here. I'll be home. She's coming to my bed again.

"Tonight, honey," she whispers, her cheeks coloring as I lean in to kiss her there before heading out for the Seed & Soil.

As Judd did not appear at the family meal—he opted out of

a few too many for my liking while the rest of us honor the day —I hoped to catch him first thing this morning. He often works from home although he has an office here, and he sneaks in on Mondays to gather whatever he might need to run reports and mind his charts. He's a geek about spreadsheets.

Judd has also been dating Heather Remington, a local beauty queen and daughter to the owners of Remington Autos, a wealthy set of car dealerships in the area and he uses her as his excuse to miss weekly dinners. He's been with Heather for a while now and hinted earlier this summer he might ask the woman to marry him.

No one in the family responded, each of us biting our cheeks to keep from voicing our unfavorable opinion. Heather's personality is as superficial as her beauty. She's narcissistic and has a need to show off her wealth and small-town prestige. If she proved she loved our brother to distraction, her flashiness and materialistic tendencies would not have bothered anyone half as much. However, we never see Judd and her interact. He doesn't bring her around us. And from an outsider's perspective, she's everything opposite our sensitive, reserved, almost reclusive, brother.

Thankfully, I see Judd before he slinks out the back exit of the Seed & Soil. He's dressed casually in dark jeans and a dark tee with a hip, crossbody computer bag over his chest.

"Come into my office." I clap his shoulder.

"Why do I feel like I'm being summoned to see the principal?"

I chuckle, knowing that never happened to Judd. He was the least likely to cause trouble in school. Quiet kid, often flying under the radar. Good grades. Teachers liked him. Not a jock, not a druggie, never an issue. He was almost boring, if you didn't know him like I do. Being directly below me in the birth order of our family, separated by two years, we were close despite his distance from the family.

Judd takes that silly extra desk chair in my office, wedging the bag strapped to his body beside him in the chair. I can't seem to get rid of that seat, even when I try to pawn it off to others.

I take my own chair and swivel so I face my brother.

"You missed another dinner." I lean forward and clasp my hands together, resting my elbows on my thighs.

Judd looks away. "Is that it?" He doesn't want a lecture. Hell, he's too old to have one, but I still want to know what's going on with him.

"Let's chat about Saturday night."

While Judd had been sitting upright in the desk chair, he slouches into the seat and tips back his head, staring up at the ceiling. "Can we count my attendance at Halle and Knox's as my weekly check-in?"

His tone is one I don't recognize, almost petulant, definitely dismissive. I should be complimenting his arrival at Halle and Knox's place. Should be thrilled he accepted the invite and showed. And I am, but I want to know a bit more.

"Explain that punch."

Judd's head tips up. His blue eyes aimed directly at me. "He insulted Dutton." A hint of a growl mingles with his explanation. A fire dances in his eyes. Judd might understand better than anyone how much words can hurt, especially when the insults imply a young boy isn't acting masculine. Or masculine enough for a small-minded dickhead. Our father had plenty of slurs for his son who cried easily and complained often about missing our mama.

Tears aren't bringing her back, you baby.

Our mother was as gone as our father's compassion.

"And I appreciate the defense of Dutton. But seriously, where did you learn to hit like that?"

Judd's position the other night was next to me. One slip of that left hook and he would have gotten me in the side of the head instead of that jackass's face. His aim was impeccable. The hit direct. A punch like that took practice and skill, not beginner's luck.

Judd shrugs. "I took self-defense classes." The corner of his mouth curls upward, reminding me of Sebastian.

"When?"

Judd's expression falls, giving away that he's trying to be cheeky. He hasn't taken a class. He doesn't need protection like that.

"A while back." His eyes lock onto mine and for the first time I'm stunned by him, and it's not his ability to hit someone.

"Why are you lying to me?" I lean back in my chair, setting my elbow on the arm rest and leaning my cheek against two fingers. Watching him, I'm trying to puzzle him out. What's he thinking? What's he been doing? Because there is a good chance, he isn't going to tell me.

Judd turns his head, giving me his cheek, so I can't see his eyes. He sits straighter in the chair. "So, I learned to fight. No big deal." His tone isn't as dismissive of the thought as he intends it to be. Instead, he's quiet, uncomfortable.

"Why?" I might have understood when he was a kid. God knows, our dad provoked him enough, but Knox and Sebastian often got in the way to protect Judd from the violent stuff. Even when Judd was nearly a man and bigger than our dad, it didn't stop the old man from going after Judd, often accusing him of looking too much like our mother. His hair was lighter than the rest of ours, like Vale's and Mom's. He had mannerisms like hers, like the way he tilts his head or the way he laughed, a sound he quickly learned to mask as a child.

"I just did." With his elbows perched on the armrests at his sides, he continues to stare off toward the window in my office. His answer might be as good as I get.

"You okay?"

Judd turns his head, bringing those sad eyes back to me. He

never seemed to recover from Mom's death. Not like any of us had, but he just took the loss of her harder. There has been an emptiness in all of us that we've struggled to fill. Most would say our father stripped us down, making that void within us. But the hollowness started with our mother passing away too young, and those of us who remember her have a special place in our hearts reserved only for her memory.

"I'm good."

He's lying again but this is a fib I've heard for a long time.

"How's Heather?"

Judd snorts, knowing I don't actually care, I'm just being polite because I care about him, and I want her to treat him right. I also think he should be fair to her. If he doesn't love her, he should let her go. The last thing he should do is ask her to marry him.

"Still getting hitched to the auto sales princess?" I tease. "Get it? Hitched. Autos."

"Good one. You practicing up on your dad jokes?"

I purse my lips. "Never know."

Judd arches a brow at that answer. "Something you want to share with the class, principal."

"I'll page you over the intercom when there's something to announce."

Judd chuckles. I don't know that he knows what an intercom is, even if he is only two years younger than me.

"Now get out of my office," I joke, shoving up from my seat at the same time as Judd stands from his. I open my arms, wordlessly demanding we embrace. He rolls his eyes like a child but hugs me hard.

"Good talk," he mutters, pulling back fast but I catch his shoulder.

"And you'll come talk to me if you need something, right?"

"Yes, Dad," he groans.

"I think I like being called the principal better."

Judd tips up his chin. "Yeah," he mumbles before straightening the crossbody computer bag against his chest and leaving my office.

I collapse back into my chair and stare after his exit, hoping he really will be okay one day.

As I'm crossing through the merchandise section of Sylver Seed & Soil, Perry nearly knocks me over, stepping into my path. We stare at one another for a hard minute. His mullet hairstyle is dated and a mess. Underneath his eyes are purple bags, like he hasn't slept in days. His flannel is wrinkled and open, exposing a white t-shirt with a coffee stain on it.

Perry Foster and I became friends by default. When Stone first went off to college and I remained behind, I'd needed an occasional break from Dad. Like me, Perry took over his family's business, renaming it Perry's Towing. His farm property hosts an annual country music festival every June. Because we didn't do the college thing, living in our small hometown while others our age left, we gravitated together, becoming tighter friends than we'd been before.

"I'm gonna need some time from you," I tell him.

"Time." He snorts. "That's all you've taken since that woman came into town."

I blink at his edgy tone. "Didn't know you and me were dating, Perry?" I bitterly joke. "And that I owed you an explanation of where I've been."

Perry and I spent plenty of time together, shooting the shit and drinking at Milton's, especially on a Friday or Saturday night. He was good people, most days. And like me, he didn't have a steady woman in his life.

"How'd you know that guy?" I tip my chin, implying the dickhead hanging out with him at Knox's place. I'd been surprised to see Perry there. He didn't live in town, so he wasn't exactly a neighbor of Knox and Halle. He also wasn't one to frequent family-centric parties, preferring the public, single scene of the local bars.

"Just met him at Milton's." Perry shrugs, glancing to the side a second. "He was asking around about Mavis and the kid. Told him I'd been invited to the party, and he could find them there."

"What's his name?" I snap, hoping I have something I can give Stone to follow up on.

"I can't remember." Perry lowers his head, eyes avoiding mine, his answer implying he was too drunk to remember. I'd like to hope he realizes how stupid his decision had been to invite someone he didn't know to a community party.

"Why would you do that? Bring a stranger to a neighborhood affair, one with families and kids?" Why hadn't he told me how he felt about us not spending time together, and then told me about some random guy inquiring about Mavis and Dutton?

Perry awkwardly looks left again, twisting his lips side to side, making his moustache wiggle. He might not be the brightest, but he wasn't typically this reckless, careless, stupid.

"Where is the guy now?" I straighten, suddenly concerned for both Dutton and Mavis. Who was this guy? What did he want with them? What's he doing here?

Perry shrugs again, hanging his head. "I haven't seen him since the other night."

I shake my head, so disappointed. Perry doesn't have a mean streak in him, but this is kind of low for him. And I need him out of my space for a while, like I said.

"He's only a little boy," I remind Perry. "That a grown man nearly drowned in an apple barrel."

Perry closes his eyes, hopefully realizing how bad things

could have been. Picking up strange men to hang out with can be just as dangerous as picking up strange women for a night.

"I'll call you, Perry," I state, dismissing him, passing him with a stiff clap to his shoulder.

"But will you?" The question stills my retreat and I spin around, facing him once more. "You're different with her."

"That's what a good woman can do for you."

Perry scoffs. It's not like either of us has avoided love, just didn't think it was in the cards for either of us. Perry had his heart broken hard when we were younger and he's hesitant about the emotion.

"You're serious." He stares at me, like he can't believe what I've said.

"As a dead horse."

Perry gasps, knowing I'd never be sacrilegious about an animal or wish ill-will on a living creature.

Another moment passes between us, staring at one another, maybe wondering who the other is anymore, before I mutter, "I've got to work."

Perry nods, twisting a worn ballcap in his hand before replacing it on his head. "See you around, Clay." Melancholy fills his tone. Unfortunately for him, he might not see much more of me if he keeps bringing strangers near Mavis and Dutton.

Once Perry leaves, I head to my office and call Stone. "We need to talk."

23

———

[Mavis]

I hadn't forgotten about the man I'd seen across the street from Halle and Knox's house when we left the party. I just needed some time to gather my thoughts.

Plus, I needed Clay to not be around when I made the call I had to make. I didn't want to disrupt his life anymore than I already had. I also wanted to keep him from the darker parts of my past. I wanted to protect him, and that meant taking care of my concerns on my own.

"Daddy." I sigh into the phone when he answers with a grunt. "You got someone following me?" Too easily, I fall into the broken vocabulary he uses so he'll understand me. I'm angry.

"Well, hello to you, too, prodigal girl."

I huff. I wasn't a prodigal. I'd returned home, I just didn't want to stay.

"Hi, Dad. How are you? Who is tailing me?" I pause as he

chuckles, deep and hearty. My father is a proud man, and his attitude matches his large stature.

"I wish we had men to spare, baby girl, but we don't. What's going on?" His tone becomes tighter, and I hear the creak of a desk chair through the phone. My mind casts images of his office. The dated paneling. The walls hung with road memorabilia. The scent of worn leather, cigarettes and cheap cologne permeating the air.

I don't really want to tell him what happened with Dutton. He'll demand I bring his grandson to him where he can keep an eye on Dutton. *Make him a man*, which was no different than what the guy the other night said, even if their means are vastly different. Dutton didn't need to be a man. He needed to be a six-year-old child for now. He needed space to roam and a safe place to live.

"I'm not certain. Maybe it's nothing." However, whoever was lingering across the street that night, I'd bet money I didn't have that he was the same person who bumped into me at the Harvest Festival a week ago. *And* that he was somehow connected to my dad's club. A friend or foe, or otherwise.

"Tell me what happened." His voice turns more commanding, and I cave, because this *is* Dutton we're discussing. Despite our differing opinion on how Dutton should be raised, we both loved him. He was a constant reminder of Cecilia and our last connection to her.

"Son of a bitch," Dad bellows once I'm finished. "I'm sending someone up there."

"I thought you didn't have anyone to spare?" I sigh. "Plus, I don't want any trouble." I'm in Sterling Falls to be away from club business and trouble. It's the reason I went off to nursing school and then stayed away, working long hours at the hospital before Cecilia fell under the spell of a not-so-great guy, had a child he refused to claim, and then lost her life.

Good riddance to Scar. The name earned by a giant gash to his right cheek.

My thoughts momentarily flit to Clay. He's so . . . normal . . . compared to how I was raised. The things I've seen and wished I could scrub from my memory. I just wanted a quiet life, a *good* life, and then I'd made some poor choices, like trusting Wesley.

"Sounds like you're in trouble anyway, baby." My dad's voice intends to soothe. However, he doesn't say anything I haven't already been thinking. Trouble might be here. Again.

And the worst part, is I don't want to hurt Clay in the fray.

NOVEMBER STARTS OUT SURPRISINGLY MILD. Clay comes home every night, and we hang out like a family. I'm in his bed every night as well, and life is good. Too good. I'm comfortable with us, and where I'm at, and the arrangement is dangerous as we don't discuss the future. I refuse to make the same mistakes as I had in the past, and every once in a while, I worry I'm on the same destructive path. Having faith in someone so quickly and easily.

Dutton and I should really get our own place. I can still date Clay, spend time with him, with the three of us, but I should give Dutton and I some space that's all our own. We need a home. Not that Clay's house isn't great. It's small but cozy and there is so much land around the place.

The following Saturday, Dutton is up early and I'm making him breakfast when Clay enters the kitchen.

"Dutton, my friend, how do you feel about spending the day with Violet? Do you remember meeting her last week? She's Halle and Knox's girl."

The newly seventeen-year-old is a high school lacrosse star and steady babysitter among the Sylver family. She also works part-time at Sylver Seed & Soil. She's a sweet girl from what I've seen of her interactions with the younger set of kids in the Sylver family.

"What's going on?" I ask, a bit put off that Clay hasn't asked me if it's okay that Dutton spend a day with Violet, and for what purpose.

Leaning against the back of a kitchen chair, Clay glances up at me, a twinkle in his icy blue eyes. And I remind myself this is Clay. I can trust him.

"I want to take you somewhere."

"Can I go?" Dutton asks, his eyes hopeful as he looks up at Clay.

Clay offers him a reassuring smile. "Maybe another day. But today, I'd like some time with just your mom." He winks at Dutton.

"Like a date?" Dutton's face turns pink.

"Maybe." Clay draws out. "That okay with you?"

Asking Dutton's permission sort of wins me over, even if I wish he'd asked me first. I can't remember the last time I was on a date, with Wesley or otherwise.

Dutton shrugs. "Sure." He lowers his head, returning to his French toast.

"Maybe you and me could have a special day, too. Soon. If that's okay with your mom?" Clay's attention turns to me.

"Oh, now you're asking *my* permission?" I giggle.

"Am I doing this backward?" His brows cinch before releasing, realizing he might have forgotten a step. He crosses the small space and leans into the counter near the stove, placing his hand on my lower back.

"Want to spend the day with me, beautiful?"

I smile back at him. Who can resist that face, and the sudden hesitation in his eyes? As if I'd say no.

"Of course, honey."

He smiles, lighting up his entire face. Without a care for Dutton's presence, he leans in and kisses the corner of my mouth. I glance at Dutton when Clay pulls back, but my son hasn't noticed, or he doesn't have a reaction if he did.

"And what about a day with Dutton?" Clay raises a brow. "Something just for us."

"That sounds nice, too." Dutton would love it and it would be good for him. Like father and son time.

The thought hits me so hard I almost drop the spatula I'm holding. A brief moment of panic sets in.

Is that good for Dutton? Is it fair to Clay?

As his hand coasts up my arm and squeezes the back of my neck, I settle into the warmth of his touch. He's been so good to us, to me. With a deep breath, I smile back at him. His brows pinch again, knowing something concerned me when I was lost in my head a second, but he lets it go, noticing it was only momentary on my end.

"Okay then. A date with Mom. And then one day soon, a date with Dutton."

Dutton chuckles. "That's what mom calls special days. Date with Mom days."

Clay playfully purses his lips but sadness washes over his face. "I like that. I didn't have enough of those with my mom."

Dutton looks up, eyes wide. "You had Date with Mom days, too?"

"I sure did." Clay helps himself to the coffee and notices my cup is half full. He tops it off.

"Where is your mom?"

"She's in heaven." Clay rests his backside against the counter near me while addressing Dutton. "I lost her when I was ten."

Dutton's gaze leaps to me, almost begging to say something. I nod, as if I can read his thoughts. We can trust Clay to keep our secrets.

"My mama died when I was still a baby. May-May took me in, and now she's my mama."

Clay softly smiles, watching Dutton. "Lucky you, you have two mamas who love you so much, they shared you with each other."

Dutton thinks about that a second before nodding. "And where is your dad?"

Clay's shoulders lift as he takes a deep inhale. "I suppose he might be in heaven as well, but he doesn't deserve it."

"My granddaddy says my father can rot in hell."

"Dutton!" I shriek.

"Well, it's true." He shrugs, swinging his legs beneath the table like he knows he said a bad word and got away with it.

Clay chuckles. "Maybe it is true."

"Clay," I turn on him, feeling outnumbered while not disagreeing with either of them. *Scar* can rot in hell, or whatever rock he rolled underneath, which is far away from here.

He laughs, leans over and kisses my shoulder then takes a fresh plate of French toast to the table to sit opposite Dutton.

"Change of subject. What are we doing today?"

"Can I surprise you?" Clay lifts his gaze, eyes hopeful.

I smile in return, finding the curve of my mouth comes too easily around him. He's comfortable.

And that scares the *hell* out of me.

24

———————

[Mavis]

"Horses?" I stare after the stable sign we passed as we pull down a gravel lane leading to a small house with a large barn nearby. The cowboy boots Clay asked me to wear along with telling me to bundle up for some time outdoors now makes sense.

The sky is slate gray and heavy with the promise of snow. The trees are bare of their leaves, prepared for winter which will be here soon enough. The second we stepped outside Clay' s house, my nose was cold, but my hands are covered in beautiful, soft leather gloves with a thick, warm lining inside them. A surprising and unwarranted gift from Clay earlier today.

Clay chuckles. "Don't sound so scared, butterfly." He pauses, running his hand around the steering wheel of his truck. "Haven't you ever been horseback riding?"

"No." I choke, before reminding him of my motorcycle

upbringing. "I grew up riding on two wheels not four legged creatures."

"Gonna make you a country girl now," he teases.

We park near the barn, where one of two panel doors is slightly open. As we exit Clay's truck, the cool mountain air hits me. Anticipation crackles around me. Clay rounds the back of his truck with a bag hitched over his shoulder and takes my hand. Walking backward a few steps, he leads me toward the barn.

His eyes dance with excitement. "I swear you'll love it."

"Being a country girl or riding horses?" I tease.

"Both." He winks before spinning around and walking beside me. When we reach the barn, he slides the door wider for our entrance and then pulls it closed behind him.

"Hey, Gilbert," he calls out to a man roughly in his forties.

"Clay." With a baseball cap on his head, Gilbert dips his chin at us while he strokes the flank of a large almond-colored horse. "Got this beauty ready for you."

He steps away from the horse and approaches us, holding out a hand to shake Clay's and be introduced to me.

"Mavis, this is Gilbert Shaw, horse breeder and boarder." Clay nods at the stoic man. "He's prepared Honey Rose for you today. I'll be riding my bay, Terra."

Clay runs his hand up my back before stepping aside to a stall and petting the nose of a horse who stuck its head through the grate as soon as it heard Clay's voice.

"Hey, Terra, baby. It's been too long." Clay leans forward and kisses the white patch between her eyes before rubbing his hand back and forth over the spot.

"Give me a minute to get Terra saddled for you," Gilbert says.

"I got it." Clay leaves me standing in the stable while he momentarily disappears and returns with a huge leather seat. Gilbert opens the stall and leads the horse into the galley way.

As for me, I just step out of the way, and watch as Clay coos at the horse, spreading a blanket over her back before lugging the saddle over her as well. She shifts and Clay softly murmurs to soothe her.

He's a different version of himself. Calm as always but clearly focused on the living creature beside him. Wearing a thick, chocolate-brown jacket with a sherpa collar, and butt-hugging jeans, he's the perfect image of a rugged outdoors-man. He's wearing a Seed & Soil ball cap on his head, one that has seen better days but also looks sexy as hell on him. When he moves, his riding jacket shifts, giving me a better view of his backside covered in form-fitting Wranglers. Every time he adjusts something on the horse, his typically rough and deep voice softens while he speaks to such a large animal. His gloved hands smooth reverently over her shiny coat.

His good looks are personified by his gentle touch and tranquil voice. He's a man who takes great pride in the creatures and people he cares about. Dutton and I are an example of that nurturing side to him as well.

He finally turns his attention back to me after tightening the harness on Terra. "Ready, butterfly?"

I blush, caught in my internal musings and blatant ogling of him. "I don't know," I admit. "I thought we'd be riding together."

"Riding double," Clay corrects. "And it isn't recommended for long journeys. We aren't going far but I still want to give you your own shot." He turns toward his horse again, stroking the white patch one more time. "Plus, I've missed my girl."

"I didn't know you owned a horse."

Clay turns back to me. "Rescued her from a farmer who wanted to get rid of her. I don't ride her often enough but she's getting older and does best with short trips. I have somewhere close by I want to take you."

I chew my lower lip, uncertain about any of this, but Clay is too excited for us to share this experience for me to deny him.

He steps closer to me while holding Terra's reins. "You've got this, butterfly."

He cups my shoulder and leans in for a kiss that lasts a little longer than it probably should considering Gilbert is waiting on us. Then, Clay leads me to the side of Honey Rose, who has been led outside the barn by Gilbert. He explains where to put my foot and helps me hoist myself upward and straddle the broad back of the even-tempered beauty. If she feels my nerves, she doesn't respond, standing still like she's bored.

Clay mounts his horse, and walks up beside me, taking over the lesson in how to pull up on the reins. With a gentle nudge of my heels into Honey Rose's side, she moves forward.

I yelp and Clay chuckles, encouraging us along.

Before I know it, we're sauntering down another gravel path that narrows into two rutted tracks along the edge of deep woods. As Clay and I ride in silence for a while, the atmosphere calms me. Cool air. Gray clouds. Quiet. The scene is peaceful, comforting even.

As we move onward, we talk about random things. Clay offers stories about learning his love of horses from his mom. He explains how the old barn on Stone's property once was filled with animals. When his mom died, his father got rid of them. Clay assumes the sight of them was too painful for his father.

"He must have loved her very much," I say.

"Hard to remember sometimes." He squints off into the distance. "My younger siblings don't remember them as a couple. How they laughed. My dad always kissing her. He'd have given her the moon if she asked. I caught them dancing in the kitchen one night. Only the radio on and the lights down low. I'd try to pull up that memory whenever Dad went on a rampage, cursing her death, or his kids. Only Stone, Judd, and me seem to remember her. Remember *them* when things were better."

His faraway look is haunted, and I don't need to ask to know that things changed, perhaps too quickly to understand as a boy. But Clay was a reflective man and despite his struggles to forgive his father, he offers compassion to him.

"He loved her so much. Made me afraid to love for the longest time. Afraid of being so attached to someone I'd lose my mind if they were gone for good."

My heart breaks for him. At the fear of love. The fear of losing it. If I'd been afraid, I would have never fallen for Wesley in the first place, something I wish I hadn't done.

"I believe love isn't something to be afraid of, though. Even if we only have it for a brief moment, that moment shines, and makes everything pale in comparison."

Clay bitter chuckles. "I think that's what happened to him. His world wasn't as bright without her in it."

"Too bad he didn't cling to the memory then and see how all the rays of her brightness flowed into her children." That's how I look at Dutton. He's an extension of Cecilia. He's the lingering streams of light after her sun set.

Clay huffs. "Yeah, too bad."

As I don't want to turn our ride into a sad song, I tease him next. "So, when do I get to really open her up and ride this baby?" I lean forward like I'm a practiced jockey instead of a novice horseback rider.

My *partner* chuckles, deep and loud, letting the sad moment wash out of him. "I'm not certain you're ready for such a ride. At least, not on a horse."

My mouth falls open at the innuendo and Clay laughs harder.

"Come on, butterfly. Just a little bit farther."

It is not long before a solitary stone structure comes into

view, low and alone in the middle of an autumn meadow. As Clay leads us toward the place, I ask, "What's this?"

"This is a place Stone and Knox rebuilt. When Knox first came home from the Navy, where he'd been a naval aviator, he had a lot on his mind. Stone found projects around the house and on our land to keep Knox's hands busy, hoping to distract his head." Clay nods at the lone building. "The back wall, made of field stones, was still intact, and Stone and Knox worked to rebuild the rest of what we assume was the original homestead on our property." Clay softly smiles. "Ironic, that Stone, and Knox whose nickname from Halle is Brick, rebuilt the stone and brick structure."

I chuckle at the connection as Clay halts his horse and slips from the saddle. He ties her up to an iron notch I hadn't noticed in the side of the small house. Then, he comes to me, holding out his hands to help me off Honey Rose. When I slide off the side of her with Clay's assistance, he spins me to kiss me hard and fast.

"Been wanting to do that since we started riding."

I blink, staggering from the suddenness. He'd kissed me only half an hour ago. But I wasn't complaining. The way Clay kissed me was like that sunshine feeling we discussed about love, because there was no doubt in my mind that I was brightly in love with Clay.

The thought should scare me. I know my track record—fall fast and hard—but everything about Clay says this time is different. *He's* the difference. The way he is with Dutton. The way he acts toward me. His gentle touch. His kind words. The only threat I feel is that Clay might not reciprocate how strongly I feel about him. Which means I still need to be on my guard because I can't risk Dutton or me getting hurt again in a deeper way, because Dutton cares and trusts Clay as much as I do.

"So why this place?" I ask, simply curious about Clay's thoughts.

"I haven't taken you on a proper date yet. I just wanted some adult time alone with you outside of the house."

"Thank you," I whisper, tickled that he wants to spend time with me and grateful for a little adult time myself.

Clay promised Dutton he'd bring him here another time, and while I'm certain Dutton will love the horses, I'm happy that I can have this experience first with Clay.

"I should be thanking you, beautiful." Clay takes the reins for Honey Rose and ties her up near Terra. Then, he takes my hand and leads me inside the tiny house.

With field stone and exposed brick walls, the space is cool like outside. A double bed rests against one wall. A wood-burning stove is in the opposite corner. A small wooden chair sits near the front window and a giant rug covers the slab floor. The place is quaint and cozy.

Clay rubs his hands together. "Just give me a minute to get the fire going. And ignore the bed. I didn't bring you here to get laid."

Running my hand over the smooth, light-colored comforter covered by a dark plaid blanket, I laugh. "What if *I* want to get laid?"

Clay stills where he's opening the front grate of the stove. "Then we can revisit the plan after lunch."

"Lunch?" There is no kitchen. No bathroom for that fact. This place is as rustic as it gets.

He hums like he holds a secret.

After tucking some logs into the stove and striking a match to light the fire, Clay stands. "Be right back." Clay exits the house, returning with the bag I hadn't seen him put in the saddle bag hanging off Terra.

"Picnic on the bed?" Because the floor might be a little cold to sit on. He holds up the sack before nodding at the bed and suggests, "Kick off your boots and climb up."

I do as he says, finding the blanket soft and the pillows comfortable as back support. The bed is cozy in general.

Clay arranges various containers with cut slices of cheese and sausage, crackers and grapes. He also has a variety of nuts. The display is charcuterie minus the board. Lastly, he pulls out a container filled with liquid.

"Going to mull this wine. It should only take a few minutes." He pours the wine into a small metal pan and places it on top of the stove, adding in some clove sticks and orange slices. Within minutes, the room smells amazing.

"This is so sweet. When did you prepare all this?" My voice bubbles over with excitement from the thoughtfulness of what he's brought with him. The care in his plan for the day. How romantic it all looks.

"I can't reveal my secrets." He chuckles, as easy going as I feel right now. "Just wanted to take care of you for an afternoon. You work so hard, Mavis. Mothering Dutton. Nursing at the hospital. Feeding me. I want you to relax. Hang out for a bit."

I hum. "I don't think anyone's ever cared for me like you do." I lower my gaze and pluck at the blanket, but I don't want the giddy energy swirling around us to burst, so I poke fun at myself by adding, "And I'm not certain I know how to relax."

"Maybe we can figure something out." He wiggles his brows as he stirs the wine in the pot.

"And here you said you didn't want to get laid."

Clay shrugs. "I do, but I don't. I'm happy to just spend time talking. If it leads to us making out, that's cool, too."

"Making out?" I tease while foolishly smiling until I see something in Clay's expression. "You're serious."

"Ever spend an afternoon just kissing someone?"

"No." My answer is a little too sharp and I soften my voice before repeating the word. "No."

"Neither have I. And I'd like a first with you."

"A first?" I whisper.

"You know. I can't be your first kiss. I can't steal your virginity."

I snort. *No, that is long gone.* "But *we* had a first kiss with each other. And a first time together."

Clay's mouth slowly crooks upward. "Yes, we did, but I want something uniquely first for us."

Us. I swallow the emotions that bloom with the thought, fighting any conflicting ideas in my head. I drop my gaze and pluck at the blanket once more. "I like us."

The wooden spoon Clay was using clangs in the pan, and I glance up to him climbing up the bed and crawling over me, knocking me deeper into the pillows at my back.

"I like us, too." He cups my cheek with one hand and kisses me, slowly, with purpose. As our mouths move together, Clay tugs me lower on the bed, shifting me beneath him. My arms wrap around him, and I'm ready for the make-out portion of our date, but the wine is simmering, and the food is spread out beside me.

I pull back and rub my nose against his. "Maybe we should lunch first."

"Your nose is freezing." He chuckles before placing a kiss on the tip. "So, yeah, lunch. You need that wine to warm you up a bit."

Doesn't he know I'm always warm around him? Hot for him? I lean up to press another quick kiss to his mouth before shoving him off me.

"Feed me, mister."

"Your commands are my wish."

I laugh as I roll to my side and perch on my elbow. "I don't think that's the saying."

"Well, I like my version better. I like when you boss me around."

"Boss you around?" I lower my head to my hand, propped

up on my elbow, and watch him pour warm wine into two camp mugs.

"I told you before. I'm always making decisions. All day long. And it's nice to be told what to do once in a while." He brings a mug to me on the bed. "I like you being bold and bossy."

I tip an eyebrow and hum, blowing on the steaming liquid in my mug. "And I like you sweet and sexy."

"You think I'm sexy?"

I laugh hard and watch my wine ripple from the exertion. "You know you are, honey."

Clay climbs up on the bed beside me. "What's fucking sexy is you calling me honey."

"What's *fucking* sexy is how you act with Dutton."

We stare at one another a long minute, each cupping the mugs in our hands, until Clay clears his throat. "We're getting weird, aren't we?"

Are we? I don't care. How often does one get an endless stream of compliments?

I sip my wine without answering him, and we fall into a quiet conversation about things we'd like to do one day and dreams we had that haven't happened yet. Clay is easy to talk to. He's also a great listener, intent and asking questions, looking directly at me. He might learn more about me than anyone ever has.

I want that kind of attention every day, not just one afternoon, and Clay is the kind of man to follow through on that desire.

As we sip wine and munch through our meal, I do relax, finding the cabin cozy and warm, and the spiced wine heating my insides. I yawn.

"Am I boring you?" Clay chuckles, sitting up to clear off the bed.

"Absolutely not. I'm just . . . toasty." I bend my knees and curl my toes, snuggling deeper into the pillows behind me. I'm not a napper, but I could easily take one here, and dream of never leaving this place.

The warmth. The company. Of course, I'd miss Dutton.

He'd been happy to see Violet when she arrived at Clay's house, babysitting backpack over her shoulder, full of activities for the day. Clay told me she'd make a great teacher one day. Violet admits she doesn't know yet what she wants to be.

Clay tops off each mug of wine and returns to the bed. After handing me my cup I take another sip, humming once more at the flavor and warmth.

"So, I did good?" He arches one brow, smiling at me with a knowing smirk.

"So far, so good," I tease.

"What would make it better?"

I tap my lower lip. "Maybe . . . you naked?"

Clay laughs, but his expression shifts from mirth to surprise. "Oh, you were serious."

"How much time do we have?" I ask wondering about the horses, the weather, and Violet watching Dutton.

"We'll take all the time you need, butterfly. No rush." He leans over and takes my mug, setting both his and mine on the floor near the stove. Standing at the end of the bed, his hands go to his belt. "Don't know if I can make out with you naked, without wanting more." He loosens his belt and starts unbuttoning his shirt and as much as I want to have sex with him here, I kind of like his idea better.

I pat the bed beside me. "Maybe we should keep our clothes on, and just kiss."

"Nothing *just* about kissing you, beautiful." He climbs up on the bed again, belt loose, shirt open, and crawls over me before leaning forward and kissing me, soft and sweet before hard and hungry.

And he's right. There is nothing *just* about kissing this man.

25

[Clay]

As we return to the horse stables, snow begins to lightly fall, like an early winter baptism. The cold air is necessary to calm my racing heart because Mavis and I kissed, *only kissed*, for an hour. And I'm fucking horny as hell now.

What a schmuck idea I had, suggesting we only make out.

Still, the afternoon had been a first on many levels. I hadn't ever taken a woman horseback riding, hadn't taken a woman to the little house, and I hadn't made out with a woman for an afternoon like I'd told Mavis.

New kinds of firsts. I loved each and every one of them because I am in love with Mavis.

This had to be it. Had to be how love felt. That desire to spend all my time with her, have her in my space. I loved kissing and talking, cuddling and laughing. I loved how *she* was with Dutton and that she saw my effort. I adored him.

And I will do whatever it takes to keep them both in my life.

A week passes, and I've never been more grateful for a Friday. Not that my business is the Monday through Friday kind, but I was trying to take off a day or two when Mavis had off from the hospital. However, tomorrow, I was taking Dutton on our 'date' while Mavis works.

When I arrive home, which my house has been for me for years, but suddenly feels homier, I'm greeted by Dutton with an absentminded wave as he's looking at something on his tablet. Mavis is a bit more enthusiastic to my entrance and tugs me into the kitchen, presses me up against the refrigerator and kisses me.

"Wow. Hello to you, too," I tease, once she pulls away, chewing her lower lip.

"Hi, honey. I'm glad you're home."

Fuck. There's just something great hearing her say such a thing to me.

"You're in a good mood." Running my hands from her shoulders to her wrists, I tug her to me again for a hug.

"I got paid today," she mumbles into my neck, pressing a kiss there before pulling back once more. "And I have something for you."

She's so cute with her excitement. Pushing away from me, she holds up a finger to signal me to wait where I am, and she'll be right back. She tips up on her toes for another quick kiss before disappearing. Anticipating her return, I help myself to a beer from the fridge finding the appliance full of groceries. Things had gotten a little slim and I had grocery shopping on my list of things to do, but apparently, I don't need to.

I pop the top off the bottle and take a healthy swallow before Mavis re-enters the kitchen with an envelope.

"What's this?" I chuckle, taking the surprise and flipping it over. Inside are several hundred-dollar bills.

"I owe you. For letting us stay here. I know it isn't much but I . . ."

Her voice drifts as I close the envelope and hand it back to her. "I am not taking your money. I don't *need* your money."

"But I should pay you something. We've been here for weeks."

Setting my beer on the counter, I lean into the cabinet as well. "Doesn't matter. You're not paying me like you're renting a room, Mavis."

She flinches at my use of her name. But I'm offended she thinks she owes me financially for being here.

"In fact, it's time you unpack that damn suitcase." She'd eventually put Dutton's things in a dresser drawer in his room, because the space went from my extra bedroom to Dutton's room.

"I did unpack."

"Dutton's things."

"My stuff is in the closet."

"And I want it in mine."

"Clay." She stares at me.

"Are you two fighting?" Dutton's small voice turns both our heads in his direction, where he's standing just inside the kitchen entryway.

"No, little bear."

"No, not fighting," I add. "Just having a healthy discussion, buddy. Sometimes we're gonna get loud when we feel passionate about something." I turn my head toward Mavis, eyeing her.

All three of us hold our breaths for a minute before Dutton rolls against the wall and returns to the living room.

I step closer to Mavis, lowering my voice only a little.

"I want you and Dutton to *live* with me, butterfly. Not like some visiting guest, but as family. I want you to unpack your bags and settle in."

"Clay," Mavis groans, her gaze a glare as if I'm not being fair. But she's the one being unfair. I don't want her to act like staying in my home is temporary. That *we* are temporary.

She's it for me. I can feel it in my bones. She warms my bed, fills my belly, and holds my heart. And right now, she's squeezing it painfully tight with the suggestion she owes me money for being here.

"If you don't want to stay, I can't force you. I *won't* force you." I glance toward the living room. "But I want you *living* here. With me. Use that money to buy some things for yourself. Spruce up my place and make it feel more like your home." I swallow hard. "Or you can use it to pay rent somewhere else. But you aren't paying me like you're a renter here."

Mavis stares at me, not responding to my outburst. I hadn't realized how loud my voice had gotten, but I'm agitated by this exchange, and I won't apologize.

"Guess you have some things to think about."

When Mavis doesn't say anything further, I announce. "I'm going out for a bit."

I don't really want to leave but I can't stand in my kitchen waiting for her answer.

Doesn't she want to stay? Doesn't she feel the same way? I thought we were good together.

Leaving my beer on the counter, I stalk toward the front door, passing the back of the couch without a glance at Dutton. If I look at him, my heart will shatter right here on the hardwood floor.

"Clay." Mavis's voice is quiet behind me. I still with my hand on the doorknob. Then her arms circle around me from behind me and her head lands on my back.

A knock comes to the door, startling me, and I pull it open with Mavis still behind me. "Violet?"

"Hi." She waves. "I'm here to pick up Dutton."

Holding open the door, I twist to face Mavis wondering

what's going on. She leans around me. "Violet, honey, why don't you come in a second? I need a minute with your uncle and then Dutton will be ready."

Mavis grips my forearm and I step back from the door, allowing Violet into my house. Dutton sits on the couch, and the tension between the three of us is thick.

"Will you excuse us a minute?" Mavis offers Violet a weak smile and tugs me toward my bedroom.

Closing the door behind her, she explains. "I was excited to get my *second* paycheck. And I thought it would be nice for another adult-only moment. At first, I was going to take you out, but you seem to like my cooking and I remembered you saying you didn't eat at home often. So, I asked Violet if she could take Dutton out and we could have some time together here."

I stare at her. She'd planned everything. Dinner. Childcare for Dutton. A date for us, and I'd just exploded on her.

"Butterfly, why didn't you say anything?"

She shrugs. "I wanted to surprise you like you surprised me last weekend."

Guilt slams into me and I swipe a hand down my face.

"If you'd still like to go out without me, I'm still going to let Dutton go with Violet. He's been looking forward to it. They might pick up Winnie and go get pizza."

Fuck. "No, I do not want to go out without you. I only said that because—" Because I want to spend all my time with her. I want her here where I know she's safe. She's *home.*

Mavis nods and turns for the door, but I catch her elbow. Glancing up at me, over her shoulder, our eyes lock. "We'll talk. Once Violet and Dutton are gone."

I definitely need a do-over for this night.

∼

With extra hugs for Dutton from Mavis, and a hug from me as well reassuring him everything is well, Violet and Dutton leave.

Mavis shuts the front door once they pull down the drive and leans her back against it.

"I messed up," I admit.

Mavis stares at me a long minute. "I'm not sure if I should be upset that you raised your voice or that you asked me to live with you during what felt like a fight."

Swiping a hand over my head again, I huff. "We weren't fighting." We just were not agreeing. "You're here. I don't want you to leave." Maybe I just assumed she'd stay.

"Then tell me that." Her voice is still hard.

"Look, butterfly. I'm not professing to be perfect. We're gonna fight. Voices might rise. But I never ever want you to feel threatened by me. I want you to feel safe. I want my home to be *our* home. And I want to feel confident that you'll stay for the long haul, just like I want you to feel confident that I'm *returning* home to you each and every night."

"Like when you tell me you're going out. You're promising you'll be back."

Fuck. Did that trigger her? I step closer to her, wishing she'd come away from the front door.

"I'm promising. I just . . . I just said that before. I didn't want to leave. I've been waiting all day to be home. With you. With Dutton." I sigh, glancing around my living room. "And I ruined your surprise for me."

Mavis purses her lips and lowers her gaze.

"Tell me what you had planned."

She shrugs. A tear trickles along her nose and she quickly swipes at it. "I just wanted to celebrate being paid. It's been a while and it felt good to make money again. Make my own money. First steps and all that."

"First steps for what, baby?"

"Regaining some independence. Feeling like I can do something. A future will happen for Dutton and me."

I close the distance between us, cupping her shoulders. "Of course a future will happen for you and Dutton. You're employed and that sounds important to you. You're making your own money. And you're safe here."

Mavis nods and a tear slips from her eye, one I kiss away.

"I'm sorry I raised my voice. And I'm sorry if I scared Dutton." The kid was definitely concerned about leaving Mavis. With a deep exhale, I slide my hands down her arms to capture her fingers. "We're good, Mavis. If you want to move out, move. Whatever you want to do. I'd never pin those wings of yours, butterfly. But I want you to stay. Forever."

I swallow around the word certain I've never said it before to anyone.

"I'm falling for you, and that might scare you. It scares me. But I'm here and if you need to leave for a while, I'll be waiting. That's my promise." I squeeze her hands. "Whatever you need."

Mavis lifts her head. Her eyes glistening. "I'm falling for you, too, honey. And it scares me as well. So many what ifs constantly running through my head."

"Tell me what they are so I can cancel them out for you."

"What if you get bored with us. What if you decide you do want us to leave. What if you think we're taking advantage of you. What if I don't need saving and you're no longer interested because I—"

I cover her mouth with my fingers, shaking my head.

"And what if I keep you. What if I want you to stay. What if I love you like I say I do and then prove it every day. What if you've never needed saving, butterfly, and I know that about you. What if *I* do."

"How can I save you?" She chokes around a bitter laugh, like she can't possibly understand what I'd need.

"By loving me back, Mavis. Every day."

Suddenly, she has her arms around me, clinging to my neck, and I'm squeezing her tight to my chest, breathing in relief and her floral scent.

"Stay, Mavis."

"Yes, Clay. Dutton and I would love to live here with you."

I pull back so I can see her face, cup her jaw, and kiss her. A kiss that is tender at first. An apology for how things went down earlier. But quickly, the meeting of our mouths turns hungry. We move on to making up for the fight.

Within seconds, Mavis's back is plastered to the front door again and my body presses into hers. The kiss hits a hundred, but I want more.

"Don't know what all you planned for tonight, but I'm gonna admit I have a new plan. And I need you to trust me."

"I trust you, honey. With everything." Her body. Her heart.

"I want control tonight, beautiful. Let me lead." I have no trouble letting her boss me around in the bedroom but tonight I want to be in charge. She's still the boss. Her pleasure is my desire.

Mavis nods and I pick her up by scooping my hands beneath her backside. She wraps her legs around my waist, and I carry her down the hallway to our bedroom. With a backward kick, the door closes behind me, but we don't need privacy. I have hours to love her like we both need, and I'm not wasting a minute of it.

Once we near the bed, I drop her and she squeals, then I climb over her, continuing to kiss her while running a hand down her chest, covering a breast and squeezing tight before pinching her nipple.

"Yes," Mavis mumbles against my mouth.

"Want it a little rough, beautiful?"

Mavis chews her lip and I tug it free with my thumb. I'm earnest when I ask, "Need a safe word? A signal that it's too much?"

"Maybe just hold my hand to reassure me."

I grin at her, willing to give her anything she needs. "Going to need both of them at times, but I'll hold your hand whenever I can."

For now, I notice the dress she is wearing. "Was this for tonight?" The maroon-colored material wraps around her body like the petals of a flower about to bloom, highlighting all her features from the curve of her hips to the midnight shade of her hair.

Mavis nods, rolling her lips again.

"Damn. You're stunning." The fabric runs neck to thighs and down her arms. Its casual while sexy and when I tug it upward and over her head, I'm speechless.

Beneath the average dress is an intricate, black bra and matching panties that doesn't leave much to the imagination. Her nipples are erect. The dusty color delicately covered by lace. Velvety straps crisscross around her breasts, trussing them up and emphasizing their size. The panties are hardly more than ribbons of fabric wrapping over her hip with a lace panel over a strip of dark hair.

"Butterfly." I choke, so overwhelmed by how beautiful she is. So precious to me.

I rub the heel of my hand between her breasts and over her belly before slipping my hand between her thighs, cupping her where she's already damp and soaking the lace.

"I don't want to remove any of this."

"You don't have to."

Lowering, I cover her breast with my mouth, sucking at the pert nipple through the lace, teasing her, driving myself wild. At the same time, I place my finger at her clit, pressing on the lace over the sensitive nub. In tandem, I work her breast and stroke her where she's needy.

"Clay." Her hands cup my head. Her back arches. She's on the edge.

I pull away from both her breast and her trigger spot.

Mavis collapses back onto the bed, eyes narrowing at me.

"I need you to trust that I'll always get you there, butterfly. Wherever, whatever, there is." I coast my hand back up her midsection and cover the other breast, palming, kneading, plucking at the nipple. At the same time, I lower my face between her thighs, which she eagerly spreads for me. I lick over the lace, flicking at that sensitive place with my tongue, pressing the material against her slick skin.

Mavis moans, arching her back again, spreading her legs wider, covering my hand at her breast.

I pull back again.

"Clay," she groans.

Crawling off the bed, I stand and remove all my clothing while Mavis watches me. She slides her hand between her legs, toying with herself while I strip.

"No cheating, baby." I warn her, growing more eager for her if that's even possible. Delaying her gratification is only delaying mine.

She removes her hand from between her legs and rolls her head against the mattress as if frustrated.

"Soon." I climb back up on the bed and run my hands around the lacy outfit, fingers tracing all the velvety ribbons, eventually rolling her over to continue the trail and experiencing another pleasing shock.

"Butterfly." My teeth grind. A velvety strip runs low at her back and through the crease of her ass, emphasizing the firm swells. Up top, the ribbons crisscross over her shoulder blades in a similar pattern to the front.

On her belly, Mavis exhales sharply as I slip my finger along the soft fabric between her ass cheeks. I climb over her, toying once more with her clit and nipping at her shoulder.

"Let me have you like this," I whisper at her ear.

Her answer is to curl her back and lift her ass. Brushing

aside the lace covering her entrance, I line up the tip of my dick to continue teasing her.

I should give her more foreplay, but she's already drenched and near a breaking point like I am.

Slipping into her, we both moan as she stretches around me, bringing me into her body until she's full. I curl my fingers into the velvet strap at her hip with one hand while reaching for her hand with the other, clasping our fingers together with my hand on top of hers.

With my fingers in the velvet ribbon, I guide Mavis back and forth while I slide in and out of her. She's so freaking wet, we easily move together. With her legs spread and me awkwardly on my knees, I won't hold out long like this, but I relish the torture of gliding in and out of her. Watching her ass lift and lower as I'm drawn into her heat.

I release her hand and wrap my arm around her waist to lift her to her knees, so her back hits my chest.

"Remember when you teased about riding me?" I nip at her neck.

Mavis groans, like she's drugged on our connection. "You teased me."

I chuckle into her skin. "I want you to ride me, Mavis. Race *with* me." I pull out of her, and she drops forward, balancing on all fours. Her head hangs, and she hisses in frustration.

I flip around on the bed, place my back to the headboard and guide Mavis over me, sitting on my lap, her back to my chest again.

"Clay," she whimpers. With her knees bent on either side of my thighs and her hands between my legs, I guide her backwards, watching as my dick slides into her, connecting us as one again. Mavis sits upright. With her hair tumbling over her shoulders, she glances at me over one of them.

"Race, butterfly." Then she's working herself up and down, taking me in this position where I'm hitting her someplace unseen that sparks her onward. Faster and faster she rocks. Her breath catching. Her head tipping back. She's losing control.

"I can feel you, beautiful. You're clenching my cock. Dripping into my lap. Fuck, you're gonna make me come."

Mavis slams down on me, almost daring me to try to leave her body before she crosses the finish line. I don't think I've ever seen something so beautiful or heard such a sound.

Mavis practically purrs, rolling her hips in my lap. I slide my hand around her front, plucking that sweet clit while catching her other hand with mine again. She covers the hand between her thighs and together we strum until she gets the finish she wants. With her head back, her back arched, she comes like she's howling at the moon. I feel every clench and pulse, causing my own release to spring free.

With one hand holding hers and the other flat against her lower belly, I go off inside Mavis like I never have before. Her squeezing me. Me filling her. The orgasm goes on and on until she collapses forward, catching herself on her hands. Running my hand up her spine, I tip my head against the headboard.

"Holy shit, Mavis." She steals my breath. She owns my heart.

With a strangled chuckle, she lifts her body and releases me, falling to her side beside me.

We remain in our separate, breathless positions for a minute. Then I slap her ass.

"Let's shower."

And we start the race all over again.

26

[Clay]

When Mavis next works, I take Dutton on the special day I promised him. Before we head to the horse stables, which Mavis approved, and thought Dutton would thoroughly enjoy, we stop at a Walmart between Sterling Falls and Huntington.

"I want you to pick out anything you'd like to make your room feel more like your room."

After our night together, Mavis moved her things into my bedroom where I'd made space in the dresser. I already had more than enough space in my closet as my wardrobe is mainly Seed & Soil t-shirts and button-ups with an occasional flannel tossed in, and jeans.

Dutton and I wandered the bedding aisles where there were almost too many choices for a kid to make a decision. While standing among the sheets and comforters, a man with shoulder length hair, wearing a leather jacket and heavy riding boots enters the same aisle. A nasty-looking scar mars his face. He stands a few feet away staring at the same set of sheets long enough, I wonder if he's really looking for kid's bedding at all.

When Dutton finally points to white bedding with polka dots in light pastel colors, I ask, "Are you sure?" The question is only meant to prompt him to be firm in his decision. My nieces and nephew have taught me kids can be fickle and I want Dutton to be positive about his choice.

Dutton nods and I reach for the bed set.

"You're a boy, son," the man states, his voice gruff like he's a smoker. I've been accused that my voice sounds similar, but this man wears the scent of cigarettes on him like a badge of honor. He's also surprisingly closer to us than he first was, and I notice that his dark hair is peppered with strands of gray. His face is weathered, and I'd put him roughly ten years older than me.

"Hey man," I counter. "The boy can have what he wants."

The man eyes Dutton up and down, taking in his pink nails and green t-shirt, something rather non-descript compared to some of Dutton's other clothing.

The lingering look makes me extra protective of Dutton and I place my hand on his shoulder, both to reassure Dutton his choice is fine and let the stranger know he's close enough. The contact also brings me comfort, making a statement to this rude man. *My kid, my business.*

"What about the blue set with planets on it?" The guy ignores me, reaching for the bed set he's recommending and pulling it off the shelf.

Dutton only blinks at the package held toward him before looking up at me.

"We're getting the polka dots," I insist, addressing Dutton to reassure him and defend his choice. This stranger is pissing me off by even talking to Dutton. I'm one breath away from telling him to fuck off, which isn't typically my nature.

The man continues to stare at Dutton before taking a second glance at the planet bedding in his hand. He grunts, tosses the set back onto the shelf, and spins on his heels. Dutton and I both watch him walk away.

Once he exits the aisle, I squat and spin Dutton so he focuses on me.

"Dutton, I want you to listen to me. Sometimes, old people can be ignorant. Hell, young people can be, too. It isn't age that defines stupidity, it's lack of knowledge and compassion."

Dutton stares at me. My explanation might be over his head.

Placing my hands on his hips, I jostle him a little bit. "I want you to know that I think you are perfect. You're smart and kind. You are loved by your mama and me." Admitting such a thing out loud should surprise me, but the words flow easily. "People who love you, respect you, and that's all that's important. Which means you can be who you want to be and have what you want to have."

I clutch the bedding package and hold it up.

"A stranger's comments do not matter."

Dutton weakly smiles, eyes lowered to the cement flooring.

"And I'm not going to let anyone ever tell you to be different than who you are meant to be. I'll never let anything happen to you. Or your mama. That's a promise."

Dutton doesn't speak but he reaches out for the buttons on my shirt, fiddling with the plastic circles a second.

"We should have a handshake for that promise," Dutton finally states.

I extend my hand for a traditional handshake, but Dutton shakes his head. "A special, secret one."

"A secret one, huh?" I purse my lips. "Got one in mind? Or do we invent our own?"

Dutton holds out his small hand. "First we slap." He holds up my hand to imitate what I need to do for my part.

"Then we tap the backs." He moves our hands so the backs connect.

"Then we make spirit fingers." He holds up both his hands, palms out and wiggles his fingers.

"Let's practice." I'm still squatting, and my knees are killing me in this position, but I hold out my hand and slap his palm, then tap his knuckles with the back of mine, and we make spirit fingers at one another.

Dutton dissolves into laughter and then wraps his arms around my neck, hugging me hard.

No one ever warned me I'd lose my heart to a kid in a Walmart.

AFTER OUR HORSE RIDE, where Honey Rose is patient with Dutton, and he falls in love with the horse, he falls asleep in my truck on the drive home.

It's been a great day, but the encounter earlier still riddles me with unease. Once we are home, I gingerly lift Dutton from his booster seat which Mavis put in my truck and carry him inside. He instantly wakes up but he's groggy, so I set the television on a horse program and step into the kitchen to call my brother.

"Hey," Stone answers on the first ring.

"Hi." We aren't much for formalities, so I break into my concerns immediately. "I wanted to check in with you about that guy Perry was with." The one I'd called Stone about after the party incident.

"We haven't found anyone yet. Perry wasn't much help. Was probably just some guy grifting through town."

Fucking Perry. The explanation does not put me at ease.

"What about Wesley?"

"What about him?" Stone counters.

"Any status updates on him?"

"Other than he's still missing and there is an APB out for his arrest? That's all we got for now."

For half a second, earlier in the day, I thought the man standing in the Walmart aisle was Wesley. However, I don't recall him having longer hair or such weathered skin. Although people can change, in only a year, he'd have to age ten and grow broader in shoulders and taller in height, a mere impossibility at over fifty years old. Plus, Dutton did not recognize the man.

Still, thoughts of the stranger, his rude comments, and near proximity to Dutton unsettle me. Hell, any stranger that gets too close to him is going to make me anxious. This fear makes me feel more like a parent than the twenty-something kid I once was while raising my siblings.

"You'll keep me posted if you learn anything new, though, right?"

Stone is a quiet a second before asking, "Is there something you want to tell me?"

Of all my siblings, he's the least likely to tease me about saving people or creatures. He knows as well as I do all we did to *save* our siblings, and we didn't always do a bang-up job. However, we kept them in school and clothed and fed, and mostly out of trouble except for Sebastian and a little issue with Vale.

But parenting is more than clothes, food, and a roof over heads. We love our siblings, but they are still that, our brothers and sister.

Love like I feel for Dutton—this desire to protect him, keep him safe and whole, assure him he's the best thing ever to exist —this feels like being a parent.

Like being a father.

"Yeah." The slow smile on my face lifts my voice. "Mavis and Dutton are living here now. With me."

We are an us.

Forever.

27

[Mavis]

Within the week, I have good news. Trudy Wallace, a local real estate agent who originally sold me my house, has found a buyer. The person wishes to remain undisclosed which is their right. He or she will actually be buying the land as there is no longer a house. Trudy thinks the person is purchasing the property for an investment. He or she will build something meeting the city's requirements for the historic boulevard of homes, possibly something modeled after the original house, then flip it for a profit.

It shouldn't matter to me what is built. I'm not gaining anything from the sale other than enough money to pay off the mortgage on a home that no longer exists.

Still, the thought makes me slightly sad. I loved the house and living in town, close to the local businesses and shops. I don't like the idea of the property being an investment, but hopefully one day a beautiful house with a loving family will reside there and enjoy the space as much as I once did.

"Are you sure you'll be happy living out here?" Clay asks me, sensing my mood about the sale as we sit on the couch, mindlessly waiting for a movie to start on the television. I'm snuggled into his side, his arm over my shoulders. His fingers toy with my hair.

As his smaller home is outside of town proper and on a large piece of land, the setting is opposite of town living but just as wonderful. The space is cozy, warm, and comfortable.

"I love it out here," I tell him, meaning it. "All the open space and the woods on the edge. It's a perfect place for Dutton to roam. I feel safe here."

Despite being in town with neighbors close by, I hadn't always felt safe in my original home. The devil lived inside my house.

Clay is an angel in comparison.

"I just want you to be happy." He presses a kiss to my forehead before turning back to the movie.

I want him to be happy as well, and the concern that one day he won't be, still rears its head occasionally.

ANOTHER SYLVER SUNDAY ARRIVES, only this one is full of excitement. Clay's brother Ford was once a famous centerfielder for the Chicago Anchors, which I already know. And his girlfriend is Cadence, a world-renown country music singer who I have yet to personally meet. She's finally home from a short tour, so she's attending the gathering. Everyone in the family is thrilled to learn she'll be making Sterling Falls her permanent residence with Ford and his three energetic girls.

Winnie has been a godsend for Dutton, and I dare say she alone has convinced me to put Dutton in the local elementary school after the holidays. They will be in the same grade and the school has honored my request to have Dutton in the same classroom as Winnie to ease the transition to the formal setting.

I'll miss our homeschooling sessions, but I'm not cut out to be a teacher. I can tackle the homework and special assignments, but any education from me is more unstructured and carefree than math problems and proper English.

As we enter the house, the noise level is louder than normal. The girls are excited to have Cadence present.

Winnie rushes to Dutton. "Meet my new mom."

Clay and I exchange glances. *Is there something he forgot to tell me?* He softly chuckles and wraps his arm around my shoulder, tugging me to him and pressing a kiss to my temple. He's become openly affectionate with me around Dutton and his family.

For the first time in a long time, I'm truly happy. A fact that unsettles me, and I can't stop the nerves jittering through me.

"And who is this?" Cadence squeals, squatting to eye Dutton. "Winnie told me she had a new best friend."

Cadence has long, acorn colored hair, a contrast to her blonde stage persona. She's expressive and friendly, and so much more than I expected a country superstar to be. She's genuinely excited to meet Dutton.

Dutton shies a bit at Cadence's exuberance, but he still smiles deeply at her attention.

"I heard you love *Princess Power*. The pink one, right?"

Dutton is adamantly nodding, confirming the information.

Cadence stands to her full height. "Then I think a *Princess Power* sleepover party is in order. You, Zelle, Winnie, and June. Soon?"

Cadence glances at me. Unfortunately, she's dangled the carrot before a rabbit, and Dutton is rolling on the balls of his feet, hands clasped together in a plea.

"I don't know," I whisper, reaching out for his longer bangs and tugging them back from his face. "Let me discuss it with Clay."

At my statement, the room slowly quiets, like I've said something the others aren't certain they've heard correctly or maybe shouldn't have heard at all.

On the verge of asking if I said something wrong, my palms grow sweaty until Clay clasps his hand around mine and lifts that hand to his mouth, pressing a soft kiss to the center of my palm. His eyes are bright, a small smirk playing on his mouth when he looks up at me. Then he glances at Dutton, giving him a smile as well.

"Mavis and I have news, too. We are officially living together. Mavis, Dutton, and me." Clay winks at Dutton who turned his head toward Clay when he heard his name.

Another roar of congratulations goes up. The family is chaos once more as the Sylver brothers step forward to hug Clay and Vale swipes at a tear escaping her eye.

"Welcome to the family," Cadence says, offering me a hug. "It's a wild ride among these Sylvers."

I've learned that Cadence is Enya's sister.

Enya chuckles next, rubbing her hand over her swollen belly. Baby number two is due in February. "You're going to scare her away."

Cadence glances back at me, eyes squinting like she's truly inspecting me. "Something tells me Mavis doesn't scare easily." The side of her mouth crooks upward before she fully smiles. "The bigger question is, how are you at baseball?"

A few groans follow the question, but other questions are asked about Clay and me, and Ford and Cadence.

And the happiness level skyrockets. This is family. With a sharp pang of homesickness, I recall the easier times that come with growing up around a motorcycle club. The family barbeques and holiday celebrations that involved boisterous male voices and soothing female ones. I miss my sister and wish she could have had an experience similar to the one I'm experiencing with Dutton.

Glancing at him, so immersed in this family as well, accepted for who he is, and embracing them all right back, I send up a silent prayer of gratitude to Cecilia for trusting me with his care. For allowing me to love him as my own.

"You okay?" Vale asks, nudging my arm while holding out a glass of wine for me.

"Yeah," I quietly state.

"Gotta love this lot, even if they can be overbearing at times. Love is overwhelming, right?"

"Yeah." I blink, something suddenly in my eye.

"It's also the best feeling in the world." Vale side-eyes me, watching her family. "Don't ever forget that, Mavis. You're one of us now."

I'm not certain if it's a warning or a reminder but I'm not likely to forget the Sylver family *if* something ever was to happen to me or them.

LATER, Clay and I tumble to his bed, a ribbon of limbs entangled and mouths meeting. I giggle, giddy from two glasses of wine when I'm not much of a drinker and the overall buzz of dinner among a family that is shifting and growing.

Slowly, Clay and I undress each other, running our hands over the other's body, exploring all the places we've already explored and yet still learning so much about one another. As I roll him to his back, climbing over him, something in my peripheral vision near the floor to ceiling windows has me turning my head, distracting me only a second from the glory of the man beneath me.

I freeze.

"Clay," I whisper. "There's someone out there."

The shadow was not that of an animal, low to the ground and walking on all fours, but a full-grown male, passing by the window. I didn't notice him looking through the glass, but he might have been. Who knows if he'd been watching us before he walked along the side of the house.

Beneath me, Clay lifts his head and glances toward the window. Then, he's sitting upright and I'm scrambling off him. He stumbles from the bed and steps into his jeans, tugging them up his legs, sans underwear, leaving them loosely open at his waist.

I climb off the end of the bed and reach for his flannel shirt on the floor. My hands shake violently as I struggle to pull the warm material on before wrapping my arms around my middle to hold the shirt closed. My spine tingles, a chill racing down it, as goosebumps settle on my skin. My stomach is instantly in knots. Fear like I haven't known in a long time wells inside me.

Clay yanks open the door to our bedroom, providing us a clear view of the hallway. Standing just outside the glass lining the wall, leaning forward with his hand shielding his eyes, is a man, and he isn't looking in the direction of Clay or me, but staring at the closed door to Dutton's room.

Clay is already rushing down the hallway toward the front door. While I fear for him because he shouldn't go outside, he doesn't know if the person is armed or dangerous, my greater concern is Dutton.

My son's name is a squeak, paralyzed in my throat as terror takes over my body. I move limbs that are heavy and weighted with fear. Finally, I cross the few steps to Dutton's door and open it, relieved to find him tucked in bed. His arms wrapped around Violet the bear. He's safe and whole in here.

Instantly, I twist toward the floor to ceiling windows, noticing Clay standing barefoot in the gravel driveway. His hair is mussed, his jaw tense. His head darts left to right, searching for the man before he runs both his hands up the back of his head, forcing his hair to stand even further upright. Obvious frustration, and maybe a healthy dose of fear, suddenly presses on his shoulders. Clay looks like he's yelling but I can't hear what he's saying through the heavy panes.

The stranger is gone.

But even without his presence, the memory of worn leather, cigarettes, and cheap cologne tickles my nose.

28

———

[Clay]

"I lost him," I repeat to Stone through the phone as I pace my living room. Stone told me to remain on the line until he gets to the house. I don't know what he thinks he'll find in the dark night. There was no breaking and entering in either the house or our vehicles. The man wasn't leaning on the glass, so I doubt there are fingerprints to be taken.

He was just a man.

And while I'm pissed he might have seen Mavis naked, been watching us like a sick fuck, I'm more upset that he was trying to glare through the tinted windows in the direction of Dutton's room.

What a fucking coward. That's what I screamed into the night. Whoever he was, if he has an issue, he should face it, face me. Because he isn't getting anywhere near *my* family.

"You shouldn't have chased him," Stone chastises.

I bite my tongue, ready to bark at him that if it had been his family he would have done the same thing. He would sprint and hunt and burn down the world to keep them protected. That's Stone.

"What the fuck was he doing out there?" I ask for the third time, as if Stone would have an answer. The better question is, "Who the fuck is he?"

His build was hard to describe. Tall. Broad. He could be anyone or no one we know. With a hood pulled over his head, I had no sense of his hair style or his facial features. Was he young or old? Clean-shaven or bearded? In the darkness of night, the lighting outside was almost null, making the man's appearance nearly impossible to decipher.

I'm left curious why the motion sensing lights I have over the driveway didn't detect his movements. But I'm most angry that I don't have cameras on my land or the camera doorbell I bought two years ago set up and functioning because I haven't taken the time to install it.

With the crunch of tires over gravel, and the glare of headlights, Stone's official sheriff's vehicle pulls up to the house and parks. His entrance doesn't trigger my motion sensor lights either, and I'll need to check the bulbs in the daylight.

I click off my phone without a goodbye and greet Stone at the front door.

"Hey." He holds his sheriff's cap in his hand. The brown leather jacket he wears is open, like he tossed it on and forgot to zip it. Stepping inside the house, he glances around the living room.

"Where is Mavis?"

When I returned inside the house, after chasing the man, my bare feet throbbed from the sharp, cold rocks in the drive. Mavis wanted to check them for cuts, especially when she saw me limping, but I was too focused on finding my phone and calling Stone.

"She's in Dutton's room."

"Are they okay?" Stone asks for the second time. Thankfully, Dutton doesn't appear to have been disturbed. Mavis is visibly shaken, though, as am I.

"You good?" Stone assesses me. I finally snapped up my jeans and threw on a sweatshirt. Mavis has on the flannel I'd worn earlier and while I want to know how sexy she might look in my shirt, I'm equally sick that someone might have seen her *without* any clothing on. Her nakedness is for my eyes only.

I didn't hesitate on the phone to tell Stone we were in a compromising position. Both undressed. The delay cost me. Tugging on my jeans gave the culprit time to move. He went right down the middle of the drive which curves in a way that protects the house from immediate view of the road. It also means it shielded his escape. Based on the intruder's heavy thuds crunching down the stony drive, he wore boots, while I'd been barefoot, and he easily outpaced me.

"Try to recall again if you heard a car? A truck? Maybe a motorcycle?"

All are questions he's already asked me, and I'm a terrible witness. The only sound I heard was the pounding of my heart in my ears.

I shake my head, letting him know I've got nothing to share.

We review once more the general size I'd estimate and the shape. Tall and broad doesn't really describe much. Dark attire head to toe does even less to help Stone.

"I'm going to have a look around, but you can go to bed. Lock up once I leave."

His warning is unnecessary. I'll be triple checking all the locks on windows and doors. Sleep isn't going to happen for me.

After checking all the latches and watching Stone's vehicle exit the drive, I return to my room and change into sweats and a t-shirt. I enter Dutton's room next, the bed covered with the new polka dot comforter he picked out. Violet the bear tucked under his arm. Mavis wrapped around him.

Her head lifts as I stand beside the bed opposite her. Her mouth opens to speak but I place a single finger against my lips silencing her. Then I climb onto the bed similar to the night of the thunderstorm when I sandwiched Dutton between us.

Mavis reaches over Dutton to clutch the side of my shirt and I reach out to her, resting my hand on her hip. Dutton is cocooned between us again, the term a better analogy than the filling of an Oreo cookie. Because, although Dutton is definitely part of the yummy goodness holding Mavis and me together, he's not the only thing keeping us connected. Loving each other, Mavis and I will do anything we can to protect him.

Because I have no doubt the person outside the window wasn't looking for only Mavis.

He wants to take my family from me.

29

[Mavis]

In the morning, Clay and I were both quiet and skittish. Dutton was in rare form. He'd been ornery and irritable, like he didn't get enough sleep when he appeared to sleep like a hibernating bear compared to Clay and me who laid awake most of the night.

"Do you have any idea who he could have been?" Clay had asked me, keeping his voice low as we stood side by side in the kitchen sipping coffee, waiting for the jolt of caffeine to kick in. Dutton stirred his oatmeal in his bowl, hardly eating. Clay had skipped their oatmeal routine.

I didn't want to lie to Clay, but I also didn't have any truths to share. I had speculations, so I shook my head, afraid words would betray me. One thing I was rather certain of was the man was not Wesley. The size of the person didn't match his stature. That didn't mean it wasn't a creditor, legal or otherwise, wanting money from Wesley. Or a person affiliated with Wesley somehow. I refused to believe the man was from the club. Dad told me he didn't have anyone to spare for West Virginia, and he wouldn't allow someone to go rogue.

Still, whoever he'd been, he was somehow familiar with Dutton and me, and I didn't like that he'd been lingering in Sterling Falls. I didn't want to put Clay in danger and not for the first time did I consider either returning to Florida or taking us on the run. However, a life hopping from one place to another, always looking over our shoulders, wasn't how I wanted to raise Dutton.

I'd encouraged Clay to go to work. I had to be at the hospital. A sense of normalcy was what we needed. There was no other way to act around Dutton, who had gone into sloth mode when told to get dressed. Clay didn't have the heart to challenge him, so he simply wished Dutton a good day and gave me a quick kiss on the cheek before he left for work.

We'd both been disappointed last night hadn't concluded the way it started, but other things took precedence. Dutton would always come first.

After Clay left, I tried to hustle Dutton along, but I was losing my patience. "Put your shoes on."

"I want to wear the pink ones."

I couldn't find the left shoe of the pair, and I was running out of time. I needed to get him to Meredith's before I went to the hospital for my shift.

"It's got to be the blue ones today, little bear," I said, attempting to loosen the clench of my teeth.

As Dutton fell back on the couch, his feet came upward, and he kicked my phone out of my hand. It landed somewhere near the fireplace.

"Dammit, Dutton." I didn't have time or patience for his attitude this morning, but my outburst had nothing to do directly with his behavior. I was on edge because I had decisions to make when I didn't want to implode our lives again.

Wrestling with his feet to slip on the blue gym shoes, Dutton laid back on the couch, unflinching at my hasty movements.

"I'm sorry," I muttered. "I didn't sleep well last night and clearly you didn't either. I'm in a mood, little bear, and you need to give Mama a break today."

Dutton didn't reply but his expression shifted, chagrin for his actions. He stood once his shoes were on and helped himself into his coat as I slipped into mine and grabbed my tote bag.

Once we were out the door and heading toward town, a light dusting of snow fell from the gloomy sky.

"Look, buddy." The winter holidays were a favorite of mine, and the sprinkling of snow hints how close they are. Ducking my head to peer out the windshield better, I glanced up at the clouds beautified by the soft flakes softly drifting downward, covering the car but not sticking to the road.

So, I was surprised when the car suddenly jerked, skidding toward the edge of the road, then hitting the shoulder despite my effort to control the Jetta.

The tires spun in the narrow strip of gravel before we pitched downward into a ditch.

When the airbag explodes, the force knocks into me so hard, I think I passed out a second. I definitely cannot right my bearings at first.

"Dutton," I scream, battling the deployed bag to turn and confirm he is still safely inside the car.

With his booster seat shifted to the right, Dutton is pressed up against the door, but thankfully, he appears unscathed. The front of the car is aimed nose first into the sharp dip off the side of the road.

Dutton's eyes are wide when he looks at me, and I reach behind me to make physical contact with him. The movement pinches my shoulder, but I need him to touch my hand. I need him to speak.

"Tell me if it hurts anywhere, little bear?"

"The seatbelt choked me." His fingers shake as he reaches for the thick strap over his shoulder and near his neck. A red rash swells along the right side of his throat. I'm still concerned he hit his head.

My own shoulders and neck will be stiff later. My face stings from the airbag impact. I'm certain to have some bruising or raw skin in places as well.

"Anywhere else? Did your head jolt forward? Did you hit it on the window? Does your tummy hurt?" I'm trying to think of anything I might miss as the seat belt and booster seat held him tightly in place.

He shakes his head.

"I need to call 911." Reaching for my bag, my own hand visibly trembles. I rustle through the large tote one handed, moving around items, realizing I never made myself lunch. When I don't feel my phone inside the bag, I awkwardly dump the purse upside down, allowing the contents to scatter on the passenger seat. Frustrated when I don't see my phone, I shakily unclip my seat belt, and struggle around the airbag, leaning toward the passenger seat.

Maybe the device fell into the foot well? Then, I remember Dutton kicking outward this morning when I was struggling to get his shoes on him, knocking the phone from my grasp.

Did I retrieve it off the floor?

I can't remember but I'm leaning toward the possibility I did not when the driver's side door opens.

A man with a weathered face and dark, shoulder-length hair stares back at me. The scent of cigarettes, worn leather, and cheap cologne conflicts with the freshness of new falling snow.

I scream before finding my voice which comes out raspy and stressed. "Darren."

"Scar," he reminds me.

Instantly, I shift in my seat glancing at Dutton strapped into the back. I quickly turn toward Darren. *Scar.* Fear fills me.

"Looks like you're in a pickle, Mavis." He bitterly chuckles. "And I realize I'm not exactly your knight in shining armor."

"I've called 911." I lie, unwilling to admit I don't have my phone and have no way to call for help.

"I have a better idea. Why don't you come with me for a while?"

"Darren," I plead. "We've just been in an accident. Dutton might need medical assistance." I don't want Darren looking at Dutton. Don't want him anywhere near the boy, but I'm also hoping he might find a pinch of pity in his measly heart.

Compassion for the child he deserted.

"I'll take you to an urgent care."

This small town doesn't have one nearby. "The hospital would be better." Soon, I'll be considered missing from work and entering the emergency room is our best hope of getting away from Darren.

The man gives me a long hard look. The scar on his face accentuated by the ruddiness of his skin in the cold temperature. He's a long way from Florida or wherever he's been hiding.

"I'll take care of you."

I could argue, questioning if his version of care was like how he took care of my sister, a woman he claimed to love? But arguing with him would not be in my best interest, or Dutton's.

When he clutches my arm, I know better than to fight him. A struggle will only make him grip harder, and I don't want to frighten Dutton. I need to be with Dutton at all times. I need to be cognizant for him.

I awkwardly slip out of the Jetta, discovering my legs are trembling like the rest of me. Shock on two levels is kicking in —the slip into the ditch and Darren's presence.

He leaves me beside the open driver's door, knowing I won't run. I won't leave Dutton, and I follow behind Darren, not wanting his hands on Dutton. He easily opens the rear passenger door, and picks up *my* son, tucking him into his chest. Dutton doesn't struggle, but his eyes remain on me.

"It's okay, buddy. He's going to take us to the hospital." I don't address who Darren is. Dutton has no recollection of a father in his life. He *didn't* have a father. Darren was simply a sperm donor.

When Darren places his hand protectively on Dutton's back, the gesture startles me. Carrying Dutton, he slips once in the wetness of the ditch wall before finishing the climb to the road. He doesn't have the proper boost seat for a child, and I want to suggest we should just wait for the 911 call I *didn't* make to dispatch emergency vehicles. But it's cold this morning, and as the call is a lie, I don't have time to waste hoping someone else will pass our location. I'm surprised no one noticed us slide into the ditch.

"Hate these cages," Darren mutters about his pickup truck, setting Dutton inside the cab. I practically push Darren out of the way, ensuring I enter the truck as well, and Darren doesn't shove me out of the way, then drive off with Dutton.

Being paranoid, I'm overly cautious for good reason. You don't grow up in a motorcycle club with potential kidnapping survival training for nothing.

As Darren circles around the hood of the truck, I glance around the cab for anything that can be used as a weapon or protection. Then Darren hops easily into the driver's seat and I tug Dutton to my side and buckle us together in one seatbelt.

If I thought Darren honestly meant he was taking us to the

hospital, that he had a momentary lapse into being a good man, I was a fool. And as we drive out of town, away from both Sterling Falls and the direction of the hospital, I know Dutton and I are in trouble.

30

[Clay]

"I have news," Stone tells me through the speaker phone in the morning as I tip back in my office chair, staring mindlessly at my computer screen.

"The authorities found Wesley."

I jerk forward, causing the chair to almost hop, and pick up the handset, holding it to my ear as if I can hear him better.

"Where?"

"Minnesota."

I tug the phone away from my ear, realizing the speaker phone is still on. Turning it off, I return the device to the side of my head. "Tell me what happened."

"A woman posted on social media that she was looking for him. His wife in Florida. She wants a divorce, and that abandonment petition timeline is closing in. As he's been missing for over a year, this was her last-ditch effort to have him come forward. Another woman recognized him as her boyfriend, although I imagine he isn't her boyfriend any longer. And now he's in jail."

"So he was in Minnesota," I confirm, piecing two and two together to note it might have been impossible for Wesley to be outside my house last night. The possibility would include late night flights, and Wesley didn't seem like the type of guy to be so frivolous as to book a plane ticket to haunt a kid. He'd moved on to destroying someone else's life.

"That's great news." Although my voice doesn't portray the extent of my relief because that only means *someone else* is out there looking for Mavis and Dutton.

"I called you because I can't get ahold of Mavis."

"She's working and probably doesn't have her phone on her." She told me she keeps it at the nurse's desk most of the day while the younger set often have the device in their pocket. "I'll give her a call."

"Nothing from last night, I'm afraid."

I nod. "Sure. But this is good news," I state, trying to find the silver lining in the stormy clouds above our heads.

Only . . . when I phone Mavis, the call goes to voice mail again and again and again.

By the end of the day, I'm irritated she hasn't answered me, called me back, or responded to any of my texts asking her to call me.

Toward late afternoon, something tells me to call Meredith, Dutton's childcare provider. Sometimes Mavis lingers a bit with the older lady, having a past relationship with her.

Meredith doesn't answer either.

Eventually, I call it a day when it's roughly around the time Mavis should be getting home.

Home. I've never been so excited or eager to get to my place as I've been the past few months. I love my house, but it's become more important to me knowing Mavis and Dutton are there waiting for me.

Stepping outside the Seed & Soil, I'm surprised to see the first dusting of snow covering the grass area to the side of the building. The snow is wet, clinging to cars, but not the gravel lot. Being from Florida, Mavis once told me how much she loves snow and the holiday season which is quickly approaching. The Seed & Soil will be extra busy, and I normally lose myself at work during this time of year as I don't have a wife or children like many of our employees. But this year, I'll be making more of an effort to give time to Mavis and Dutton.

I'm thinking of the unusual activities we can do in the winter and what a romantic snowy night horse ride might be like for Mavis and me when I pull into my driveway and discover her car isn't parked where it normally would be.

Trying not to let panic take over, I park and enter the house to the eerie silence of an empty space.

"Mavis," I call loudly, as if she might be in our bedroom, the furthest point away from the front door. However, with no lights on anywhere, and Dutton not in his room, I already know I'm going to find our room vacant.

For some reason, I check the closet, relieved to see all her clothes still hanging amid mine.

As I walk back to the living room, then stand in the middle, turning in a slow circle like I don't know what to do with myself, something black and shiny catches my eye. Stepping closer to the fireplace, I discover Mavis's phone on the floor, face down, thankfully not cracked. Tapping the screen, a few notifications pop up, showing my last text and the one before that, but I need her passcode to enter the device for further information.

From my phone, I call Meredith again.

"Hey. It's Clay. I'm just checking to see when Mavis might have left your place. She isn't home yet." I don't want to sound like an overbearing lover or controlling man in her life, but I'm uneasy, especially after last night.

"Oh, I'm so glad you called me. I've been trying to reach Mavis all day."

I chuckle, the sound coming out more like I'm choking. "She left her phone at home. Is Dutton okay?" My hand tightens on the device at my ear.

"That's why I was calling. Mavis never dropped Dutton off this morning."

A lump immediately forms in my throat. My heart drops to my stomach.

"Did she call you this morning? Tell you she wasn't coming?"

"She didn't. And it's not like her to *not* call me if plans change. Is she okay?"

I want to say she's fine. I want to say she's home with me. She's safe. But I can't lie, and the truth socks me in the gut.

"I don't know," I whisper. "But I need to go." I click off the phone before Meredith even says goodbye, and call Stone.

"Mavis and Dutton are missing."

Stone inhales sharply before asking a barrage of questions. *When did I see her last? Did she report to work? Was Dutton at Meredith's?* I can only answer two out of three before telling him I'll call the hospital, already fearing what they'll tell me.

When my suspicion is confirmed—Mavis did not report for her shift—I stare at her phone in my other hand, glaring at the ten digits in circles on the home screen, willing the passcode to somehow reveal itself.

I try her birthdate. *Fail.*

Dutton's birthdate. *Fail.*

I wish I knew her sister's birthdate. Maybe her death date. I even try my birthdate, but I'm quickly running out of options before the phone will lock on me.

I try to think of any other number that might be of significance to her.

Then I take a lucky guess as I only need six digits.

7-9-5-8-3-7

Sylver.

The phone unlocks, and I breathe out a deep sigh of relief. Scrolling her favorite contacts for someone I don't know and probably hasn't heard about me, he's the third person I can think of who might know where Mavis and Dutton are.

I click on the contact for Mavis's Dad.

31

[Mavis]

When Darren pulls into the motel parking lot, roughly an hour outside of Sterling Falls on some obscure highway, I have no sense of where we were. The seedy, rundown location screams motel rooms that rent by the hour.

I complained at first. "Dutton needs medical attention." I wanted him checked for a concussion better than the brief scan I've done in Darren's truck. Plus, he needed ointment for the seatbelt burn on his neck.

"The kid looks fine."

The kid? Was he kidding me? *His* kid. Although, Darren had no claim to the boy he created.

Inside the dark room, a musty smell lingers. Darren keeps the blinds closed.

For the longest time, we are quiet. All three of us.

Darren took a seat in a chair two sizes too small for him. He's been staring at his phone but not necessarily scrolling.

I don't have my phone to distract Dutton with *Princess Power* videos, and the television doesn't offer any streaming services. Not that Darren has bothered to turn it on. Instead, I sit on the lumpy double bed against the headboard with Dutton curled into my side. Stroking his hair, I attempt to keep him calm while my heart hammers in my chest.

Eventually, Dutton naps, and I stare at my reflection in the mirror opposite the bed. Black and blue marks are forming beneath my eyes from the pressure of my nose slammed by the air bag. The tension of gripping the steering wheel is starting to settle in, making my upper back and neck stiff. I briefly close my eyes.

When Dutton wakes, he whines, "I'm hungry."

Darren's head shoots upright as if he'd forgotten Dutton is in the room. His large mouth falls open, before he snaps it shut. His gaze fixates on Dutton tucked into my side.

"He's turning soft," Darren grunts.

"He's six," I remind him, not certain Darren can count that high. Or has bothered to recall how much time has passed since he denied this child was his son and dumped my sister. "And he's hungry. There's a difference."

Darren is really referencing Dutton's appearance. A time, or five, he's eyed Dutton's peach sweatshirt with a gold-colored crown.

"He didn't eat breakfast," I explain. "And we missed lunch as well." The digital clock on the nightstand tells me it's after five. Clay must be coming out of his skin at my absence. While he might not have noticed I was missing during the hours of my shift, we do communicate often with text messages and an occasional phone call, and by now he'd notice I haven't responded to any.

It's also well past the time I would be home, making dinner for the three of us.

We'd settle onto the couch for episodes of *Princess Power* we'd seen a hundred times or maybe watch the new horse program Clay found as Dutton's newfound interest leans toward wanting a horse of his own. We'd fall into the routine of getting Dutton ready for bed, tucking him in, and then maybe resettle on the couch for some adult time together. Or we'd head to Clay's bed and—

"I'll order something," Darren huffs, typing away at his phone.

"Why don't you just let us go?" I haven't tried pleading with him yet, knowing a man like Darren needs time, not pressure, to make a decision. Especially as he doesn't appear to have thought anything through. If he wanted to disappear with us, we'd still be on the road. If he wanted only Dutton, I'd have been ditched, or worse. And if he wanted to go back to Florida, and the club, we'd be heading south by now.

"What's the plan here?" I snap.

"Don't ask." His dark beady eyes narrow at me.

"Because you don't know," I argue, knowing I'm pushing him.

"Shut it, Mavis."

When my sister and I were teens, Darren was in his twenties, and I might have talked back to him then, telling him to make me shut up. Knowing he couldn't touch me because of Dad. But at some point, once we aged, Darren thought he'd get away with fooling around with Cecelia. Her body and her emotions. Then again, with Cecilia in her late twenties when she made the mistake of getting involved with Darren, they were both consenting adults. Being pregnant when she turned thirty wasn't how she saw the next decade of her life going. At thirty-one, her life was cut short.

Many in the club blamed Darren. My parents had. I

certainly did. And I wanted him to disappear again, like he'd been missing for the last six years.

Within forty minutes, greasy fast food that I wouldn't typically feed Dutton arrives. He balks at the burger, dripping with ketchup and mustard.

Darren points a French fry at Dutton. "Eat the meat, boy, so you grow up big and strong."

Dutton bends his thin arm, attempting to make a muscle when there is hardly a bulge. "I'm already strong. Clay tells me all the time."

My brows lift. I don't recall Clay saying such a thing but then again Clay is always complimenting Dutton. Telling him how smart he is with his schoolwork. Telling him he can be anything he wants to be, even a Power Princess. Clay doesn't stifle who Dutton is, because he's *six*. And Clay cares about Dutton. I see it in the way he watches him, marveling at him. I hear it in the way he talks to him, like he's not only a child, but a person with thoughts and ideas, feelings and emotions.

"That your man now?" Darren's eyes lift, locking on mine.

"Yes." I don't want to put Clay in any danger as I don't know who Darren is working with, if anyone. But I also want him to understand something. "His brother is the local sheriff, and considering we should be home by now, he'll be looking for us."

The warning is a shot fired. Our absence is not going to go unnoticed.

"You should have stayed in Florida."

"I felt safer here." *Until this moment.*

Keep your friends close and your enemies closer. The idea of keeping my enemies close meant Wesley might be drawn back to Sterling Falls. Darren was the last person I expected to lure to this small town.

"That old man of yours was worthless."

"Daddy?" How dare Darren speak about a senior member of his former club like that?

"Wesley."

How does Darren know about Wesley? Darren was long gone around the time my sister's death happened, and Wesley came into the picture for me.

"Have you been following us?" My brows heavy cinch.

Darren tips his chin at Dutton. "He's my—"

As Dutton and I are sharing a chair, I cover his ears, like Darren is about to swear in front of a six-year-old. His intended statement is worse than any cursing.

Dutton is not Darren's. He's mine.

Darren drops another fry from his fingers and sits back, narrowing his eyes at me.

"He's *my* son." I lower my hands from Dutton's ears. "You have no claim on him."

"Biologically, he's mine." Darren continues as if Dutton isn't present. *Little ears with big listening power.*

"And in every other way, he's *mine*. Cecelia wanted it that way."

"Don't mention her," he growls.

"Don't you," I warn.

He dropped my sister like she was some sweet butt, a woman hanging around the club easily offering up sexual favors in hopes of a higher status within the club ranks. But Cecelia was better than that, and I never understood what she saw in Darren in the first place to make her start sleeping with him. Or how he thought he was worthy of my sister.

"I could take you to court."

This is one of my biggest fears, as Darren does have paternal rights, even if the birth certificate is blank in the box that reads *Father's Name*. However, I can't imagine a court in America that would give rights to an absentee father who has had no recorded address for six years. I doubt he's employed.

And I don't care. I also know Darren has lived a lifestyle that prides itself on living outside the law. He won't take legal action, but he could try to kidnap Dutton and disappear on me.

"What would you do with him?" I sneer at the flat burger bun dripping with sauces that Dutton hasn't touched. "What's his favorite meal? His favorite book? His favorite shirt?"

"He wouldn't be wearing no damn girl sweatshirt, that's for sure." Darren nods at the one Dutton wears.

I tug Dutton into my side. Everything in me wants to shut this conversation down, while I'd love nothing more than to continue defending Dutton . . . just not in his presence.

"He is who he is," I snap. "You accept him as such, or never see him again." Just like he hasn't seen him in six years. "What do you really want, Darren?"

Because I don't think it's his son or the right to claim who is biologically his.

"I want back in the club."

Ah, there it is. I lean back in the chair and run my hand up Dutton's little back.

Going rogue can be dangerous for a member. Going rogue is also rough when the club is all you've known. They are family and friends, camaraderie and competition. Being a member is everything to some.

Not me. I'd wanted out, and being a woman, I wasn't ever officially in.

"You want me to call Dad." It isn't a question.

"I want to explain myself."

"Explain it to me." Darren isn't getting anywhere near a conversation with my father if he can't tell me first what he wants to say. Daddy won't give him a breath of a chance, especially if he knows Darren has Dutton and me held as hostages. And if I can't help Darren get what he wants, so I get what I want, which is no contact with him ever again, we're at a stalemate. Or worse.

Darren might be a coldhearted man, but I'd like to hope he doesn't have the emotional strength to harm his kid. As for me, I'm another story.

Darren and I stare at one another, eyes narrowed, neither willing to look away.

"Not in front of the kid."

"And what do you suggest I do with him?" I'm not letting Dutton out of my sight.

Darren shrugs. "What do you do when you need a minute?"

I might let him watch television as a distraction, a guilty form of babysitting. Or I could stick him in the tub, the running water drowning out a conversation. Turning to Dutton, I swipe a hand through his hair. He looks tired, and I know he's still hungry. Maybe a bath will distract him.

"How about a bath, buddy?"

He looks up at me. "Are we spending the night here?"

I glance at Darren. "I hope not."

Darren simply shakes his head. He doesn't have an answer. Hasn't made up his mind.

"Let's give you a bath for now." Gently, I nudge him off our shared seat and guide him to the bathroom. While the water runs, Dutton steps into the tub, swiping his hands underneath the stream coming from the faucet. I check out his thin neck again, angry once more that Darren didn't stop at a pharmacy for ointment or pain meds.

Leaving the door slightly ajar so I can see Dutton in the tub, I step back into the bedroom area, leaning against the door jamb, and purse my lips while looking at Darren.

Hoping the water drowns out Darren's story, I tip up my chin. "So speak."

Darren moves to the edge of the bed, eyes fixed in the direction of the bathroom where I've closed the door as a shield from Darren but can still see Dutton myself. I'm working double time here, watching Dutton out of the corner of my eye while keeping my sights on Darren.

"I loved her," Darren states.

A fire rushes up my belly. "You had a funny way of showing it."

"Denying I did was my way to prove it. I had to protect her."

I glare at him. How dare he think denying his kid and pushing my sister to the side was protecting her?

"If I'd claimed her, she'd have been marked." He swallows hard, hands clasping together between his spread thighs. "But not claiming her damned her anyway."

He blinks rapidly before clearing his throat. I don't offer him any sympathy. I'd been there when my sister found out she was pregnant and there for the aftermath of Darren's rejection. I was there as she held her son for the first time, and there when my sister was discovered, her last breath gone.

"I thought I was doing right by her."

"Save it," I snap. "You broke her heart." Thankfully, not her spirit, though. My sister was a vibrant force which I imagine might have caused Darren's attraction to her. Not that Cecilia wasn't also beautiful in body and mind, but her energy was contagious.

"It broke mine as well," he admits. The large man before me, a wall of strength and pride, looks ready to crumble. "And I hate myself every day for what I did to her. What happened to her."

"You killed her."

"I didn't." He sits up straighter.

While he hadn't been the one to pull the trigger, my sister was dead because of him. Someone had it out for him and took my sister out as a warning.

I check on Dutton, my eyes filling with tears at his loss. My loss. He'll never know what he's missing, and many days I consider myself a poor substitute. But we are all each other has, and I've come to terms with that.

Me and Dutton . . . and Clay.

I close my eyes, once more thinking about him, and how he must be going mad. I hope he understands I didn't leave by choice. I'm hoping someone found my car in the ditch, and he found my phone at his house. I'm praying he takes each clue as a sign that I'd never willingly let him go, unless the decision was made for me.

"What does this have to do with Dad or the club?"

"I want a meeting. I want to explain."

I turn my gaze toward him again. "And you're holding us hostage?"

"Collateral."

"What if Dad refuses?"

"I have faith he won't."

I equally hope that's the case.

"I don't have my phone." Surely, Darren's noticed by now, especially as he didn't give me time to gather my things.

His brow arches, but he sits up straighter. "You can use mine."

I'm afraid Dad won't recognize the number. Or he will. Or it's blocked. But I'm willing to try anything.

I step into the bathroom and turn off the water, allowing Dutton to simply soak and play with a thin washcloth and a plastic drinking cup that had been wrapped in a protective cellophane cover near the sink.

Stepping out of the bathroom, but still keeping my eyes on Dutton, I hold out my hand. Darren sets his phone on my palm but pauses, keeping his fingers on the device.

"No funny business, Mavis. Straight talk. No locations. Nothing yet. He agrees to a chat."

"Or else?"

Darren drops his gaze. He doesn't want to answer me, but I already know what he might do, what he is capable of.

While my heart hammers, I'm equally calm. Maybe too calm. Maybe this is shock, or fear on the most base level. I'm numb.

"And if he agrees?"

"Then I'll tell him where and when."

Being that my father is in Florida, some five states away, and Darren isn't likely to let us go until he talks to Dad, we're stuck.

"Let me call Clay. I don't want him to worry. Plus, his brother, Stone, the sheriff . . ." I let the thought linger. The authorities will be looking for us and that's more trouble for Darren.

"Hammer first."

Hearing my dad's road name stiffens my back, but when Darren releases his phone in my hand, I make the call. It goes unanswered. I'm positive dad lost this number and won't answer a random one he doesn't recognize.

My next hope is my mom. "Let me call Mom. She can pass this number to Dad."

Darren eyes me suspiciously before nodding. It takes a minute to recall my parent's house phone number. Shocking they still have a house phone, but mom feels safer with the landline service. She answers on the second ring.

"Hello."

"Mama." My voice cracks and my gaze catches on Darren. He shakes his head slowly side to side, warning me to keep it together. He also lifts his hand, holding it close to my ear, before capturing my wrist and pulling the phone downward. He clicks on the speaker button.

"Mavis, baby. It's been too long. How are you? How's Dutton?"

"We're both . . . okay. Mom, I don't have long to talk, and I really need to get in touch with Daddy."

"He's not here, honey. Got a call and said he needed to roll. You know how he is." She chuckles. "Before he left, though, he told me if you called, he wanted to know where you were. Ask if there was a way to reach you."

If my mother is concerned, she's giving nothing away. And if she knows more than she's leading on, she's a darn good actress.

"I'm—" Darren's hand covers the phone, ready to pull it from mine. "I need Dad to call this number." I'm practically yelling, knowing I'm running out of time because Darren is running out of patience.

"Let me get a pen." The comment buys me time. Darren takes pity that my parents are older, pen and paper is their thing.

"Okay, honey. Shoot."

I call out the number as Darren mouths the digits. Then I ask Mom to repeat it back to me.

"Are you in some kind of trouble?" she finally asks.

"A butterfly is never trapped." My voice is hushed, shaky and rough, and before Mom can respond, Darren clicks off the call.

Our eyes meet. "You're walking a fine line, Mavis."

I glance at Dutton again, my throat thickening. I don't have a choice. If the proverbial line is thin, I need to cross it to keep Dutton safe.

And the code to Mom should explain it all.

We *are* in trouble.

32

[Clay]

I pace the house, no longer able to ask the same question I've asked for the last hour.

Where could they be?

My family has rallied around me. Stone arrived first with Knox on his heels. Then Sebastian and Ford surprisingly came together as Enya and Adara went to stay with Cadence and the girls. Vale also dropped Hudson off with Cadence, and my sister is here keeping the coffee pot full. Even Judd is present.

As Ford had an incident this summer with his little June, he understands my fears for Dutton. Sebastian also sympathizes as a lunatic had once cornered Enya and Adara.

"Shouldn't we be out there?" I wave toward the wall of windows. "Doing something."

Stone has already made the all-call for a missing child and mother, both potentially in danger. He told me the first forty-eight hours are crucial. Being that it's after five at night, the

November sky is dark, the mountain air is cold, and I'm struggling not to fear the worst.

"Perry?" Stone glances at me as he answers his phone, which turns my head.

Perry called me a few times earlier in the day, but as I'm still not speaking to him, I didn't answer.

I signal Stone to put Perry on speaker phone. As I'm amped up, I'm itching for a fight with my old friend because I'm thinking that *mothertrucker* he brought to the Halloween party has something to do with this situation.

Stone clicks the phone over to speaker, and before I talk, I hear Perry in mid-sentence. ". . . the contents of a purse were spilled in the front seat. Didn't look like anything was taken. Leather bag on the floor. Wallet still present. Cash in the side pocket. No cell phone, though."

I glance at the phone that has been laying on the peninsula counter between my kitchen and living room area. I plugged it into the charger, hoping Mavis might call her own phone for some silly reason.

"Any sign of struggle in the car?" Stone asks, calm and professional.

I close my eyes at the thought and swallow hard.

"As I told Harris, we didn't notice anything. He inspected it for traces of blood or injury."

Bile rises up my throat.

"Airbag had exploded, so that might have hurt. Cracked windshield. Kid car seat still intact in the backseat."

"Where are they?" I snap, rushing toward Stone, who holds the phone away from me as if I'll try to snatch it out of his hands.

"Clay?"

"Perry, I swear to God if this has anything to do with—" Knox's hand on my bicep shuts me up.

"You need to let Stone handle this," he mutters beside me.

"Thanks for the update, Perry," Stone interjects.

"Yeah, I'm sorry I didn't get to it earlier. With the black ice this morning, there's been a slew of vehicles off the road. I'd been trying to call Clay all afternoon once we pulled this one from the ditch and found the wallet."

I close my eyes again. *If only* I'd answered my phone earlier. *If only* I'd insisted we stay home today. *If only* I'd told Mavis and Dutton I loved them.

The idea of loving hard and then losing them was exactly what I feared most. That I wouldn't survive the loss, but I wasn't giving up. Mavis was coming home to me. With Dutton.

I don't hear the rest of the conversation between Perry and Stone as I head to my room, step into the closet and find Mavis's butterfly shawl hanging on a hanger. She told me she'd been fortunate not to lose it in the house fire. Something about having it professionally cleaned as the fabric was so delicate, so it wasn't in the house fire.

For about five seconds earlier in the day, I thought that Mavis might have left me. That living out here wasn't enough for her, like I'd asked her only a few nights ago. Or that the man who'd peeped in the window had something to do with Mavis's past and she ran. Or that she simply had a change of heart and didn't love me.

But I didn't want to believe any of those things about her, about us, and the butterfly shawl hanging in the closet, which is something so precious to her, and the findings of her scattered purse, tells me Mavis is in trouble.

"Butterfly," I whisper, pulling the flimsy fabric to my nose and inhaling Mavis's intoxicating floral scent that lingers in the fabric. "Please be safe. Come back to me."

Or better yet, I'll come find you.

With newfound determination, I return to the living room. "I'm going out. I need to do something."

Stone is still standing where he took the call from Perry.

"You aren't going anywhere. I know it's hard to sit still, and you feel cooped up, but Mavis needs you here." Stone points to the floor. "If that guy comes back—"

"What guy?" Vale asks, her head lifting and swinging in my direction.

"Or if she calls your phone," Stone continues, ignoring Vale. "I can coach you through how to help her give us information."

The implication is clear. *If* Mavis is in trouble, Stone knows we need to work fast to get any info we can from her, to help her.

"What guy?" Vale asks again and I realize my family isn't up to speed on everything. Although many of them know about the house fire and Wesley being on the run, they don't know about last night's situation or my suspicions that Mavis's past might be catching up to her in a different manner.

Stone knows the details about Mavis not being Dutton's biological mother. The detail felt too important not to share, despite betraying Mavis's trust. He also knows Mavis's history. Her motorcycle club upbringing in Florida. She hasn't told me much. Not a name. Not a location. But her dad was still labeled as a favorite in her phone, and I told Stone about the call I made.

Mr. Grant was just as concerned as I was about his missing daughter and grandson.

Stone told me the less I knew about her past lifestyle, the better, although I suspect he knows a few additional details as he was in contact with Mavis after the house fire and with Wesley's disappearance.

However, my only concern is getting Mavis and Dutton back.

Come on, butterfly. Send me a sign.

33

[Clay]

Nearing the twenty-four hour mark since the discovery of missing persons, I'm lying awake on my bed, staring at the dark ceiling. Nearly one full day since I've seen Mavis and Dutton, and I'm coming out of my skin.

I'd wallow in sadness if I wasn't so angry. Angry that they are gone. Angry that I'm certain someone took them. Angry that it isn't Wesley which means I have no idea who it is, other than the possibility of some mysterious man peeping through my window two nights ago.

I've failed Mavis. Accepting that failure, though, means I've given up and I'm not giving up.

She's out there somewhere with Dutton, and until they are safely returned to me, I won't rest.

I've never wished daylight to appear so quickly as I have lying on my bed, waiting for the seconds to tick by.

Unfortunately, the new day is just as gloomy as yesterday. Snow is lightly falling again this morning. The weather is cold, although I don't think I feel the temperature. At the moment, I'm numb. Frozen with fear.

At first light, a crew has been assembled to start searching the woods closest to where the car skidded off the road. If a second set of tracks had been apparent in the gravel shoulder, it was covered by Perry's tow truck, through no fault of his, when his truck pulled up and then backed into the ditch to pull Mavis's car out.

Mavis and Dutton won't have set off on foot without being coerced. Still, Stone thinks a group should scope out the closest woods. He doesn't let me go.

And Mavis and Dutton could be anywhere, and nowhere near Sterling Falls by now, if someone picked them up. Someone I don't have a clue to recognize.

I'm kicking myself once more that I don't have a better description of the man who stood at the window. In my head, he keeps merging with the dick in the Walmart aisle but that doesn't seem right or fair. Not that a stranger insulting Dutton deserves fairness, but I don't want an innocent man apprehended for a crime he didn't commit.

Still . . . I can't quell the niggling sensation that the two men might be the same person.

Roughly an hour later, the rest of my family convenes at my house again. While Sebastian and Ford wanted to be part of the search crew, Stone asked them to come here instead. Which I'm assuming is for moral support, but I'm starting to feel suffocated by the concern of my family.

Knox is with the fire department, volunteering his time, while Stone is manning the situation from my kitchen table instead of his office.

And while all this is happening, I'm hiding in the long hallway, in the place opposite where a stranger stood the other night, staring outside. Eventually, I press my forehead to the glass and close my eyes a second. I breathe in the emptiness. The silence without Mavis and Dutton filling my home. The loss of Mavis and Dutton will crush me. There is no simple way to describe the pain.

Like a shattered piece of pottery, the pieces of me will be unrepairable.

The sensation is something I've always feared. Watching my father lose the love of his life, then drown himself in bottle after bottle, I never wanted to know love like he felt because I didn't want to know such heartbreaking loss. It didn't stop me from wanting to help people. To save *them*. I just never wanted to feel saved myself, for fear the rescue would end.

As I open my eyes, a figure is walking up my drive. A woman wearing a coat I don't recognize, carrying a child. A child with a blanket wrapped over him.

"Butterfly," I whisper, pulling my head back from the window for a clearer view.

I blink once, drawing them better into focus as they continue toward the house.

"Mavis." I yell, like she can hear me through the glass. Then I'm running for the front door, ignoring the shift in my family as people stand from the couch and Stone enters the living room from the kitchen.

I'm out the door without coat or hat or care as I race toward Mavis and Dutton. My vision blurs but I keep my sight on them until my arms are around them both and I'm kissing Mavis's head.

"Oh my God, butterfly. Thank God." I pull back, hands on her arms, scanning her face, looking for injury while at the same time focusing on her standing before me. She's here, beneath my hands.

Then I notice the blue marks beneath her eyes and the stiffness in her shoulders. I have so many questions and they all tumble out at the same time.

"Are you okay? Is Dutton?" I place my hand on the back of his head, and he turns toward me, reaching out his arms for me. Tugging him to me, I press kisses in his hair while still addressing Mavis. "What happened? Where have you been? Who hurt you?"

Tears roll down Mavis's face, her mouth falling open and then closing again. She trembles while shaking her head. I'm asking too much too fast.

Unable to be another second without touching her, I wrap my arm around her again. And then, she's hugging Dutton and me at the same time. The leather jacket over her shoulders smells like stale cigarettes and cheap cologne, and it slips to the ground with her embrace.

Suddenly, the deep rumble of several motorcycles hits my ears, followed by the crunch of gravel as three imposing metal machines roll up my drive. The noise is deafening until they stop only a few feet from us. My brother Judd rides, and Sebastian owns a bike, but their rides are nothing like these powerhouses.

After the first man shuts off his engine, he kicks the stand and climbs off the motorcycle. For a moment, Mavis and I stare in the same direction, our arms wrapped around one another until Dutton whispers, "Granddad."

Recognition slowly happens. The eyes uncovered by sunglasses are the same as Mavis's. Dark hair is released from the helmet. He lowers a scarf that covers his nose, mouth, and neck.

Time stands still as Mavis doesn't move forward and the man keeps his distance.

"Baby girl," he states, his voice rough from age.

"Daddy?" She steps out from underneath my arms and stares back at her father. "What are you doing *here*?"

She doesn't sound surprised to see him as much as she's bewildered he is in my driveway.

"I got your message." His gaze transfers to me. "You must be Clay."

Mavis turns only her head, an apology as well as stark vulnerability on her face, but she has nothing to apologize for. Or anything to fear.

However, I am a bit concerned. I don't know what this man and his biker brothers are doing here either. While I'd called him with my concerns for Mavis's safety, he was short with his responses, ending our call with "I'm on it."

I had no idea what that meant. Yet, here he is.

"Thanks for the call," he offers me.

Mavis's brows lift. "You called my dad?"

"Butterfly, I would have gone to the ends of the earth to find you."

"Butterfly?" Her father chokes and we both turn back to him. The large man's hard eyes soften a bit as he looks at his daughter. "He knows your nana's name for you?"

Her nana called her that name? I had no idea. It hits me as I stand here, there is so much I still don't know about Mavis in the a few short months I've known her, but I want to know it all like I once told her. I want *time* to learn everything.

I slip my arm around Mavis's waist, gently tugging her so her back hits my chest while Dutton clings to my neck and side. I don't know if the move is my fear that Mavis will go off with them, or a protective statement that I won't let her go without a fight.

Her father catches the movement. I'm staking my claim.

"This what you want now?" He nods at us, while his eyes remain on his daughter. Then his gaze shifts over my shoulder. I don't dare turn for the house or my family whom I'm certain are flanking me protectively as they watch this play out.

"This is what I've always wanted," she tells him.

"Always were a little different."

I'm not certain if the comment is an insult or compliment, or simply a statement that Mavis wanted something other than the lifestyle she'd been brought up in. Either way, she stiffens beneath my arm, and I squeeze, hopefully reminding her I love her as she is.

"Not shacking up with him like you did with that fool Wesley." Her father wants confirmation.

"Daddy," she groans.

"With all due respect, sir." I begin. "Speak to her again like that, and we'll have a problem."

He eyes me like he can't imagine what sort of trouble I'd make. And while I'm not a fighter by nature, I'm also easily twenty-plus years younger than him and I'll hold my own until the last strike.

Slowly, his mouth ticks up and I see the similarity to Mavis's smile.

"Got some big balls." He chuckles.

"Daddy," Mavis chides. "Not in front of Dutton."

His thick brows lift, as if something crossed his mind.

"How come my grandson isn't giving this old man a hug?" He tips up his chin, waiting for me to release Dutton, but Dutton isn't letting me go, burrowing his face into my neck. His cold nose against my skin reminds me we are outside in the November chill. I should be inviting everyone inside but all I really want is to collect Mavis and Dutton and take us to my bed, where I'll keep them wrapped in a protective cocoon.

"It's been a long twenty-four hours," Mavis answers.

"He hurt you?" Her father isn't talking about me anymore, and I want to know who he references.

Mavis shakes her head, lowering it. "He just wants to chat."

"We're going there next, but I wanted to see for myself that you were safe and whole." Her father pauses a second. "I love you, baby girl."

"I know, Daddy." With that, she uses her hand to remove my arm from her waist and she slowly walks to her father. There's no rush in her steps, more like she's hesitating, but the second he opens his arms, she melts into them, letting his leather-covered limbs engulf her. He kisses the top of her head, mutters something to her, and she looks up at him.

With a slow smile on her face, she responds, glances at me, and then pulls out of his arms.

"Dutton." Her father's tone is sharp. "Give Granddad a hug and then I'll let you be."

Dutton wiggles from my arms and rushes to his grandpa, whose entire demeanor changes. He smiles wide as he hikes Dutton easily into the air, tossing him upward and catching him before tucking him into his side. He says something to Dutton as well and Dutton wraps his arms around the man's neck, but quickly releases him.

"Look after your mama," he says, patting Dutton's behind before setting his grandson on his feet and watching him rush back to Mavis.

The motorcycle man does another swiping gaze over me and whomever is behind me.

"I'm still gonna be available whenever you need me," he states to Mavis.

"*If* I need you," she replies, but slowly smiles back at him.

"Don't get sassy like your sister," he teases. "And call your mama again. She'll want to know you're safe."

He nods at me, with no other acknowledgement, and climbs back on his bike. Mavis walks with Dutton back to me and curls into my side. I wrap both arms around her again, squeezing her tight as her father and his two men turn in my drive and then disappear down my driveway, the crunch of gravel softening, the scream of motorcycles picking up as they first hit pavement.

Then silence.

I kiss the top of Mavis's head. "Let's get inside."

Releasing her, I reach down for Dutton and hike him up to my hip. When I turn around, my family is standing in a straight line. Ford and Sebastian both stand with arms crossed over their chests. Judd has his hands lowered behind his back. Stone has his hand hitched into his belt, fingers near his holstered gun. Even Vale is standing in the cold without a jacket, hands tucked into the back pockets of her jeans.

A man who has siblings who love him cannot do worse.

Families come in all combinations. Siblings with no functioning parent. A mother to her sister's child. An orphan with an aunt that loves him. A set of men collected by a common interest. And yet, love is no less in any form where family is concerned. The desire to keep the ones we love safe and protected, comforted and claimed is no different.

And this is my family. My siblings and their extended families.

Mavis and Dutton.

The two who have claimed my heart. Forever.

34

———

[Mavis]

Clay has so many questions, and I want to tell him everything. While I am exhausted, I am also wired.

Once we are ushered inside, I am still trying to mentally catch up with all that happened. Plus, there was my dad suddenly in the driveway flanked by two men I didn't recognize. The club is changing. I don't want the details.

Unfortunately, the audience in Clay's house quickly closes in on me when I know his family means well. They'd rallied to be here for him, and they deserved my story for the worry it caused their brother.

Still, I feel uneasy and pressured.

Sensing my hesitation, and maybe recognizing that Dutton and I need food and a hot shower before anything else, people slowly peel away from Clay's place. From *our* home.

First, Sebastian and Ford. Then Judd. Vale told Clay about some dish she'd made and was ready to be heated up while

Stone gathered papers and equipment off the kitchen table. As local law enforcement, he'd linger to hear what happened.

Before each family member left, I am given a tight hug and encouraging words.

Glad you're back.

Glad you're safe.

Gave him quite a fright.

Happy nothing happened to you.

Had nothing happened?

With only Stone and Clay remaining, I set Dutton up in his room with another *Princess Power* video, explaining I needed a few minutes to tell them what happened. Still, I hesitated before closing his door.

"Can you leave it open a sliver?" he asks, eyes wild. He's been through a lot in the last twenty-four hours as well as me, and I worry about the emotional damage this latest incident will bring him.

"Of course, little bear. I'll only be in the living room with Stone and Clay."

I blow him a kiss and he weakly smiles, settling into his bed when it's only mid-morning. We are definitely calling today a snow day from school and a sick day from work.

I hadn't forgotten that I'd missed yesterday and should be at the hospital today. Vale told me she'd called Trinity, hoping she could help with my sudden absence. Vale explained about the accident and then said I had a family emergency. I hadn't called in because I'd left my phone behind in my haste.

I was going to owe both Trinity and Vale for their help, which I'd said to Vale.

"Family doesn't owe. We love," Vale assured me.

The thought nearly brought me to tears. I suspect more tears would come later.

Entering the living room, Clay has a fire burning in the fireplace and he motions for me to take a seat beside him on the couch. Wrapping his arm around me, he tugs me to slouch back into the familiar cushions.

"Want some tea? Coffee?" Stone offers.

Coffee would be great, but I shake my head, wanting to get this interview over with.

"I'd like to bring you into the station to take a statement, but I thought it might be best to chat here first. I know you've been through an ordeal, but I want you to tell me everything while it's still fresh."

I nod and Clay presses a kiss to my temple.

Starting at the beginning, I tell them about the accident and how my phone was left behind. I tell them about Darren's arrival, where he took us, and our long stay in the motel.

Stone holds up a hand. "Did he hurt you? Or Dutton?" His gaze falls to the bruising beneath my eyes.

"They're from the accident. The airbag."

Clay relaxes beside me.

Then, I explain who Darren is in relation to Dutton.

"He's his father," Clay gasps. "Where the fuck has he been for six years?"

I appreciate Clay's upset on Dutton's behalf and even Stone gives a tight smile of support, but then he clears his throat, warning his brother not to interrupt me.

"He'd disappeared. Gone rogue, is what the club calls it. He didn't confirm or deny my suspicion that he might have been trying to find who killed my sister."

"Butterfly," Clay hums in sympathy, pulling me tighter to his side.

"He *claims* he loved her and rejected her to protect her. Her and Dutton. He worried that if he took Cecilia and Dutton as his family, they'd always be in danger. It hadn't mattered." I swallow hard, tears filling my eyes.

"Maybe we can talk about this later?" Clay looks at his

brother who is watching me. I shake my head, knowing I need to get it out now.

"What did Darren want with you and Dutton?"

"He wanted a meeting with my dad. Wants to explain his absence. I'd told Darren the less I knew the better." I didn't want to know where he'd been or who he'd seen or what he'd done.

Stone nods in understanding.

"So he held you as hostages? Kidnapped you?" Clays voice rises. "You need to press charges."

"No charges." I stare at Stone instead of Clay. "This is club business and I'm letting Dad handle it."

While my father isn't always reasonable, or even just, for that matter, I gave him my word that I believed Darren had legitimate information the club would want to hear. And that made it club business, not mine.

"I'm never going to really be free from them," I whisper. "They are my family. But again, the less I know and the further I am from them, the better we are. Dutton and me."

Stone keeps his gaze on me. Clay is shaking his head.

"I return to them and live in fear. Or I live my life." And maybe still live in fear. But I'm not looking backward. I'm not going backward. I want the life I'm hoping I still have with Clay.

"He simply let you go when your father agreed to meet him?" Stone asks.

The most shocking concept, and one I'm still concerned will come back to haunt me, is that Darren let us go. "He did."

"I don't like this," Clay argues, stiffening once more beside me. "Will he be back? Will he use them again? Will he try to take Dutton from us?"

"He won't be back." While I wouldn't normally believe a word Darren said, he gave Dad his word he'd never come near us again. *If* the club took him back, and it was a strongly worded *if,* along with a few other expletives, then Darren forfeited any claim to Dutton. The club would always be more important to Darren, and he didn't know his son. He had no rights to him.

But I stumble after explaining all this on what Clay has said and turn my head to look at him.

"Us?" I question.

"Us?" Clay's brows pinch. "You and me. Dutton is *ours*." He says is so plainly, so easily, like it's something we've already discussed and agreed upon. *Ours*. He isn't asking; he is claiming. And I am not complaining. I don't have the bandwidth to think or argue or make more decisions.

Clay kisses my forehead before turning toward Stone. "So now what? What else do you need?"

Stone straightens where he's been seated on the ottoman. "I don't think I want to know where their meeting is being held." He sighs. "And I'm going to send out a call that you and Dutton have been found."

Returned.

"What will you say about that?" I ask.

Stone purses his lips, thinking long and hard. "You had an accident. Didn't have your phone. Thought you were headed toward town on foot and got turned around. Let's say you spent the night in an abandoned barn and then figured out where you were in the morning. Closer to home than you thought."

Stone is good.

"What about Dutton?" Clay asks, turning his head from me to Stone and back.

None of us want him living a lie, or feeling he needs to tell one.

"What's most important for him is he is home. Safe and loved. And he won't ever see this Darren again." There isn't a question in Stone's voice. His furrowed brow hammers home the thought.

I shake my head. I don't intend to return to Florida, and if my parents want to see Dutton, they can come to Sterling Falls.

"Don't forget to tell her about Wesley," Stone states and I glance at Clay.

"What about him?"

With a slow smile, he states, "They found him. He's been arrested in Minnesota."

What a relief, but also one more thing I can't process yet. For now, I'm simply *free*, knowing justice will be served by Wesley and Darren will pay his dues to the club.

Stone stands, and Clay shifts to his feet as well. They clasp hands and pull each other into a hug.

"Thank you," Clay states. "For everything."

Stone simply shakes his head, cupping the back of his brother's neck. "This is what we do for each other."

Clay nods and I stand, too. Holding open my arms, Stone pulls me into a bear hug of an embrace.

"Thank you for looking after him," I mutter to his chest.

Stone surprises me by kissing the top of my head. "Now you look after him."

Our voices are not quiet, so I'm certain Clay hears all. His hand comes to my lower back as I step out of Stone's embrace.

"I plan to."

THE REMAINDER OF THE DAY, we are simply lazy, sticking close to one another. Clay keeps the fireplace lit, and we watch kid movies and horse videos. We eat Vale's casserole, and Dutton and I nap on the couch pressed into Clay. When bedtime arrives, Dutton had already taken a real bath in the middle of the day, and eagerly climbs into his bed, happy to be back in familiar sheets with his beloved Violet bear.

"Sleep tight," Clay says smoothing the covers over Dutton,

which are pulled up to his neck. "Violet bear is here to keep you safe. Just like your mama and me."

"Mama bear and papa bear," Dutton says, keeping his gaze on Clay.

"Papa bear." Clay swallows hard, before lowering toward Dutton, and pressing a kiss to his forehead. "You need anything, we are right down the hall."

If I asked, Clay won't mind sleeping with Dutton between us. He wants both of us as close as I want both of them. But I need some alone time with Clay as much as I think he wants that time with me.

"Love you, little bear." I say, taking a turn to kiss him again.

"I love you, too, Mama."

Tears burn my eyes again.

"Love you, buddy," Clay adds as I swipe at my cheeks as they spill over.

"Love you, buddy." Dutton rolls his lips inward while a grin curls his mouth, fighting back a little hint of sass.

He's such a good boy, and with Clay and I here for him, he's going to have a great life.

35

[Clay]

Stepping into the hallway, we both stall after I close the door, leaving it open enough to paint a thin sliver of light across the floor of Dutton's room.

Tonight, there will be no man peeping through the window. Dutton let it be revealed the man in Walmart was the man who took him and Mavis, and I'm certain he was the same man outside my house.

And Wesley is behind bars on a number of criminal charges.

However, I don't want to think about either man. My woman and her son are safely back inside my home.

"What do you need from me?" I ask her as we remain in the hallway. I gingerly reach for the skin beneath her eyes. The black and blue marks mixing with exhaustion. "I want to be with you. Hold you tight against my body and be one with you, but I understand if you need space. Time and patience before we touch like that again."

Mavis stares at me.

"You need control, butterfly." Her life has been chaos in the past twenty-four hours. Past year. Past *years*. But not the last few months, because she's been with me, and I want her to see that we are as stable as it can get. "You tell me what you want from me right now."

Mavis steps up to me, close enough to be hugged but not reaching out for me. Swallowing hard, she lowers her gaze. Her eyes brim with tears. "I need you to take care of me, Clay."

Reaching up for her hair, I brush it over her ear.

"Always, baby. But tonight, be specific." Not more than a second passes when an idea strikes me. "Take a bath with me?"

Her head pops up and she nods once, blinking those normally lustrous eyes which are presently sad and dark. I take her hand and lead her to my guest bathroom, which has a soaker tub. The basin is deep and large enough for two, so I set the water to a comfortable temperature and while the tub fills, I strip her of her clothes before removing mine. The way she wraps her arms around her middle, she comes off as shy, but I don't want her ever hiding from me.

"Where does it hurt?" I question, knowing not all her bruises are visible.

"My shoulders and neck are stiff," she admits, reminding us both that she endured an accident first.

Taking her hand, I step into the tub first, then help her over the edge. "Feel good?"

She nods, and I lower us both, settling her between my bent, spread legs. In this position, I pepper her upper back and shoulders with kisses, tenderly covering all her aches.

Then, I press her forward to wash her hair, taking my time to rinse the long locks. I sponge her back with a washcloth and stroke down her arms before settling her against my chest.

I want her to relax, and we sit in silence for a while, soaking up the warmth of the water and the comfort of our closeness.

"If he'd hurt you . . ." I swallow the thickness in my throat. "I don't know what I'd have done."

Mavis runs her hands over my arms around her middle.

"I might never be free," she finally whispers. "I might have to always look over my shoulder. Always worry double time about Dutton's safety or mine. I don't want to bring danger to your door."

"Hey," I murmur, wrapping my arms around her and pressing a kiss to her shoulder. "You didn't bring danger here. And I'll always have your back, butterfly. I'm always going to be equally concerned about you and Dutton. Your safety. Your happiness."

"I don't know that I've ever been happier than being here with you."

"Then why do you sound so sad about it?" I chuckle, cupping her chin and turning her head so she'll look at me.

"I don't want to be a burden."

"Mavis." My tone strengthens.

"You heard my dad. I'm different than them."

I did hear him and he's an ass for saying such a thing to his daughter. I still didn't know if it was meant as an insult. He could have intended it as a compliment, meaning she's smarter, stronger, better in some way. But the comment clearly hurt her. "You're perfect."

Her gaze lowers. "When I was younger, I just wanted a simple life. A nice, quiet house. A stable income. A job that made me feel good about myself."

"You have all that," I remind her.

"But I also wanted the fairy tale. A man by my side. The wedding and dress. A family to call my own." She doesn't look at me while she talks.

"Who doesn't want the fairy tale, butterfly? Growing up I

wanted my mom to be alive and my dad to love his kids. I wanted our beautiful, growing family to stay the way it was. Life happens, and I don't say that as an excuse. Life is the fairy tale, if you look in all the little cracks and corners."

Mavis still doesn't look at me.

"One day, you meet a woman in your store, and you want her, but you can't have her. And still, you long for her. Your day brightens when you catch a glimpse of her in town, or when she smiles at you like you are old friends."

"Clay," she whispers, her hands tightening around my wrists over her chest.

"And you don't give up faith that you'll deserve a smile like that from someone, if it can't be her." I kiss her neck and murmur near her ear, "How lucky am I, that one day, the queen became mine?"

Mavis twists a little more, giving me a glare like she doesn't believe me.

"Those smiles became mine." I kiss her shoulder. "And she still brightens my day when she looks at me." I press the softest kiss to her jaw.

Then I pull back so we can look at one another better. Only, she shrugs. "Seems silly to still wish for the fairy tale at forty, though."

"Why?" My brows pinch. I'm truly puzzled. "So the story might change a bit, but it has no less value to *you*."

Mavis doesn't look up, her hands coasting over the smooth surface of water in front of her.

"There's nothing wrong with wanting normal, whatever normal might be. Quiet. Security. Stability." I emphasize each word. "If that's your fairy tale, then so be it."

I take a deep breath. "And if you want a wedding, I'll give it to you."

"Clay." Her voice is a warning, pinched with hurt. She thinks I'm joking.

"Butterfly, I told you I was falling for you, but the truth is I fell a long time ago. On a stolen smile, and kind words. Not to mention, you're stunning. And by some lucky star, you became available. And I'm not letting *my* fairy tale pass." I pinch her chin and make her look me in the eye. "I love you, butterfly."

Her eyes well with tears again.

"And just to confirm my feelings for Dutton, as I'm the lucky guy with a package present. I love him, too."

The tears tip over the rim of her eyes and her hand comes to my jaw. "I love you, too, honey." Then her mouth is against mine, and while the kiss is slow, love fills every press and suck that turns to nips and licks, and then tongues coming together, until Mavis is twisting to straddle me.

With her hands around the back of my neck and my hands on her hips, she settles in my lap where I try to ignore how hard she's made me, and we kiss and kiss, like that afternoon in the old cabin. Taking our time to let our mouths speak without words.

I love this woman. I love her child. And I want her to be my wife. They will be my family.

As the kiss heats, Mavis begins to move. Her center covering my length. The water sloshing around us.

"Let me just touch you, beautiful," I beg against her mouth. Sliding my hand around her hip, I intend to slip it between us, get my fingers on where she's slick and sensitive.

Mavis gently moves my hand back. "Let's just be one." Then, she's wrapping her hand around me, holding my heavy shaft upright and positioning herself on the tip.

"I'm not—" My voice catches, as Mavis lowers herself, taking me into her body. Raw. Real. With nothing between us.

She gasps at the intrusion into her body, as I fill her full, until she settles on my lap. Glancing down first at where we are joined beneath the water, she then snaps her head up and our eyes catch.

"This is the best feeling in the world, baby. *You* are the best thing to ever happen to me."

"That's my line," she whispers. "You're the best person I've ever known, honey. And I never want to lose you."

"You won't." I stretch up to kiss her, hard and deep, until my dick twitches inside her, needing more from her.

She pulls back and chuckles, glancing down where we connect. "It's never been like this, felt like this." She looks up again, her eyes filling with tears once more. "I love you so much, Clay."

"I know, butterfly. I love you that much, too." My mouth is on hers again, and then we move. Slow and rhythmic at first, like a practiced dance, until our mouths turn more frantic. We break apart, catching our breath as our bodies take over.

I dive into her. She takes me deeper. We move together and we love each other with her arms wrapped around my neck and mine around her lower back.

The water is a tidal wave within the tub as our bodies rock. Mavis's breath starts to catch, hitching higher and higher.

"That's it, baby. Let me take care of you." Let me be her fairy tale come true.

"Always," she whimpers, dragging up and down my dick, pistoning herself, until she stills, and tips back her head. "Oh, Clay."

The cry sets me loose, and I move her up and down a few more times, drawing out her release before tugging her down and going off inside her, filling her more ways than one.

Like she has filled me.

With her love and her trust and her commitment.

To stay mine.

36

[Mavis]

When we finally collapse in bed, after a check on Dutton, Clay holds me against his side, stroking down my hair and over my shoulders. I'm sleepy and warm, and so unbelievably content. I don't want to close my eyes, afraid I'll miss a second of this bliss.

I've been thinking about what Clay said about fairy tales and how they live in the cracks and corners of our lives. For some reason, my mind leaps to the book Dutton and I were reading together some months back, about the princess who collected sand in a jar, thinking it was magical and could save her kingdom.

Clay was filling in the cracks and corners of my life. He wasn't fairy dust, but those magical grains of sand. And our kingdom was us, saved by our love.

"When I was ten," Clay interjects on my thoughts. "I found

my mother bent over beside my parents' bed. The pain unbearable for her."

"Clay," I murmur, attempting to sit upright, but he tugs me tighter to his side.

"She died in childbirth, something practically unheard of in the modern era, and yet not as uncommon as one might think. Pre-eclampsia."

Oh my God. How awful for him.

"I watched as my father fell apart. The love of his life gone. A new baby in her place."

I hear Clay swallow.

"And I was afraid to love." His voice isn't more than a rough whisper. "Afraid of the pain it causes when you lose that *someone* you love more than anyone else."

He clears his voice, but the volume doesn't rise. "I've never been afraid to help someone or save a hurt creature. But I've been terrified to make someone mine."

I remain quiet, sensing Clay has something more he wants to say, something he needs to get off his chest.

"Before I was into girls or understood that love was what my parents had. Before my mom's death, my mom once said, *find your person, Clay.*" He pauses. "*Love her hard. Let her love you hard, too.*"

He's quiet again, his fingers tickling down my arm in a lulling motion. "I don't think I understood what she meant until now."

He kisses my head and I shift so I can look at him better, but he isn't looking at me. He's staring off at the opposite wall.

"Did you know that each of us were named after something related to the earth?" He softly chuckles. "Stone and Clay are probably obvious. Our father's name was Flint. Mom said he was a hard man to love at first, but when he gave in, when he embraced the love he was given . . . Then she'd just deeply sigh like it was the best feeling."

I smile, pressing a kiss to his bare chest.

"You're my deep sigh, Mavis."

I press up on his chest, so I can look directly at him, and he'll look at me. "That's the most beautiful thing I've ever heard."

"You're the most beautiful thing I've ever seen. And I meant what I said earlier. I want a fairy tale, too, Mavis. Let *us* have that wedding."

"Clay, are you asking—" I didn't feel I could tempt fate to ask him for clarification. My hope couldn't take the letdown if I was jumping ahead of this conversation.

"I'm saying I want more firsts with you. But I also want to be your last. The last man you ever kiss. The last man to ever love you as fiercely as I do."

His eyes lock on mine which are overflowing with tears of joy.

"Marry me, butterfly."

"Clay. Yes. Absolutely yes." Leaning down, I kiss him with all I have, and then he's rolling over me, filling me once again.

And that content feeling, which is pure happiness, leaves me breathless once more.

He's *my* deep sigh.

IN THE MORNING, we wake to a visitor in our bed. In the early morning hours, Dutton climbed between us. Clay didn't seem to mind the intrusion, slipping his arm over Dutton and reaching out for me, wrapping us both underneath his protection.

Thankfully, he slipped on his boxer briefs and I'm wearing a Seed & Soil t-shirt after our second round of love making last night.

In a groggy voice, Clay mutters. "What's the plan for today, buddy?"

Dutton lays on his back, staring up at the ceiling. "First, oatmeal."

"On it," Clay says, tossing back the covers and standing beside the bed to stretch.

I admire his back as he lifts his arms over his head.

Dutton stands on the mattress, jostling the bed and imitating Clay, adding an extra groan to the stretch. Clay chuckles and spins toward Dutton.

"Whatcha doing', little bear?"

"Stretching like Papa Bear. Gotta limber up before the dismount."

"What dismount?" Clay asks but before he finishes, Dutton is doing a cartwheel across the bed and landing off the end of it. His little feet hit the floor before he snaps his heels together, tosses his arms into the air, and dramatically tips back his head.

"Whoa," Clay says, staring at Dutton.

"How'd I do on the dismount?"

"A perfect ten."

Dutton beams, lowering his arms and staring at Clay. "Really?"

"Absolutely." Clay nods in confirmation.

Dutton pumps his thin arm beside him. "Yes!" Then, he rushes off for his room or the kitchen. All things considered, he's definitely in a good mood this morning.

I perch up on my elbow, drop my voice to sound as gruffly masculine as it can go, and say "Whatever happened to *not doing him any favors by making him think everything he does is perfect*?"

Clay laughs, hands on his hips as he looks at me. He points toward the door. "Did you see that, though? It was perfect."

"You're a sap." I toss a pillow at him which he easily catches.

"Yeah, well, that's my kid. He's always going to be perfect."

Clay kneels on the mattress coming closer to me, and I fall back on the bed.

"So now you get it," I tease.

"Nope. Now I get you and him. And that's a perfect ten."

I laugh. "Oh my God, I love you, Clay."

"I know." He smiles. "That's a ten, too." He kisses me fast and quick before pulling back. "And I love you, too, butterfly. Now get up. We have oatmeal to eat."

EPILOGUE

May

[Mavis]

I f it's even possible, Sylver Sundays have certainly gotten a lot more exciting with the addition of Annabelle Valentine Sylver, born to Sebastian and Enya in February. We are all excited for the second time parents.

Clay and I discussed babies. I won't mind having one, but Dutton is also more than enough. Clay is content as he's done his duty as a brother raising siblings. For him, he wants to concentrate only on one kid, *our* Dutton. We're perfectly happy in our little family of three.

Filling up Stone's backyard on the season's first beautiful spring afternoon, people are playing pass the baby and uncles are arguing over who is the favorite for a newborn.

As an official member of the growing number of women in this family, we're off to the side where Enya is taking a break from holding her own child. The official sisters are sitting in a new addition to the backyard, a two-seater swing, while Vale, Halle, and I sit in Adirondack chairs facing Cadence and Enya.

"I'm just not liking this," Vale states, speaking about Judd and his decision to ask his long-time girlfriend Heather Remington to marry him.

The weird thing about this woman is he never brings her to family events. He hardly attends Sylver Sundays himself, much to Stone and Vale's dismay.

From family discussions, it's evident they don't care for Heather, the daughter of a local car dealership owner, who is both wealthy and a bit crooked, according to Sebastian. She's pin-up worthy in the looks department, but the family thinks she's full of hot air. And somehow, she has Judd swindled into thinking he loves her, and she loves him. None of the Sylver women, nor men, are convinced.

Clay especially doesn't like it, thinking his brother is making a huge mistake. Not that marriage is the issue, but he wants his brother to have that deep sigh sensation, and he believes Judd is experiencing more like a can't-catch-his-breath feeling. As if he's suffocating under some hidden pressure that he *should* get married when he doesn't need to settle down.

Cadence once let it slip that Judd told Ford he was tired of being alone, and I think many of us can attest to understanding that feeling.

When I'd been with Wesley, I was still lonely as hell. Before that, I'd been working so often, I didn't have time to think until I was alone in my condo after shifts, wishing there was someone to greet me and ask me about my day.

Glancing over at Clay, I catch him watching me and he winks. He's standing by the grill which Stone mans and uses during almost any season. I smile back at Clay, loving him more every day, if that's even possible.

"I love how you look at him," Cadence interjects, drawing my attention back to the group of women.

"Is it any different than how you look at Ford?"

"I don't know, is it?" She glances over at him, almost glaring at him a second, before her cheeks turn a soft pink.

Enya chuckles beside her sister. "I don't think any of us are safe from the Sylver magnetism. Sorry, Vale."

Vale already has her hands over her ears, *la-la-la*-ing when it comes to us discussing the men in our lives. As for me, I glance down at the ring Clay gave me near Christmas as a promise of that wedding we'll be having soon. Something simple. Mainly family.

"Anyway," Vale drags out. "I keep telling everyone, if Judd loves her, we need to love her, for him. But I still don't love how this is playing out. Him and Heather? I don't see it."

"The problem is we never see them together," Enya states.

I'd only met Heather once and it was last fall when Clay had me pick out an SUV from Remington Auto. While the Jetta wasn't fully wrecked in the slip into the ditch, he didn't like the idea of simply replacing the airbag. Plus, he thought it might be triggering for both me and Dutton. *And* he wanted a bigger, more stable, protective vehicle around us. He was very persuasive in his presentation about why I deserved a new car, that he purchased. The argument included sexual pleasuring as well.

Clay made amends with Perry Foster, but their friendship is more distant than it once was. I feel guilty about that, but Clay assures me I shouldn't. He'd rather be home than hanging out at the bar, watching men over forty make fools of themselves trying to pick up younger women.

He's so domestic.

A shift in attention from the guys near the grill, and the two picnic tables now needed to hold the family, causing us ladies to look up, wondering if the kids have gotten into trouble somehow.

Hudson and Zelle are tight, at the moment. Tim joins them when they are willing to play soccer with him.

Winnie and Dutton are thick as thieves while complete opposites, letting June tag along with them.

Violet is on Adara duty as the near two-year old toddles around the yard.

But it isn't the kids that causes the shift.

"Hi . . . everyone." Judd's deep voice stumbles over the greeting. He waves awkwardly before lowering his hand. However, his other hand has everyone's attention. He's holding the hand of a woman who is clearly not the auto salesman's pin-up daughter.

This woman is smaller, cuter, brightly dressed and wearing a tight, anxious smile. She's holding Judd's right hand, clutching his bicep with her left hand. And something shiny glints in the sunshine.

"Uhm . . . I'd like you all to meet Genie. My fiancée."

At first no one reacts. Too stunned to say anything. Then Stone moves toward them and Vale hops up from her seat, muttering, "Thank God," before she rushes toward her brother.

Slowly, the rest of us rise, making our way over to the reclusive brother, wondering what this story is all about, because we're certain there's a story here.

～

Thank you for taking the time to read this book.

Please consider writing a review on major sales channels where ebooks and paperbacks are sold and discussed.

Want a little more of Clay and Mavis?

Bonus - Sterling Clay

Up next in Sterling Falls.
Reunited friends in a fake relationship (or is it?)
STERLING FIGHT.

Turn the page for a sample.

STERLING FIGHT
CHAPTER 1

Nineteen-years old

[Genie]

As I round the stacks in the university library, my gaze catches on a lone student sitting at a dark wood table amid the numerous empty ones. The hour is late, nearly closing time. The lights are low. The scent of leather bindings and old paper is more prominent in the emptiness, and I'm on my final stretch of reshelving books. Work-study for financial assistance isn't glamorous, especially when it cuts into your Saturday night plans.

From where I stand, I simply admire the man I know is a senior. His head is bowed. His wet-sand colored hair is shaggy and flopping forward against a prominent forehead. He dresses in dark colors giving off a broody vibe, like a poet from the 1960s. He's quiet, reserved, and often alone.

But he didn't have to be.

The first time I met Judd Sylver, I was in third grade. It was

February 11, National Make a New Friend Day, and I wrote him a note on lined paper decorated with a unicorn.

Do you want to be my new friend? Check yes or no.

With eyes the same shade as the brilliant blue sparkles on the cover of my notebook, he looked up at me from underneath that disheveled hair and stared. An entire conversation went on behind those eyes, like he was actually considering being my friend, then he blinked once, narrowed his gaze, tugged one of my French braids, and said, "Why would I be friends with a girl?"

I might have only been a skinny eight-year-old, but my arms had enough strength to push him right off the low desk chair.

Judd was a reading buddy in the elementary school program that paired fifth graders with third graders. I don't know why third graders needed reading buddies. I'd known how to read since I was six. While at first, I'd been excited to have Judd as my buddy, hopeful of a new friend, I'd wished for someone else after that encounter.

Then, there was a brief period in middle school when I had a crush on Judd. He wasn't the most popular kid in Sterling Falls, our small mountain town in West Virginia. He was considered shy and aloof. Sometimes he looked a little dirty with matted hair, pants too short for his long, thin legs. He had the saddest blue eyes, and that was something which constantly drew my attention. A time or two, I caught him glancing over at me across the crowded lunchroom or in the library where I'd wait for my mom to pick me up after school. An eighth-grader rarely looked at a sixth-grader, but I'd feel those eyes on me and glance up, knowing exactly who was watching. My innocent heart would flutter in my chest, like the wings of a majestic bird taking flight. A slow pump on liftoff before the thumping wings gracefully flapped faster and faster. Sometimes, I'd ship Judd's name and mine together in a pretty floral notebook where I kept all my precious thoughts and important dates.

Such a silly girl back then.

Finally, Judd and I connected for a while in high school. Being two years ahead of me, seniors didn't often associate with sophomores, but we were in Math Club together. By then, Judd was no longer a scrawny mountain rat but a young man on the verge of adulthood. He'd bulked up but kept his head down. He was in the extra-curricular activity to beef up his college applications. He was so smart. He was also quiet but polite. Teachers adored him. He was your average good guy, and that was the best of compliments. I dare to say, we were friends. My secret crush on him was renewed.

And I made the bold move to ask him to *his* senior prom.

I have an obsession with national dates, the odder—*the quirkier*—the better, and I'd been a trendsetter when I hadn't even known it. National Promposal Day, which takes place on March 11, would not become a thing until years after I graduated from high school. Back then, I thought I was so clever, finding that old unicorn notebook from third grade in the bottom of a dresser drawer, and ripping out a blank piece of paper, then handwriting my promposal question in a similar fashion to how I asked Judd to be friends when I was a child.

Finally, in high school, Judd checked yes.

Excitement brewed with every minute I stood in my living room, twirling around in the dress that I'd picked because it matched the bright blue of Judd's eyes. He was special to me. Important even. He'd be my first kiss, and I couldn't wait.

Until those minutes added up to an hour, then two, and then the clock struck midnight.

Judd never showed. He never called either.

He missed his prom. He even skipped his high school graduation.

After finally winning his friendship, which I did consider a rare prize, the hurt I'd experienced from his absence was unbearable. I already had an aversion to being abandoned, as in, I didn't want it to ever happen again.

Judd had been that *again*.

Next thing I knew, he was here in Tennessee. Maybe I should have known he attended the same university I did, but I didn't. Then one day, I spied him working in the dining center. After that, I noticed him a time or two, or twenty. *Who was counting?* And each time I saw him, my opinion of him changed from anger to grief to confusion.

The quiet of the library, on late Saturday nights, was the place I found him most often.

He never noticed me.

Head down, book in hand, he wasn't the boy I'd pushed off a chair or the teenager who stood me up for prom. He was solid, refined, haunted-looking, like ghosts followed him, and he was determined to ignore their presence. That buzzing energy also suggested I keep my distance.

I'd learned my lesson with Judd long ago and swore he'd broken my fragile heart for the last time.

But as I watched him at the ripe age of nineteen on another National Make a New Friend Day, despite all that happened between us, I wished silently Judd Sylver and I were friends.

He looked like he could use one.

Continue reading STERLING FIGHT.

MORE BY L.B. DUNBAR

<u>Sterling Falls</u>
Seven small-town siblings muddle their way through love
over 40.
Sterling Heat
Sterling Brick
Sterling Streak
Sterling Clay
Sterling Fight
Sterling Touch
Sterling Stone

<u>Chicago Anchors</u>
When your eyes are on the silver fox coach more than the ball.
Elevator Pitch
Catch the Kiss

Parentmoon
When the mother of the groom goes head-to-head with the
single father of the bride.

Holiday Hotties (Christmas novellas)

Holiday novellas certain to heat the season.

Scrooge-ish
Naughty-ish
Grouch-ish

Road Trips & Romance

Three sisters. Three destinations. All second chances at love over 40.

Hauling Ashe
Merging Wright
Rhode Trip

Lakeside Cottage

Four friends. Four summers. Shenanigans and love happen at the lake.

Living at 40
Loving at 40
Learning at 40
Letting Go at 40

The Silver Foxes of Blue Ridge

Small mountain town, silver fox brothers seeking love over 40.

Silver Brewer
Silver Player
Silver Mayor
Silver Biker

Sexy Silver Foxes

When sexy silver foxes meet the feisty vixens of their dreams.

After Care
Midlife Crisis
Restored Dreams
Second Chance

Wine&Dine

<u>Collision novellas</u>
A spin-off from *After Care* – the younger set/rock stars
Collide
Caught

The Sex Education of M.E.
The original sexy silver fox.
When a widowed professor decides she'd like to date again,
and a local fireman volunteers to give her lessons.

<u>The Heart Collection</u>
Small town, big hearts - stories of family and love.
Speak from the Heart
Read with your Heart
Look with your Heart
Fight from the Heart
View with your Heart

A Heart Collection Spin-off
The Heart Remembers

BOOKS IN OTHER AUTHOR WORLDS

<u>Smartypants Romance (an imprint of Penny Reid)</u>
Tales of the Winters sisters set in Green Valley.
Love in Due Time
Love in Deed
Love in a Pickle

<u>The World of True North (an imprint of Sarina Bowen)</u>
Welcome to Vermont! And the Busy Bean Café.
Cowboy

Studfinder

THE EARLY YEARS

<u>Legendary Rock Stars Series</u>
A classic tale with a modern twist of rockstar romance and suspense.

<u>Paradise Stories</u>
MMA romance. Two brothers. One fight.

<u>The Island Duet</u>
Intrigue and suspense. The island knows what you've done.

<u>Modern Descendants – writing as elda lore</u>
Magical realism. Modern myths of Greek gods.

ABOUT THE AUTHOR

www.lbdunbar.com

L.B. Dunbar loves sexy silver foxes, second chances, and small towns. If you enjoy older characters in your romance reads, including a hero with a little silver in his scruff and a heroine rediscovering her worth, then welcome to romance for those over 40. L.B. Dunbar's signature works include women and men in their prime taking another turn at love and happily ever after. She's a *USA TODAY* Bestseller as well as #1 Bestseller on Amazon in Later in Life Romance with her Sterling Falls, Lakeside Cottage, and Road Trips & Romance series. L.B. lives in Chicago with her own sexy silver fox.

To get all the scoop about the self-proclaimed queen of silver fox romance, join her on Facebook at Loving L.B. (Dunbar) or receive her monthly newsletter, Love Notes.

+ + +

CONNECT WITH L.B. DUNBAR

www.ingramcontent.com/pod-product-compliance
Lightning Source LLC
Chambersburg PA
CBHW060900210726
48293CB00006B/1891